Aisle

COME BACK

to you

CONTENTS

Playlist

Aisle
COME BACK
to you
THE OFFICIAL PLAYLIST

1. THIS TOWN | NIALL HORAN
2. WE DON'T TALK ANYMORE | CHARLIE PUTH, SELENA GOMEZ
3. FORTNIGHT | TAYLOR SWIFT, POST MALONE
4. WHEN YOU'RE GONE | SHAWN MENDES
5. WE CAN'T BE FRIENDS | ARIANA GRANDE
6. EVERMORE | TAYLOR SWIFT
7. LIE TO ME | 5 SECONDS OF SUMMER
8. BACK TO YOU | SELENA GOMEZ
9. LET ME | ZAYN
10. AT YOUR WORST | CALUM SCOTT
11. CAN I HAVE THIS DANCE | JOSHUA BASSETT, SOFIA WYLIE
12. NEVER LEAVE | BAILEY ZIMMERMAN

To Kaele:
Thank you for being my platonic soulmate, a shoulder to cry on, my unwavering cheerleader, and my most delightful chipmunk bestie.

Authors Note

While most of this book contains pure sweetness and fluff that will hopefully have you kicking your feet and giggling, please be advised that this book contains mature themes that include: spicy, and open door scenes, explicit language, on page drinking, emotional and mental abuse by a partner, emotional cheating, mentions of physical cheating, mentions of alcoholic parents, and mentions of absent and neglectful parenting.

1

BLAIR

WHEN I ASKED MY older brother to pick me up from the airport, this was not what I had in mind. Instead of welcoming me home in style like I'd jokingly suggested, with him in a suit and tie and a small sign with my name on it, I'm met with a large poster board that reads, '*Welcome home from prison, Blair!*'

I should roll my eyes, but instead I lift my hand to stifle the laughter. This is so out of character for Miles, and not something I'd usually expect from him. He's always been my lovable yet grumpy older brother, which is precisely why I can't hate it or be mad. If anything, I'm impressed.

Scurrying past security, I practically leap into his arms and pull him into a warm bear hug. "Don't you worry. I'm a changed woman, Miles. I'm never going back there again," I loudly proclaim as a few nearby lurkers uncomfortably glance our way.

"Well, uh, make sure you don't." He tries to play along, running a nervous hand through his tousled blond locks. As he pulls away from my grasp, he seems to make a conscious effort to let the sign drop to his side, its message concealed against his body.

"So, did that one backfire on you or what?" I tease, adjusting my camera bag as he places a friendly arm around my shoulder and guides me toward the baggage claim.

"Honestly?" he asks, before letting out a loud sigh. "Yeah. I was getting the weirdest looks as I stood there waiting for you. Pretty sure that was the longest twenty-minute wait of my life."

I laugh, shaking my head. "Well, that's what you get for trying to make a joke. Did all these years apart make you forget that I'm the funny one in the Bennett family?"

"Maybe if I didn't have to wait so long between visits, I wouldn't have to forget," he playfully chastises, a smile tugging at his lips.

"Hey now," I say, giving him a light shove as we walk, his arm falling from around me. "Planes fly both ways. You're more than welcome to come and visit me, too, you know?"

"Not all of us are as lucky as you and can fly home at the drop of a hat. And even when you have breaks in your schedule, you hardly ever make the trip. I can barely even remember the last time I saw you."

He's not wrong. Being a concert photographer for some of the biggest bands in the world gives me the freedom and flexibility to travel, allowing me the opportunity to occasionally fly home or the ability to explore new destinations—I always choose the latter. Returning home has never been something I particularly look forward to, which means vacationing elsewhere will always be my number one choice.

When it came to being an older brother, Miles was truly one of a kind and everything I needed and more, but our childhood was anything but idyllic. We were primarily raised by our eccentric grandmother after our mom not only ran out on our drunken father, but on us as well. Our father's drinking habits only intensified, making it almost impossible to have any real sentimental feelings toward my childhood or hometown. If it wasn't for Miles and my two childhood best friends, I don't know how I would've made it through.

"I've been busy." I shrug, not really in the mood to explain myself. Plus, it's complicated.

"Yeah, yeah," he says with a roll of his eyes, clearly not buying what I'm selling.

"I'm home now. That has to count for something, right?" I frown up at him, giving my signature puppy dog eyes, putting my big baby blues to work. If you've got 'em, flaunt 'em, and you best believe I know how to put 'em to use.

"I would hope so. I'm pretty sure Veronica would kick your ass if you didn't come home for her big day."

I let out a much-needed laugh. "No kidding. It's not every day your best friend gets married."

"Now that I think about it, wasn't it Ford's wedding that brought you home the last time?" he asks, his chin lifting in thought as we continue down the long hallway, maneuvering through the small crowd of travelers.

I attempt to hide my body's physical response to hearing my other best friend's name. Or who knows, at this point? I'm not sure if you could still consider us friends.

Miles isn't wrong about my last visit home. What he may not realize is that after I discreetly slipped away during the reception to deal with my emotions with a mixture of tears and alcohol, I haven't exchanged a single word with Ford since. Okay, maybe that's not *entirely* true, since he has reached out with the occasional text message, but that was the last time *I* personally chose to communicate with him.

Instead of delving into the truth, I offer a curt nod. "Yeah, I think you're right."

"Holy shit," he says, shaking his head. "That's way too long for you not to come home and visit," he scoffs, once again using his free hand to pull me into his side for a quick hug.

"What can I say? I've been busy," I lie, twisting out of his grasp as we reach the baggage claim area. Unfortunately, my suitcase is nowhere to be found on the carousel, which currently sits motionless and devoid of all other luggage and bags.

"Let me guess, you've been too busy with Max Storm?" he asks, raising a judgmental brow while looking anything but amused.

I fold my arms, refusing to look his way. "I'll have you know, we're on a break."

"Oh, so that's why he's not here?"

"Can we please not talk about Max? I'm not in the mood," I huff and pout simultaneously. Since the start, my brother has made it clear he disapproves of my on-and-off relationship with Max.

My hunch is that Miles has always resented my ex for taking me away. After all, he was the one who offered me my ticket out when he suggested I tour with him and his band ten years ago. Obviously, I said yes and haven't looked back since.

"Oh, touchy subject, huh? What did he do this time?" He bristles, clearly not getting the hint. Then again, I guess this is the downside to having an older brother. Or maybe it's the downside to having Miles as an older brother, since he's always been relentless and nosey.

"Who says it was him? Maybe I'm the one in the wrong this time?" I challenge, tilting my head.

"The fact that you even have to say the phrase *'this time'* just goes to show how toxic he is. However, if I'm going to play along, I'll go with the usual: 'because it's always him.' He's an asshole, Blair. Always has been, always will be. Don't let him make you question that, because I'm sure as hell not."

"Alright, alright." I give up, throwing my hands in the air. "It was him, and I'm done—or at least I want to be, but you know how it is—it's complicated. We work together. It's not the band's fault that me and their drummer can't seem to get our shit together."

"It's not like you aren't in demand, Blair. Everyone loves your work. You don't have to work for Heartstrings Riot when one of their members treats you like complete shit. They can find a new photographer, and maybe they deserve to have to work with someone less talented for putting up with one of their members' bullshit when all he has to do is keep it in his pants."

"Miles!" I squeal, my eyes going wide as I reach out and smack his arm. "I'll have you know, he didn't cheat this time." I understand it's a bit pathetic that I have to emphasize he didn't cheat *this time*, but it's the honest truth.

He holds up his hands in defense. "Oh, okay. My bad. Since he didn't cheat *this time*, then I have to like him and let all the other shit he's put you through go," he grumbles, his tone a bit too sarcastic for my liking.

Luckily, I'm given a distraction as my phone pings in my pocket. Even though I'm still irritated, a smile spreads across my face. "It's Ronnie," I announce. I'll always be happy to receive a text from my best friend, but the timing from the bride-to-be is beyond impeccable. "She wants to know if you can drop me off at SalsaLeedo Sal's for Margarita Monday."

I don't even wait for his response as I immediately text her back that it's a date. Not only will he not say no, he knows he has no choice in the matter.

"So you're already going to ditch me on your first night back?" he asks. While I do sense a tinge of annoyance and perhaps a hint of jealousy in his voice, I know he understands. Ronnie's wedding is less than two weeks away, and why I've come home in the first place. I may not be thrilled to be back in town, but for Ronnie, I'd do just about anything. Hell, if the girl asked me to bury a body, I'd do it in a heartbeat. There'd probably be a lot of questions and judgment, but I'd still do it.

"You can always join us," I point out, looking up from my phone, even though I already know the answer.

"A night out with Veronica Prescott? No thanks," he answers, proving my initial instincts right. We may spend the majority of our time countries apart, but I still know my brother. I can still read him like a book, despite the passage of time and distance. "I'd rather follow a scary-ass clown into a storm drain."

"Oh, come on. She's not that bad. I don't get what you have against her."

"Well, first off..." he starts, but I interrupt.

"Hey now," I caution, my voice laced with warning as I lift a threatening finger in his direction. "She's my best friend and I will not accept any best friend slander from you, mister."

"Well, you see," he starts up again, his voice competing with the sound of the carousel as it begins to operate and spin, but that doesn't seem to deter him. "That's part of the problem. That girl can do no wrong in your eyes, but she's trouble, and has been since you were kids."

"She is not," I scoff, taking my eyes off the carousel as I roll them in his direction.

"You can't tell me that whenever the three of you got into trouble growing up, she wasn't the mastermind behind each and every dumb and dumber idea the three of you took part in."

"You're exaggerating," I say, attempting to downplay our juvenile antics, but deep down, even I can't deny he's right. Whenever the three of us got caught doing something dumb or ridiculous, it was always Ronnie's idea. Sure, I was right there to egg it all on, but she was most certainly the mastermind working behind the scenes.

"Am I exaggerating about the time you guys broke onto Mr. Holstead's property, stole his tractor, and rode it down the middle of Main Street? Or how about the time you thought it would be a smart idea to..." he continues, but I lift a hand to interrupt.

I don't need any reminders. Every one of those memories is etched vividly in my mind, and I have to say, the majority of them hold a fond place in my heart. While much of my childhood was marred by negative memories, the ones I created alongside Ronnie and Ford will forever be my favorites.

"Okay, fine. We did some stupid stuff, but it's not like we ever went to jail or did anything too crazy. They were all silly and harmless pranks."

"You do realize that the only reason nobody ever pressed charges or why the three of you got out of trouble each and every time was because Veronica's dad was the mayor and Ford's dad was the sheriff? If anything, it always made the two of us look worse, since most people assumed *you* were the bad influence."

I hate that he's right, when your dad is the town drunk and you do something stupid, you're only playing right into their built-in negative stereotypes.

"Miles," I say, placing my hand on his arm. I know he's sensitive about this stuff, and it's probably been a lot harder for him since, unlike me, he's never had the luxury of escaping the relentless gossip of Evergreen Grove. "I'm sorry if I made it harder for you growing up, but that was a long time ago. We've all matured since then. We aren't the reckless kids we used to be. Hell, Ronnie is a high school teacher, for goodness' sake, and is marrying the town councilman. If that doesn't scream grown-up, then I don't know what does."

"Maybe she's older and has somehow managed to get a big-girl job, but considering her first order of business when you come back into town is to get you drunk on margaritas, I'm not exactly inspired to see her in a new light."

I understand that he's only saying this out of protectiveness, as our father's history with alcohol has always made him extra cautious. However, this isn't something I want or need him to worry about. He's already spent way too many years playing the responsible adult in our lives. Now that I'm a grown woman, it's no longer required, nor is it wanted.

"I travel with some of the biggest rock bands in the world. Believe me, I've been around much crazier drinkers than Ronnie. If anything, we'll only have a drink or two. Don't worry, we have no intention of losing control or causing any trouble tonight. We just want to hang out and catch up. That's it."

He doesn't look all that convinced, but luckily, he also doesn't look like he's going to fight me on the matter. "Just be smart, Blair. If you need me to pick you up afterward, you know I'm always just a quick phone call away."

"Believe me," I assure him, giving his arm a reassuring squeeze, "I know I can always count on you." Yes, he can be a protective pain in the ass, but he's my pain in the ass and I can't imagine life without him, nor would I want to. "Oh, look," I continue as I tug on his arm and do my best to steer his gaze in the right direction. "There's my bag." I point out with my other hand, thankful for the distraction as he moves to grab it, effortlessly pulling it off the belt.

"Well, I guess it's time to get you to Sal's," he says, his tone lacking enthusiasm, but at least he's no longer opposing the idea.

"To Sal's!" I cheer, lifting my hand as I gesture toward the parking garage. As good as it's been to see my older brother, Ronnie is the reason I'm here, and I'm dying to be back with the one person in this world who knows me better than anyone else.

2

BLAIR

A S MILES DROPPED ME off at SalsaLeedo Sal's, it was obvious he was still annoyed with my bailing on him, but luckily all seemed to be forgiven once I suggested lunch tomorrow at his mechanic shop. Plus, it's not like I'm not planning to stay with him at his apartment for the duration of my visit. There will be plenty of brother-sister bonding time to be had in the next two weeks.

As much as I love my older brother, there are times when a girl craves and needs the advice of her absolute best friend in the entire world. I completely understand why Miles worries and why he despises Max, but it's just different with Ronnie. Sure, she dislikes my on-and-off again fling as well, but at least she can relate and empathize with the difficulties and knows firsthand what it's like to be a woman dating in this modern world.

I love Miles, but he doesn't get it. He can be a grumpy and brooding asshole, and women still flock to him, regardless. It's different for us ladies, and if there's ever someone I can vent or complain to without the fear of judgment, it's Ronnie. The girl knows how to give it to me straight without making me feel worse about myself or my situation.

That's precisely why girl time and margaritas are the much-needed distraction I crave tonight. Despite the limited options for great cuisine in Evergreen Grove, Sal's restaurant delivers some pretty damn good Mexican food, which is quite impressive for a small town such as this. My love for this place only grew after turning twenty-one, as it fully allowed me to take part in the grand tradition of Margarita Mondays.

As a kid or teenager, it was common knowledge to steer clear of this place on Mondays because of the infamous and unbearably long wait. The adults of Evergreen found it impossible to resist the temptation of the town's worst-kept secret of cheap margaritas. Sure, the chips and salsa are tasty, and the tacos are top-notch, but it's the drinks that keep this place in business.

The moment I step inside, the irresistible aroma of warm tortillas greets me, mingling with the energetic rhythm of mariachi music playing from the speakers. Despite it being a few years since my last visit, the vibrant purple, red, green, and orange decor immediately transports me back in time. Nothing has changed, not even the familiar voice calling my name.

Sitting in our favorite booth, my absolute best friend catches my eye as she pushes her way out and barrels toward me. I do the same, meeting her halfway, enveloping her petite frame in a bear hug, immediately feeling the surge of comfort and security that only she can provide. Given that we're both short, me at five foot two, and her at five foot three, as we pull away, we're standing practically eye to eye as our grins mirror one another.

That is where the physical similarities between the two of us end. While I have long, golden blonde hair that drapes down to the middle of my back, Ronnie's chic and stylish short brown hair falls just an inch above her shoulders. "Wow, this is new," I compliment, letting my fingers lightly comb through the ends of her short locks.

"What do you think?" she asks, wrinkling her nose as she swishes it from side to side. "It was Pete's idea. He thought it'd make me look more professional and help people take me more seriously."

"It's gorgeous," I assure her, reaching for her hand as I lead her back toward our booth. "But for the record, you don't need to change anything about yourself or your appearance to present yourself in any particular way. You're perfect and always have been. Plus, screw looking professional. You don't need to look like anyone other than yourself."

While I never found it hard to set myself apart in this small town, one thing the two of us have always prided ourselves on was the fact that we didn't stick to the status quo. We did our own thing, and even though it only added to the gossip about me and my family, being true to ourselves was always the top priority—or at least I'd always assumed so.

"Said like a true best friend," she says through a small laugh, as we both slide into our usual seats.

While she thankfully made a few trips to visit me this past summer as I toured with Heartstrings Riot, it definitely wasn't enough. However, like usual, the familiar warmth and ease of our connection takes over, making it feel as though no time has passed at all.

Growing up, there had been plenty of people who didn't understand our friendship or connection. While Ronnie is sunlight personified, with the demeanor of a real-life Disney princess, I'm essentially Wednesday Addams, exuding the aura of a rainy day. In so many ways, that's exactly why I think we work so well. We balance each other out. She's the peanut butter to my jelly, the moon to my night sky.

Even when it comes to our styles, we couldn't be more different. I stick to darker colors and black clothing with a more edgy and rebellious style. My closet consists mainly of various band T-shirts and raw distressed jeans. If I had to categorize it, I'd say I prefer to be bold, yet also very laid back.

Ronnie's style, on the other hand, is vibrant, girly, and playful, with a fearless approach to color. She's constantly mixing and matching bold and bright hues with different patterns and isn't afraid to try something new. She also tends to wear a lot of skirts and dresses that are not only sweet and playful, but fun and flirty, with elaborate prints, lace trimmings, and ruffles. While a lot of people see me as unapproachable, everyone constantly seeks out Ronnie's attention, yet somehow mine is always the most important to her.

Then again, it's crazy to think about where our lives have gone and how much has changed since we were kids, especially with her having a huge rock on her finger, only days away from getting married.

"Well, what are best friends for if not telling the truth?" I ask before holding my hand out and wiggling my fingers, gesturing for her to give me her hand. "Now let me see that ring of yours in person."

After using a month of her summer break to tour with me, she'd returned home to a surprise. Her then boyfriend, Pete, proposed the day after her arrival. Apparently, he'd said that the time apart made him realize just how much he loved her and how he never wanted to be apart from her again. With that, he'd gotten down on one knee and asked her to marry him in front of their friends and family. As sad as I was to miss it and bummed that Pete hadn't even thought to invite me, I'd like to think it was a blessing in disguise, since it gave me even more reason to avoid coming home until now.

Pete is a couple of years older than us, so I'd never paid him much attention growing up, and honestly, had never really felt like I had a reason to. Sure, he'd been on student council and was known for his loud and charming ways, but I'd been perfectly content with my small, tight-knit group of friends.

Following my lead, Ronnie sheepishly offers her hand, allowing it to settle in my palm.

"Wow!" I exclaim. The pictures don't do this thing justice at all. I knew that it was big and shiny, but I'm practically blinded by the sight of it—this ring exudes pure opulence. "Do you love it?" I ask, my eyes moving to meet hers from across the table.

"Yeah." She shrugs, a flicker of embarrassment crossing her face as she hastily retracts her hand, letting it fall underneath the table and out of sight.

"Yeah? That's all you have to say?" I ask, my eyebrows furrowing as I reach for one of the chips and dip it into the salsa. When I imagined the ring that would sit on my best friend's hand, I had always pictured something fun and unique—just like her. While the size alone gives this the upper hand on being different, there doesn't seem to be anything particularly special about it. It's just a giant diamond surrounded by a few other ginormous diamonds.

"It isn't what I personally would've picked, but Pete was so excited, and he loves it, so I love it too." She shrugs, also reaching for a chip, seeming to grab it purposely with her other hand.

Unfortunately, I know my friend better than almost anyone. She's far from being honest here. However, I'm not going to make anything about her special day uncomfortable, so I keep my mouth shut—which, for someone like me, is extremely difficult.

Luckily, I don't have to worry about it as the middle-aged waitress comes to take our order, saving us from any ensuing awkwardness. We both order tonight's special blackberry margarita, and their signature three-taco plates.

"Since we have the next week and a half to discuss wedding stuff, let's change the subject and talk about you," Ronnie suggests before chomping into her chip. She's not fooling anyone here, let alone me, but since she's the bride-to-be, I let her have this one.

"Well, what about me do you want to talk about?" I ask before taking a bite of my salsa-covered chip. Although, I suspect I already know the answer. Max had promised to be my date for Ronnie's wedding, and given that he isn't here, I'm pretty sure she gets it without either of us having to say it out loud—Max and I are on yet another break.

"Oh, I'm pretty sure you already know the answer to that," she assures me, a mischievous glint in her eye, reminding me once again of our uncanny connection.

"Unfortunately, I think I do," I sigh.

"Well, in that case, what happened this time? And *please* don't tell me he cheated again," she pleads.

I shake my head. "No, nothing like that," I assure her, just as two drinks are placed in front of us. With the tense topics that have already been brought up, it's no surprise that both of us immediately dive in and take some much-needed sips.

"God, that is good," Ronnie hums as I nod my head and close my eyes while I fully take it in.

Given that this is a tiny town, and even more, I've been all over the world and had some of the best and most unique drinks out there, I've yet to find anything that competes with the heavenly taste of a margarita from Sal's. It might just be the fact that I'm home and sitting with my best friend, but even with the conversation being what it is, this moment feels perfect.

"It really is," I agree, savoring another sip, the blackberry infusing a delightful tang and kick.

"While the drink may be good, don't go thinking I forgot about what we were talking about. Spill it, missy."

I let out a frustrated breath of air. While I'm not annoyed at Ronnie, it sucks that I'm having to deal with this, especially during what should be a fun and easygoing week. "It's the usual," I sigh, waving it off as I try not to make it into some huge thing. "He's too busy, and despite promising to come with me and taking time off, he's convinced that he needs to work on new music since the guys are supposed to be heading back into the studio in a few weeks."

"Oh, so this isn't a true break, then? He just didn't come?" she asks, leaning down as she wraps her lips around her straw once more.

"Oh, no. It's *definitely* a break," I assure her as I let out a less than amused laugh. "I told him that if he didn't have the time to come with me to my best friend's wedding, then he didn't have time to be my boyfriend, either."

"Damn, girl!" she giggles, nodding her head in approval. "I obviously hate that you're sad and upset, but I love that you're standing up for yourself. I mean, come on, what piece of shit lets their girlfriend go to their best friend's wedding all alone and dateless? Doesn't he know that a single maid of honor is going to be a hot commodity and that all the groomsmen are going to be fighting over who gets the honor to hook up with you?"

"No offense, but I don't picture myself being into any of Pete's friends." I shiver before letting out a soft laugh as I lift my glass to take another sip, realizing that I've already drunk almost half my margarita. Sure, from what I can remember, Pete had some cute friends back in high school, but pretty boys that exude frat guy energy aren't exactly my type.

"Well, what about a hot bridesman?" she asks, wiggling her eyebrows in my direction.

"What the fuck is a bridesman?" I ask, trying not to laugh.

"Ford. He obviously has to be in my line, so that's going to be his honorary title from here on out," she explains, as if it's all so obvious.

"Yeah, married men aren't exactly my thing either," I point out, not sure why she's bringing him up, given all of our history. Obviously, she knew of my feelings for him all throughout our teenage years, but I'm not that desperate, even if it would be a nice way to stick it to Max.

Wrinkling her nose, Ronnie softly chews on her bottom lip. "I actually probably shouldn't say anything, since I know Ford wanted to keep it on the down low, but you know me," she says, waving it off, "I've never been able to keep anything from you." She hesitates but finally gives in and spills. "But, uh, he and Jenny are officially separated and going through a divorce."

My mouth gapes open. I'm not sure what I'd been expecting her to say, but it certainly wasn't that.

"You won't say anything though, right? I sort of think he wanted to be the one to tell you, but you know how I get when I drink." She sheepishly winces, even if I can sense the relief she feels at finally being able to drop that big of a bomb on me. She's right, we don't keep secrets from each other, but in this case, I'm still debating whether this is news I wanted to hear or not.

"Ronnie, you haven't even had a full margarita. I don't think you get to blame this one on the alcohol," I remind her, nodding toward her glass that is still over halfway full. "But uh, wow. I'm not sure what to say to that."

I've never exactly been the biggest fan of Ford and Jenny as a couple, and every time I saw them together, I was plagued with an embarrassing amount of jealousy. However, this is the last thing I'd ever want to happen to one of my good friends. Given that he was the third member of our best friend trio growing up, I'd always wanted him to be happy. While it's taken some time for me to be this mature about it all, I'd reluctantly realized that even if his happiness didn't include me, if that was what it took, then the two of them should be together.

Okay, I'll admit it, *at least to myself*. His being single does capture my attention, but considering how recent this all is, I don't see anything happening between us, and *I don't want it to either*. I have way more respect for myself than that—or at least I hope so. I'm not about to be someone's rebound girl, especially not Ford's. I have way too much experience feeling like his second pick, especially since that's exactly how it felt when Jenny moved into town during our freshman year of high school and stole his attention straight away. I can't let myself go down that road, *not again*.

I've already let myself get hurt by all of this back in the day, and I'm too grown up and too far removed to let myself get entangled in this sort of thing ever again. Dealing with Max's never-ending drama is overwhelming and exhausting enough.

"So, uh," Ronnie begins, cutting through my thoughts as I realize just how nervous she appears as her eyes dart behind me, and my eyes narrow. "I probably should've warned you earlier, but uh, I maaaaay have invited Ford tonight, and he may have just walked in."

"Wait, what? What do you mean?" I ask, my heart rate quickening as I sit up straight. The temptation to turn around in my seat and follow Ronnie's brown-eyed gaze is strong, but fear keeps me rooted in place.

I haven't seen Ford since the night of his wedding just over two years ago. I'd known that coming home meant I'd run into him and see him at some point, but nothing could have prepared me for the bomb she'd just dropped, especially so soon. I'd figured I'd at least have a few more days before we'd be forced to interact.

"I invited him to Margarita Monday. I mean, he is the other important part of this friendship trio," she explains in an annoyingly casual fashion as she reaches for a chip to dip in the salsa, like she hadn't just tipped my world upside down.

Before I can say anything else, Ford's familiar timbre rings out as he approaches our table. "If it isn't Tweedle Dee and Tweedle Dum," he teases as I finally brave looking up at him.

Damn! How does he still look this good? He's somehow grown even more attractive. This isn't fair. Why couldn't life have treated him to a dad bod or something? Okay, so maybe he's not actually a father yet, but a round belly or *something* to take away from that handsome face of his would be nice.

Instead, many of his boyish attributes have faded with time, giving way to a more mature appearance with a sharp, chiseled jawline that has the perfect amount of well-groomed stubble. His short, dark hair curls in just the right way, adding even more appeal. While I'd guess he recently got out of the shower and let his hair air dry, instead of looking like a mess, it looks effortlessly tousled and perfectly styled.

He still has on his signature pair of black glasses, but instead of looking goofy or dorky, they give him a distinguished sophistication. I'm so not ready for this, especially as his gorgeous dark chestnut eyes fix directly on me. How am I ever going to make it through the night now?

3

FORD

"WHICH ONE OF US is Tweedle Dee and which one is Tweedle Dum?" Blair asks, her eyes locking with mine, causing me to temporarily freeze and lose track of what I'd just asked. It's clear I hadn't thought it through when I'd made that stupid joke, and now, being back in her presence has me feeling completely off-center and out of sorts—something I haven't felt in a really long time. She's always had a way of keeping me on my toes, but between our two years of separation and limited contact before that, I feel like I've forgotten how to act around her.

It doesn't help that she looks just as gorgeous as ever. Her eyes, a piercing shade of baby blue, never fail to captivate me, no matter how many times I've gazed into them. Then there are her plump, heart-shaped lips that don't do me any favors either, as I do my best not to look their way. If anything, I train my eyes to look at her hair, which, even after spending the afternoon traveling, looks flawless as it falls in long silky waves over her shoulders.

Ignoring my instincts, my eyes wander as I fully take her in. Blair's style has always set her apart from everyone here in Evergreen Grove, as if she's always known she was destined for something bigger—something neither I nor this town could offer her.

From what I can see, she's wearing jean shorts and a black lacy crop top that accentuates her perfect curves, teasing just the right amount of skin, with a blue and orange flannel worn over it. She's absolutely stunning, and it takes all my self-control not to gawk, or worse, openly confess just how damn much I've missed her.

I get why she never texted me back after the night of my wedding, but that doesn't make the loss of contact hurt any less. We grew up together, and she was most definitely my person. While I'm happy she and Ronnie stayed close, it sucks that all my knowledge of her life now comes via secondhand gossip from our mutual friend.

"Well?" Ronnie asks, tilting her head as she presses for my answer. "Which one are we?" she prods, pursing her lips, loving the fact that I've clearly backed myself into a corner with this one.

"How about we all pretend I didn't start off with a stupid joke and you let me off the hook?" I beg with a hopeful smile.

"I don't know, Blair. What do you think? Do we let him off the hook this time?" Ronnie asks, as both of our gazes shift toward our blonde counterpart.

"I think I may be willing to let it go. *This time*," she sighs. "Plus, we all know I'm Tweedle Dee, and Ronnie is Tweedle Dum."

Ronnie scoffs. "You wish. I'm totally Tweedle Dee, right Ford?" she presses, as they once again put me on blast and in the middle. As familiar as it is to be in this position between the two of them, so much has changed since then, making any sort of answer feel practically impossible.

I just have to hope it isn't obvious how nervous I am as beads of sweat begin to form on my forehead. "How about you're both Tweedle Dee and I'm the Tweedle Dum?" I offer, figuring the name is pretty fitting right about now.

"I suppose we shall accept your offering, now take a seat before you have a heart attack," Ronnie teases as she thankfully shuffles further into the booth so I can slip in next to her.

Once upon a time, I would've eagerly chosen to sit next to Blair, hoping for any accidental contact, but things have definitely changed, and not for the better.

"So, what've I missed? Besides the two of you starting the fun without me," I muse, taking in the fact that they are both seemingly ready for margarita number two. At least it doesn't look like I've missed dinner, as the table only holds their drinks and the complimentary chips and salsa.

"Not much," Ronnie casually shares as she reaches for a chip and coats it in salsa. "Although, Blair did mention that she and Max are on yet another break," she adds, before stuffing the bite into her mouth.

"Oh," I say, an odd mix of guilt and happiness swirling inside me at the news. I've never liked Max, especially since he was the one who got her to leave Evergreen Grove in the first place. "I'm sorry," I offer, looking toward Blair as I do my best to convey genuine sympathy, even if it's all forced and completely fake. While he might have changed since I first met him, my gut instinct has always been that she deserves someone far better. Nobody merits being with a cheating asshole, especially not someone as special as Blair.

"I'm sure we'll get back together when I get home. We always figure it out, so no need to feel bad." She shrugs, brushing my words off as she lifts her glass and slides her lips around the straw. I hate myself for noticing just how perfectly full they are, as well as the dangerously wicked thoughts about where I'd like to have those lips go next. While I've only felt them against my own once, my body somehow seems to remember just how amazing that kiss was and how soft and pillowy they were, aching to experience it all over again. Perhaps it wasn't the wisest choice to sit directly across from her, as I now have a completely unobstructed view of her unmatched beauty.

"Well, we definitely didn't get that far into the conversation," Ronnie half scoffs, shooting Blair a penetrating stare.

"It's not like it should be a big surprise. Plus, I never hinted at anything different." She shrugs, purposely avoiding not only my face, but Ronnie's as well, as she stares down at her practically empty glass and swirls her straw in it.

"I'm not looking to ruin dinner or your first night back by explaining why I think getting back with him is a bad idea, and I hope you know I'll always support you in whatever you decide, but you have to know my opinion on the matter. You deserve so much better than what Max offers you, which we all know isn't much, so I have to imagine the bar isn't set very high."

Blair's jaw clenches and her lips fall into a straight line. God, what is wrong with me? Why can't I stop staring at her damn lips?

"Well, we can't all have a Pete now, can we?" Blair shoots back, in what I'm assuming is supposed to be a playful manner, but misses the mark, especially as Ronnie's shoulders slump.

"I promise I'm not trying to make you feel bad. I'm sorry. Can we start over and change the subject please," Ronnie pleads, pouting her lips.

"I know," Blair sighs, sounding a bit more sincere this time as she reaches a hand across the table. Ronnie takes it, seeming to settle their differences with that simple touch.

Being in the middle of this should probably have me feeling weird and uncomfortable, but if anything, it only takes me back. As the middleman in their friendship, I often found myself reluctantly involved in their conflicts, as they had their ups and downs. However, they've always found a way to make up rather quickly.

"Speaking of Pete, I don't even remember much about him," Blair adds as she pulls her hand back to grab a chip. "If I'm being honest, he was never someone I paid all that much attention to."

"That's how I felt too," I chime in, Blair's eyes meeting mine for a brief moment before she averts her gaze just as quickly and dips her chip in the salsa.

Before I can fully analyze it, the waitress interrupts, placing their tacos on the table and multitasking by taking my order and fetching more margaritas for the ladies.

"But you like Pete now, right?" Ronnie asks the second we're left alone, pulling us right back into the previous conversation.

"Yeah, sure," I shrug, not sure what else to say. "I mean, we aren't close, and I don't expect us to be, but he seems to make you happy, so I have no complaints," I lie, doing my best to hide all of my worries and suspicions. Besides, I'm not in the mood to open that can of worms, especially since I've always taken my role as the group peacemaker rather seriously.

Perhaps, as one of her closest friends, it falls upon me to step in and advise her against someone who doesn't seem to compliment her in a way that I think she deserves, but it all feels so complicated. My ongoing separation from my ex has left me feeling jaded and skeptical about love, likely altering my perspective on things unfairly. It just doesn't feel right to project my own issues onto Ronnie and her relationship.

The only problem is that both of these women know me better than anyone else. Even Blair seems to sense something up with my answer, despite the two of us not having spoken in over two years.

"I think you both just need to spend some more time around him." Ronnie tries to assure us. "I know that he seems a bit too serious and can come across as being rough around the edges, but once you get to know him he's awesome," she adds as their drinks are placed on the table, along with my usual Dr Pepper.

While I'm not opposed to drinking, letting loose, and partaking in the age-old tradition of five-dollar margaritas, I have a feeling that since it's a special night with Blair finally coming home and Ronnie's upcoming nuptials these ladies might benefit from having a designated driver.

"Well, I have the next two and a half weeks off, so I'm hopeful that we can fit in some future-husband bonding time." Blair nods as she pushes her empty glass toward the waitress before immediately diving into margarita number two.

"Well, I'm saving my leave for my two-week honeymoon after the wedding, and I'm pretty sure Ford here," she says, nudging her elbow into my arm, "has to work these next two weeks as well, but during the nights we are all yours. Right, Fordy?"

"Oh, uh yeah. Sure." I nod. As a newly single man, my responsibilities these days are limited to work, and that's about it. However, I can sense Blair's disapproval through a cold stare, making me doubt she wants me to be a part of her nights in town. Despite everything, I continue on. "I also suspected that I'd be needed this week, so I planned ahead and have all of my lesson plans figured out for the next few weeks as well, so I'm all yours for whatever you need," I assure Ronnie, glancing her way to a much warmer smile.

While I was a groomsman in my older brother's wedding, I can't say I've ever been part of a bridal party before or know what all is involved. However, I've always been someone who likes to be prepared, and since I know Ronnie, I figured it's best to be there for whatever she needs. She's always been the bossy one of the group, and honestly, we love her for it.

"Ugh, that's so smart," Ronnie whines, blowing out a breath of air. "I'm constantly flying by the seat of my pants and can't plan more than a day or two ahead."

"Why does none of this surprise me, yet also fits you both so well?" Blair interrupts with a soft giggle—a melodic sound I hadn't realized how much I'd missed until now. Growing up, I'd practically made it my life's mission to make her laugh, especially since it was always so unique and just so *her*.

"Well, I'd offer to help plan, but art isn't exactly my forte. There's a reason I teach science and stay as far away from the arts as possible," I say with an apologetic shrug.

"I guess I'll just have to plan my own lessons then," Ronnie sighs, adding an overdramatic gag as she sticks out her tongue. "I really mean it, though. We need to plan some night outings. Pete is going to be a big part of my life now, and since the two of you have always been and will continue to be some of my favorite people, I need you all to get along."

"Whatever you want and need. You know I'll do it," I assure her, reaching an arm around her shoulders as I pull her into a small side hug. I meant what I said earlier. While I don't see Pete and me becoming super close, I'm open to giving him a chance.

"Oh, I know!" Ronnie perks up, sitting up straight as some of the liquid from her glass sloshes over the edge. I quickly dodge the spill, moving back into my spot. "Maybe tomorrow night we can have a barbecue at Pete's place. He's got this gorgeous house just off Main Street, and well, I suppose it'll be my house soon too. That way you can all see it."

"Yeah, sure," Blair agrees, taking another long draw from her straw.

"I'm in too. Just let me know what to bring," I add.

"Oh man, you're still such a suck-up, aren't you, Hastings?" Blair teases with another small giggle.

"What?" I ask, an amused grin tugging at my features.

"What are you? An actual adult? Offering to bring something to a barbecue," she further scoffs.

"I hope I'd be considered an adult. We are twenty-eight now, after all. I even have a nice big-boy job to prove it." I try to play along, not really sure where she's going with this. I also suspect that the now almost-empty second glass might be playing its part a little too well.

"Are you saying I don't have an adult job?" she asks, her eyes narrowing.

"Whoa!" Ronnie thankfully chimes in, seeming just as taken aback as I am by the direction this conversation has taken.

I hold up my hands. "No, not at all. If anything, you should know how proud I am of you. We're a bunch of high school teachers while you travel around the world taking pictures of some of the biggest and most well-known bands out there. Believe me, if anyone has a reason to be jealous, it's us," I assure her as Ronnie eagerly nods along next to me.

Maybe I shouldn't care so much about making this up to her, especially since she was the one coming at me with this weird hostility, but despite the distance and the way our friendship has grown apart these past few years, I find myself wanting and needing her approval. One thing I've unfortunately realized about myself is that I'll always care a bit too much about what Blair Bennett thinks about me.

"Yeah, no need to get upset. In fact, I think this calls for another round of drinks," Ronnie not so helpfully decides as the waitress sets down my plate of food before nodding her head as she goes off to put in their next order of margaritas. Something tells me I have a long night ahead.

4

FORD

TURNS OUT NOT DRINKING was the right decision, especially when it became clear that neither woman was capable of driving home. But now, as I carefully maneuver the two women up the stairs toward Miles Bennett's second-story apartment, I'm questioning all the life choices that led me to this point. They definitely aren't making this easy on me, especially as they keep giggling and insisting that they need to rest every few steps.

The fact that I have to deliver them to Miles in this condition makes it even worse. While being three years older than us may play a part, his overprotective nature has always been intimidating as hell. I may have surpassed him in height with my now six-foot frame by an inch or two, but that doesn't stop me from shaking like a leaf. The dude is not one to mess with, especially when it comes to his younger sister.

I've always suspected that Miles is capable of knocking me out with just one punch, and has only been waiting for me to give him the perfect opportunity to get away with it. Then again, I've also had a feeling he appreciates the way I look out for the girls. However, I can't help but feel apprehensive that if I take one step out of line, he won't hesitate to make me pay for it.

Considering his sister's short time in town, I doubt he'll be pleased to see her in such an intoxicated state, especially on her first night back. But who am I to be the one to determine how much someone should or shouldn't drink? Given our complicated history, I also imagine she wouldn't have been all that happy if I were to make any comments about how overboard she went tonight. Once upon a time, it probably would've been fine for me to say something, but I suspect those days are long gone.

"It's this one, right?" I ask Blair, pointing toward the door on our right.

Miles and I have never been close, so I've never been to his place. But in a small town like Evergreen Grove, it's common to know everyone's business and know where they live. It's both a blessing and a curse. Sure, it's nice that I didn't have to drive around town aimlessly while we tried to figure it out, but I suspect by tomorrow morning everyone in Evergreen is going to know that I drove a very drunk and giggly Blair and Ronnie home.

I know I no longer need to care or think about what Jenny and her family will have to say about this. However, my mind definitely goes there, especially since I know how much she has always hated and resented my tight-knit friendship with Blair Bennett.

"How am I supposed to know?" she asks through another loud giggle. Ronnie follows suit and the two of them fall into each other as if I just asked the most hilarious and ridiculous question in the entire world.

"Well, I guess there's only one way to find out," I decide as I release a defeated sigh. I raise my hand and give the door a firm knock. Thankfully, it isn't too late, and if I'm mistaken and we're in the completely wrong place, they shouldn't be too upset about the weird intrusion. However, Miles opening the door with a disappointed and hardened stare is equally intimidating—pretty sure I'm in a lose-lose situation.

I'm not sure if I'm relieved or not when I hear barking and shuffling behind the door, as someone comes to open it.

"Uh, hey Miles," I say with an optimistic smile as I awkwardly raise a hand in greeting. Thankfully it is his face that greets us. "I have a special delivery," I add, as he looks behind me to find Blair and Ronnie still snickering away.

It's clear he and Blair are related, with their strikingly similar blond hair and piercing blue eyes, and I'm once again reminded why I've always found the guy intimidating. I may be taller, but he's certainly not short. Instead of being on the lankier side like me, he's got muscles, which are very pronounced at the moment in his gray sweatpants and white T-shirt as he crosses his arms and shakes his head.

I silently will him not to kill me as he puffs out an annoyed breath of air, seeming to do everything he can to hold his frustration in. "Do me a favor and help me get them inside," he finally says. He walks outside and grabs his sister around the shoulders with a small, but hefty bulldog in tow, and does his best to guide her through the door. Clearly leaving Ronnie for me to handle.

I'd offered to take both girls to Ronnie's place, but they'd decided Miles would be upset if Blair didn't come home, and since they wanted to spend the night together, I went along with it. I've long since learned that if Ronnie and Blair have something in mind, you do it. Once they make a joint decision, it's set in stone—there's no changing their minds.

Yes, Ronnie and I have work tomorrow, and while I considered reminding her about this, neither of them seems worried about it, so I do my best not to care either. If they're not worried, then why should I be? Then again, it's always been my role to be the caretaker for the three of us.

"Come on, Ron," I softly encourage, as I place a hand on the back of her shoulder and follow Miles and Blair's lead.

Walking into his place for the first time, I have to admit, this very much feels like a Miles sort of place. It once again makes sense that he and Blair are siblings. The majority of the room is furnished with black, metal, and industrial-style furniture, with a huge leather couch in the middle of the living area. It exudes a strong bachelor aesthetic, especially with the various use of old car parts and license plates as decor. The atmosphere is exactly what you'd expect from someone who owns an auto-body shop.

"Ooooh, doggy," Ronnie coos as she clumsily pulls away from my grasp and falls to the ground, her legs spreading into a v-shape as she moves to give the bulldog some love. He practically jumps on her, covering her in wet, slobbery dog kisses. Luckily, this dog seems like a big softy, unlike his grumpy owner, who seems pretty annoyed that his dog is loving on Ronnie, of all people. "I didn't know you were a *daddy*."

"Ew." Blair shivers as she pushes herself out of her brother's grasp before plopping down onto the black leather sofa. "Please don't *ever* call my brother daddy again, and definitely not in *that* tone of voice."

"Yeah, I think I'd appreciate that too," Miles echoes as he heads into the kitchen, where he retrieves two water bottles from the fridge.

"Hey, I'm only calling it as I see it. Plus, come on, if he's worried about it, he shouldn't go around flaunting it in those sexy-ass gray sweatpants. Doesn't he know that we ladies go feral for that?" Ronnie asks, her attention still on the dog.

"Okay, ew." Blair gags. "That's my brother you're talking about."

"Not to mention the fact that you're engaged," I add as a final reminder, as Miles shifts uncomfortably. I understand that I'm not the ideal person to call anyone out, given my own circumstances, but it still feels important to point out.

"Oops, my bad," Ronnie giggles as Miles takes it in stride and instead focuses on handing out the water to the women.

"Drink," he commands, and luckily, they both seem to comply, at least for now.

"So, uh, sorry about this," I apologize, as I rub at the back of my neck. "Didn't mean to drop them on you like this."

"No, it's fine. I'm just glad you were there to drive them home." He brushes me off and folds his arms across his strong chest once more.

"Oh, well, yeah. Of course, I'd never let either of them drive home in this condition," I say, trying to hide my confusion.

I came in expecting a lecture. Instead, he's acting surprisingly relaxed.

"I know, and that's why I've always appreciated you being her friend," he says, giving my shoulder an unexpected pat as Blair moves to join Ronnie and the two of them continue to give that lucky little bulldog even more love and attention. It's crazy how envious I am of a dog right now, especially as she leans down to kiss the top of his head. What the hell is wrong with me?

"Really?" I ask, trying not to get distracted by the ladies as I turn to look over at Miles. "I always thought you hated me."

"You? No," he assures me with a shake of the head. "Others, perhaps," he continues, his gaze dropping toward Ronnie in a less than subtle way. "But with you, I always knew you had her back and would always look out for her."

A massive wave of guilt crashes over me. I haven't always been the friend she needed or deserved. More recently, I was likely one of the people who hurt her the most. As much as I hate it, I understand why she stopped answering my calls and texts—I also have to imagine it was my presence tonight that had her drinking so much more than usual. Maybe I'm giving myself way too much credit here, but in this case, I don't think I'm wrong.

"I try, but as you know, these two can often make things a little difficult," I add with an awkward chuckle.

"Oh, I get it. It's certainly not easy when Blair constantly has that little devil on her shoulder," he huffs, shaking his head.

"Are you talking about Ronnie?" I ask, my head rearing back in shock. "Because those two definitely play off each other. It's a combined effort," I add with a nervous laugh. Sure, Ronnie produces some ridiculous ideas, but she doesn't come up with them on her own, that's for sure.

"Maybe it is a combined effort, but she never seems to get herself into the same kind of trouble when Veronica isn't around. Hell, as much as it sucked having Blair move and be so far away, at least I know she isn't getting into the same stupid shit she gets into with *her*," Miles shoots back, once again nodding his head in Ronnie's direction.

I'm caught off guard by the obvious tone of annoyance and resentment. Admittedly, the girls did do some stupid shit over the years, and often tried to involve me in their crazy plans, but none of it seems worth holding that level of resentment and bitterness.

"Ronnie may have helped cause some of the trouble, but she always got us out of it. Even more importantly, it's obvious she'd do anything for Blair. As close as we are and as much as she'll always be one of my best friends, we'll never share the same kind of connection that they have. You have to know that Ronnie would never let anything bad happen to Blair," I say, doing my best to have my friend's back. Sure, he's made a few good points, and he isn't totally off base here, but it's also wrong to discount all the amazing things Ronnie has done for both of us. Hell, I wouldn't have agreed to be in her bridal party and embarrass myself in such a way if I didn't feel like I owed it to her.

"Maybe, but I'm still never going to be her biggest fan." Miles shrugs, and while I wish he'd take it easier on her, I figure that when it comes to Miles, this is as good as it's going to get.

"Well, I should probably get going," I decide, taking an awkward step back. "Ronnie, Blair," I call out to them. They both look up at me from their spots on the floor. "I'll see you both tomorrow night," I say with a nod as Blair all but ignores me and goes back to loving on the dog.

"Don't forget the coooooookies," Ronnie reminds me in a sing-song voice. I'm no baker, but I've always found those pretty hard to mess up, which is why they felt like the perfect thing to bring to the barbecue tomorrow—even if Blair had continued to give me shit for it all night.

"I won't," I promise, shaking my head in amusement. "And good luck to you," I say one last time to Miles as he rubs a palm over his face.

"Thanks, I'm going to need it."

Unfortunately, I don't think he's wrong.

5

BLAIR

THERE'S NOTHING MORE EMBARRASSING than waking up to realize that past you made some really questionable choices, especially when those choices involved you getting drunk in front of your childhood crush. Sadly, or maybe on the bright side, he's seen me do much worse. I'm pretty sure his wedding day will forever go down as my worst decision ever.

Unfortunately, this was not exactly how I envisioned spending my first night back in Evergreen Grove. It doesn't help that I likely disappointed Miles in the process. As a twenty-eight-year-old woman, I shouldn't care what my older brother thinks of my decisions and choices, but I also know how much he worries, and I completely understand why.

Growing up, we were all each other had. Sure, there was my grandma, who provided for us financially, but that was about all she did. More often than not, we were made to feel like burdens as she constantly reminded us that those were her golden years. She had already done her time as a parent, and she shouldn't have to be taking care of her son's kids too.

Although my father was more present than our mom, it can't be said that he did much for us—unless you count the terrible reputation he saddled us with. Everyone knew he was the town drunk and couldn't stay sober for the life of him.

He was extremely unreliable, getting fired from every job he applied to, and that was only if he didn't quit first. If there was anything you could count on from Bill Bennett, it was that he was good at quitting, or at least quitting the important stuff. The one thing he couldn't quit, or rather refused to, was the drugs and alcohol—not even for us kids, who desperately needed a caring parent.

That's precisely why I can't help but be disappointed in myself—I've always taken pride in being a responsible drinker, so this feels like a complete failure on my part.

Like Miles, I'm terrified of turning out like our father. I've also done my best to avoid drinking when I'm upset or emotional, but unfortunately, that's exactly what I did last night. While it's a horrible excuse, Ford's unexpected arrival threw me off. This was especially true given the bomb Ronnie dropped only moments before he walked right back into my life.

I'd known when I agreed to come home that I'd inevitably see him again, especially with us playing such prominent roles in the wedding party. But, nothing could've truly prepared me for the emotions I'd felt when I saw him again. It certainly doesn't help that the last time we spoke, it'd been when I was confessing my feelings as I begged and pleaded for him not to marry Jenny.

Yep! I was that girl who went all Meredith Grey on a guy, desperately pleading with him to pick me instead of her...on his freaking wedding day. Clearly, not my proudest moment.

It's also the reason I decided I needed to cut off all contact with him as I stopped answering or responding to his calls and texts. I should've just blocked his number, but I still haven't been able to bring myself to do it. As eager as my mind is to be done with him, my heart continues to fight me on this—unfortunately, my heart is a real pain in the ass, and refuses to let go.

He probably thinks this is my way of punishing him for not choosing me, but in reality, I'm punishing myself. I never should have put him in the situation where he felt like he had to choose. It'd be one thing if we'd actually dated and the feelings were mutual, but one kiss all the way back in high school is not a good enough reason to justify living in the past.

Clearly, I suck at moving on, especially after last night when my body had a visceral reaction to seeing him again. It was impossible to ignore the way my nerves hummed and buzzed with excitement, remembering just how good it felt to be in his presence.

As much as I like to tell myself that I've moved on, it became ridiculously clear that I might still be in love with my best friend. I mean, what kind of person gets excited over the news of hearing that their former best friend is going through a divorce? Yep, I'm a terrible person—this is the exact reminder of why I never deserved him in the first place.

I should've been the supportive friend he needed and deserved in that moment. What I should've done was offer a sympathetic ear and a comforting shoulder to cry on. Instead, I'd closed myself off and distanced myself from him and all the reemerging emotions I was experiencing by drinking way more than I should have. Pretty sure I gave him every reason in the book last night to remember exactly why he's better off without me. Yet, in typical Ford fashion, he showed up and made sure Ronnie and I made it home safely.

However, today, making things right with Ford is second to making things right with Miles. My first order of business was to stop by his shop with lunch. I even earned myself some additional brownie points by bringing food for the entire crew. I'm more than aware of how annoyed he was, especially since I'd not only forced him to take care of little ol' drunk me, but Ronnie as well.

I know that wasn't the easiest for him, especially since he's never liked her to begin with. Furthermore, since this is a small town with no Uber drivers, it was him who'd been forced to become her chauffeur and drop her off at her place bright and early so she could make it to work on time.

Fortunately, his love for food has always been a direct path to his heart, and although I still have some work to do, he seemed a little less grumpy afterward. I invited him to join us at tonight's barbecue at Pete and Ronnie's new place, but he not-so-politely declined, saying he got more than enough Veronica time last night. For once, he made no arguments and was more than okay with just dropping me off instead.

My next order of business is figuring out how to make it up to Ford, as the guilt over last night and the past few years gnaws at me. My heart races as I make my way up the paved pathway toward Pete West's stunning wraparound porch. I shouldn't be this worried, especially since once upon a time, being around Ford was as simple and easy as breathing. Now, a heavy weight of tension consumes every inch of me, making it now feel like work.

Instead, I try to focus on the house in front of me, as it becomes clear why Ronnie has been so eager to show it off. Being the mayor's daughter, she's always lived in a big and beautiful cookie-cutter house, but I'm completely taken aback by the sheer extravagance of this place, especially since there isn't anything else quite like it here in Evergreen.

This house is clearly a custom build, blending some of the more classic elements of Evergreen Grove with a more modern aesthetic. The white siding, black shutters, and black door add a stylish twist, giving it a beautiful contemporary vibe, one that definitely differentiates itself from the rest of the houses here in town.

While adjusting both the fresh veggie and fruit trays I'd picked up from the grocery store, I do my best to lift a hand to the doorbell and press. While I shouldn't be surprised, instead of a normal doorbell sound, a fun and playful tune can be heard. Thankfully, I don't have to wait long as the giant black door swings open.

"Blair!" Ronnie excitedly shrieks, racing out to grab the veggie tray, making my life a little easier. "What do you think? This place is amazing, right?"

"It is. It really is," I agree, stepping inside as she gestures for me to follow. Ronnie had mentioned that she had yet to move in and was waiting until after the wedding. However, the decor clearly reflects the influence of a woman, or at least someone with impeccable taste and meticulous attention to detail—even if that person clearly wasn't my best friend. It's as if this place was pulled straight out of the pages of a country farmhouse magazine. "Oh, wow. It just gets better," I add, my eyes widening as I look around.

"You hate it?" she asks, her smile collapsing.

"No, I never said that," I protest, even though I am a bit taken aback by the sheer extravagance of it all. Yes, this place looks great, but it's once again not the style of my best friend. Everything here is so...white. Ronnie's current place is a vibrant explosion of color, with cool and funky pieces adorning every inch.

"We've been best friends since kindergarten. You don't have to say it. I can read you like a book," she says, her lower lip jutting into a pout.

"I don't hate it," I say, reaching for her arm. "It's just not what I expected, but it's nice. Gorgeous even," I add, feeling compelled to do some damage control. Despite Ronnie's tough exterior, no one knows quite like I do just how sensitive she can actually be.

Even worse, I hate myself for letting her see my true thoughts. Apparently, it isn't just Miles and Ford I need to make things up to. I know I didn't have the best reaction yesterday when it came to her new hair and look, but it was such a shock to see how much has changed since I last saw her, especially since her long brown hair had always been something she prided herself on.

Maybe I'm just overreacting. Yes, we grew up together, and she's my best friend in the entire world, but it's not like I can pretend that although I've been away, everything here is going to remain the same. That's not fair to anyone, nor is it how life works, but it doesn't make it hurt any less to see everything and everyone moving on without me.

Sure, we've made a point of staying in contact through daily texts and the occasional video chat whenever we can, and she's even come to spend time with me while touring, but that still doesn't mean we know each other in the same way we once did. For all I know, maybe this is all part of her growing up. I just hope I'm not somehow getting left behind in all of this.

Thankfully, she seems to accept my answer, acknowledging it with a slight nod. Although, it's practically impossible to ignore the way her light diminishes, even with the fake smile plastered on her face.

"Wow," Ford's voice interrupts. While I'm no more than five minutes late to our agreed-upon time, it isn't a surprise to see that Ford arrived earlier. It's a comfort to know that at least some things have remained the same. He's always been the perpetual early arriver, and whenever Ronnie and I were running late, he did what he could to push us to hurry it up. "You look great," he says, his eyes sweeping over me in my midi black dress dotted with tiny white flowers, which I've paired with my favorite leather jacket and black Dr. Martens boots.

While I'm sure he isn't overthinking it like me, or if he even meant anything with those words, the butterflies in my stomach refuse to remain still. "Why do you sound so surprised?" I ask, my free hand resting on my hip as I tilt my head accusingly.

"If I drank as much as the two of you did last night I'd barely have been able to get out of bed this morning, let alone look so put together," he explains, his own cheeks warming with color as he attempts some damage control of his own. Yep, of course he didn't mean it like that.

"Oh, believe me, it took a lot of work for me to look this presentable," I assure him. "This is definitely not how I looked when I woke up, and the splitting headache didn't do me any favors either."

Maybe in the past, I could've gotten away with drinking so much and woken up like it was nothing, but as I near my thirties, I've definitely noticed a change in my tolerance level. I imagine the one saving grace was that as soon as we walked in his door, Miles pumped Ronnie and me full of water, food, and electrolytes.

"My secret weapon is the makeup. I can assure you it's doing all the heavy lifting right about now," Ronnie cuts in.

I nod my head. "That too."

"Well, either way, you both look great," Ford assures us, stepping forward to grab the final tray from my hands.

"Of course we do," Ronnie scoffs, as if it's all so obvious, knocking her hip into mine before nodding toward the doorway to the kitchen. "Come on. You need to meet Pete...or at least get to know him better since I know you've met before, but uh, you know what I mean," she rambles with a dismissive wave of her hand.

I let out a soft laugh. "I know exactly what you mean, and once again, don't worry. I'm sure I'll love him. If he's Ronnie-approved, then I can't imagine not liking him." It's obvious she's nervous, and while a part of me feels like that's probably warranted, I don't want her stressing, especially so close to her big day. "I'll love him, right, Ford?"

Ford's eyes widen, his mouth falling open before he shakes his head. "Oh, yeah. Of course, he's great," he says, giving me all the confirmation I need. He doesn't like Pete either. Maybe he doesn't hate him, but it's clear he's not his favorite person.

"Exactly, he's great," Ronnie agrees with a nod, her voice betraying her fake enthusiasm with a slight rise in pitch.

I wish I could extend my hand and reassure her that everything will be alright, but truthfully, I'm also nervous about meeting this guy. I already had one best friend whose spouse I didn't get along with, which ultimately led to a strained relationship, and I can't have that happen again.

Then again, maybe I'm stressing for nothing. The situations are completely different. Yes, I love Ronnie, but not in the same way I loved Ford. If anything, we're all likely making this into a much bigger deal than it needs to be.

Thankfully, Ford takes the lead as he walks into the kitchen first, followed by Ronnie, with me trailing at the end. Everything's fine. Tonight will be great. It has to be.

6

FORD

I'M KICKING MYSELF AS we walk into the kitchen. What the hell is wrong with me? Not only did I just tell Blair how good she looks, but I let myself get caught off guard by her question.

No, I don't like Pete. He's a pretentious know-it-all with a superiority complex. It's just not my style to tell someone that I dislike their significant other. I hated how obvious it'd been back in the day when Blair and Ronnie openly disliked Jenny, and while I now realize it may have been for good reason, I still don't want to do it back to either of them.

I fucking hate Max Storm, and while that guy is a million times worse than Pete, I've never shit-talked him to Blair—it only seems fair that I give Ronnie the same level of treatment and respect.

Okay, so maybe Blair was right. Jenny and I weren't right for each other, which is made even more blatantly obvious given our current separation and impending divorce, but that was my decision and my mistake to make. If Pete ends up being a mistake for Ronnie, then it's her choice to make as well.

Plus, they do often say opposites attract, so while Ronnie and Pete have never made the most sense to me, it doesn't matter. If Ronnie says he's the one, then I have to believe her. As her best friend, my only job is to be there for her through the good and the bad.

"So, I see they weren't lying when they said you never show up on time," Pete starts, calling Blair out as soon as we walk into the kitchen.

Pete clearly spared no expense when he had this place built. While it feels a bit cold and sterile for my liking, it must be exactly how he wanted it. The amount of white in this kitchen and the rest of the house is a little overwhelming and a bit too much for me, but he seems to like it, given his choice of white cabinets, backsplash, and countertops. The only thing that seems to break the monotony are the silver appliances. I just have to hope or assume that Ronnie will add her own artistic flair and creative touch when she moves in after the wedding.

I fight the urge to roll my eyes as Pete wipes his hand on his "Kiss the Cook" apron before moving to offer Blair a handshake.

"Oh, come on, I'm not *that* bad," she defends, seeming to play along as she gives him her hand while I set the veggie tray on the counter next to the wide array of food that's been prepared for our small barbecue. There's no way the four of us can eat all of this, but it doesn't come as a surprise that Pete has gone above and beyond. In fact, showing off has always seemed to be one of his favorite pastimes. "If this was old me, I would have been a good thirty minutes late. Five minutes is a clear improvement," she adds with a small laugh.

"Look at you growing up," I tack on, needing to defend her a bit. While it's okay for me and Ronnie to poke fun at her inability to ever be on time, it's not okay for Pete to do it.

"Well, you know me. I've always been on Blair Standard Time, so if anything, you all should be glad that it's gotten closer to the actual time," she plays along, sending a beautiful grin my way. My pulse quickens, and an annoying jolt of electricity zings down my spine. I hate how she can still send my entire body into complete disarray, all from a simple smile.

"Oh yes, I'll never forget BST," Ronnie laughs as she places the other tray on the granite countertop.

"Well, you know what they say; being on time is the first step to being respected; it shows you value not just your time, but the time of others," Pete says, clearly not joining in on the joke or the fun. My lips fall into a narrow line.

Blair's jaw flexes before her eyes harden in his direction. It's clear she wasn't expecting to be rebuked or called out, but luckily, Ronnie has her back and swiftly smacks Pete in the arm.

"Pete! Be nice," she scolds, and while there's still a smile on her face, I'm sure we all know her well enough to hear the warning in her tone. "Blair's the best, and I will not accept any slander on her name whatsoever," she adds, pointing a finger in his direction.

"Well, maybe he isn't totally wrong. I could make more of an effort. I don't want anybody thinking I don't respect the time of others," Blair says, her voice dripping with overly sweet sarcasm, clearly annoyed by being called out by this guy, despite the actual words coming out of her mouth.

"Don't sweat it, Blair. Those who actually know you know that couldn't be further from the truth. You've done nothing wrong and have nothing to prove here. Plus, you know what they say: don't make assumptions because it only makes an ass out of you and me," I blurt out before I can stop myself. I'm not normally an antagonistic person, but nobody gets to call out my friends like that, especially not some prick like Pete.

Our friendship may be strained, but as Blair flashes me a smile that's equal parts amusement and gratitude, I have no regrets. Even if Pete was the type of guy who reacted with violence and chose to take out his anger on me, I'd do it all over again. Especially if it means I get to catch another glimpse of that perfect smile of hers—the kind of smile that feels like a burst of sunshine on a cloudy day—and these days, given what I have going on in my life, that's very much needed.

"On that note, let's eat," Ronnie cuts in before Pete can say anything else, which is probably for the best.

It might seem like I'm looking for a fight, but that couldn't be further from the truth. Like Ronnie, all I want is for everyone to be happy and get along. I'd love nothing more than to be wrong about Pete, and I'd love for Blair to see a side of our friend's fiancé that I've yet to see, putting all my concerns to rest.

"Yes, I'm starving," Blair agrees, looking my way one last time, that same mesmerizing grin of hers offering a small glimmer of hope that maybe, just maybe, tonight won't be as terrible as I thought it'd be. Sure, we're going to be eating and hanging out with one of my least favorite people, but if Blair keeps looking at me like that, maybe things won't be entirely insufferable.

"This cheesecake is amazing," Blair coos as we get started on dessert, her eyes drifting back in ecstasy, a move that has me thinking way too many dirty thoughts. I shift in my seat as I wonder what exactly I'd have to do for her to make that face again, but hopefully for an entirely different reason.

"Well, we have Pete to thank for that." Ronnie smiles, placing a hand on her fiancé's shoulder. Thankfully, he has cooled it with his asshole-type commentary.

Okay, maybe not completely, since he's spent the majority of the night talking about himself and all of his accomplishments, leaving little room for anyone else to speak. I mean, how many times do we have to listen to him ramble on about how he's the youngest councilman in town history and how he plans to one day take over as mayor? At least it makes it much easier to keep control of myself and my wandering brain, since every time he speaks, it's the equivalent of a bucket of cold water being dumped all over you.

It could be that I already dislike the hell out of him, and maybe he isn't as bad as I've been leading myself to believe, but with each stolen glance in Blair's direction, it's obvious we're on the same page, as her eyes look completely glazed over, making me feel less alone in my line of thinking.

"In fact, Pete is responsible for most of this dinner. He's such an amazing cook, right?" Ronnie continues, her eyes filled with pure adoration as she looks toward her fiancé.

"Well, I've sort of been forced to take over that role since Veronica here is a disaster in the kitchen," Pete says, placing his arm around her shoulder. "I don't think she's made one meal that hasn't been burned or undercooked," Pete chuckles, his voice tinged with an annoying amount of condescension. "But don't worry. I've already got your next birthday present planned out—cooking classes." I'm sure he expected us to laugh along with him, but instead, his "joke" falls completely flat.

"I hope you're kidding, because that's the last thing Ronnie would want as a birthday present," Blair states, devoid of any and all amusement.

"Not at all. I think it's the perfect present for her. Don't you think, babe?" he asks, as we all glance in Ronnie's direction.

"I'll be happy with whatever you decide to get me," she answers as I cock an eyebrow. I get not wanting to cause any trouble, but normally Ronnie isn't afraid to voice her true opinion, and I have to say, I'm with Blair on this one. There's no way that'd be something she'd enjoy.

"Well, in that case, I'll just have to get you something *extra* special this year. Something I *know* you'll actually want," Blair counters.

"Oh hush," Ronnie brushes her off as she swats her hand toward Blair. "I'm honestly not that picky. Maybe I would enjoy learning some culinary skills. Cooking is an art, after all, so maybe a lesson or two could be kind of fun."

"Oh, babe, it's *definitely* going to take more than a lesson or two to get you to where you need to be," Pete cuts in. My hands ball into fists in my lap. Despite my efforts to see the good in him, he's making it extremely challenging to find even the slightest redeeming quality.

"Maybe you just don't know your fiancé as well as you think you do, because if anybody can do something they set their mind to, it's Ronnie," I say, folding my arms. "If she wants to be a good cook, then she'll do it. She's a beast at everything she tries."

"I'll believe it only when I see it," Pete says with an obnoxious chuckle, rolling his eyes, completely oblivious to the fact that none of us find this even remotely funny.

"That's too bad because—" Blair starts to say, but Ronnie stands up, interrupting before she can complete that thought, which may be for the best, given the way her icy-blue eyes are blazing in his direction.

"Let's take some of this inside. Pete, can you help me bring in some of the dishes?" she asks, reaching for his hand as she not-so-gently pulls him up.

Despite his lack of enthusiasm and clear annoyance, he seems to decide not to fight her on this. "Yeah, sure," he gives in, reaching for an empty plate.

In silence, we hand over our dishes, before Blair reaches for the open bottle of wine and proceeds to pour herself another glass. "So," she says, after lifting it to her lips once Ronnie and Pete are inside and out of earshot, "he's an ass, right? It's not just me being overprotective?"

"No, it's not just you. He's definitely an ass."

"Damn. I hate this for her," she sighs, setting her glass down on the table. "I want to be supportive, and I want to like him, but I don't. I'm actually worried that if I don't get out of here soon, I'm going to end up saying something I'll eventually regret."

"You don't think it's too early to dip out?" I ask, looking through the glass door to make sure they're still out of earshot. I'm not surprised it's taking a while. I have to imagine that Ronnie is inside giving him a piece of her mind, or at least that's what the old Ronnie would've done.

"I hope not. I mean, we did dinner and dessert. That should be good enough, right? Because if not, I think I'm going to get myself kicked out of the wedding party," she laughs, despite the fact that there is little to no amusement in the sound.

"Ronnie would never kick you out, but I get it. I'm starting to lose my patience with him, too."

"We're back," Ronnie calls as she and Pete walk into the backyard hand-in-hand. I want to believe it's a good thing that they seem to be okay, and that there doesn't seem to be any lingering tension between the two of them. Still, it's incredibly hard to be happy for the couple when I still can't make sense of what she sees in him.

Ronnie has dated plenty off-and-on throughout the years. Some guys were absolutely great and balanced her out really well, and some were complete duds, but at this point, I'd take the biggest dud over Pete fucking West.

"Actually, Ford here was just offering to give me a ride home. I'm starting to feel a bit guilty over not spending enough time with Miles. Instead of having my brother come and pick me up, yet again, I figured I'd surprise him."

I'm not sure her thought process on this was entirely on point, since if she wanted more time with her brother, it would make sense for him to pick her up, but I'm thankful that her excuse includes me as well.

"Oh, yeah. Of course. I understand." Ronnie nods, though a small pout forms on her face. "I guess I can't completely monopolize your time at home."

"And hey, we still have our fittings tomorrow, so I'll see you as soon as you're off work," Blair offers, doing her best to make up for our quick escape.

"Yes, definitely." Ronnie attempts to smile, even if it doesn't quite reach her eyes.

I should feel bad, and I suppose I do, but more than anything, the prevailing feeling taking over is relief as we all stand up, give hugs, and say our goodbyes. I can't pretend for even a single second longer that Pete West is even close to being a likable guy. The only decent thing about him is his cooking, and that's not saying much.

However, as Blair and I make our exit, and it's just the two of us walking toward my car, I realize that I'm about to be alone with her for the first time since she confessed her feelings toward me right before my wedding. Instead of relief, I'm now consumed by unadulterated panic. What in the hell did I just willingly walk myself into?

7

BLAIR

MY OVERWHELMING DESPERATION TO avoid being near Pete clearly clouded my judgment, since I'm now alone in a car with Ford, of all people—the number one person I planned to avoid spending any time with during my stay at home.

I'm probably overreacting. No, I'm definitely overreacting. I can't even count the number of times I've previously sat in the passenger seat next to Ford, at least whenever Ronnie didn't beat me to calling shotgun. Then, of course, there were plenty of times when it was just the two of us. However, even with my unbearable crush on him all those years ago, it never felt as awkward as this.

Why, oh why, didn't I think of using the universal "get out of jail free" card? I could have faked a headache and suggested that Miles be the one to come and pick me up. Then again, Ford could have always suggested that he be the one to take me, which would have ultimately led to me being right back here anyway, but at least it wouldn't have been me walking into the lion's den by choice.

"So, I should probably say thanks for the ride," I nervously chuckle, crossing my legs as I look down and pick at the black polish on my thumbnail.

"No problem. I'm just glad you included me in your escape plan. My usual excuse is that I need to lesson plan, but since I already told both of you how I'm all prepped for the next few weeks, I couldn't exactly get away with that particular excuse."

I heave a loud sigh. "I feel bad, but hopefully now that I know what I'm in for and know what to expect from him, I can keep myself better in check. He's definitely not an easy person to be around."

"Yeah, I probably should have warned you ahead of time," he admits, and I can't help the unamused laugh that escapes as he glances my way, raising his brow.

"I'm pretty sure that's not the only thing I should've been warned about before I came back," I mutter, immediately wishing I could take it back. It's not his fault that the thing that's bothering me most is the one thing Ronnie had told me in confidence. However, part of me feels like ever since I've been home, I've been hit with blindside after blindside. I'm not sure how much more of this I can take.

"Like what?" he asks, eyebrows raising, before realization dawns on his face and his mouth dips open. "Oh." He nods his head in understanding. "So, I'm guessing she told you then?"

"That you and Jenny are separated and getting divorced? Yeah, she told me."

Ford's hands tightly grip the steering wheel, causing his veins to visibly bulge before he finally releases a large exhale of breath. "Yeah, unfortunately, things haven't been the best between us for a while now. I know the gossip is making the rounds, but I was kind of hoping to keep it under wraps until after Ronnie's big day. The last thing I want is for any of my shitty drama to somehow overshadow her wedding."

"I know it probably doesn't sound that believable coming from me of all people, but I really am sorry. I know how much you loved her, or I guess maybe still do..." I offer, inwardly cringing at how awful of a job I'm doing, but what exactly am I supposed to say to this? *I hated your fiancé, and I never wanted you to marry her in the first place, so you're getting exactly what you deserve for not choosing me?*

"It's fine. It is what it is," he curtly responds, making it clear this isn't something he wants to discuss any further. Truthfully, I don't want to talk about it either, even if I was the one who brought it up.

However, despite knowing I need to drop it, I can't seem to help myself. "I just hope you know..." I begin, shifting in my seat as I angle my body toward his. "It was never anything against you, or really even Jenny, back then. I was stupid for doing what I did on your wedding day. That wasn't fair of me, and I hate that I did that. To this day, it's still one of my biggest regrets, and that's the only reason that I felt like I needed to cut off all contact."

I try to gauge his reaction, but I find myself at a loss. Despite our history, I can't seem to figure him out; his expression remains inscrutable as he tightly grips the wheel, his eyes remaining fixed on the road ahead.

I continue. "It wasn't because I was mad at you for not choosing me. You shouldn't have, and it was so unfair of me to even think that I had the right to do something like that. It was a me thing, and if anything, I was the one who needed the distance and the space to finally move on so I could truly get over you once and for all. I just hope that I didn't ruin everything. I know things can never go back to how they used to be, but maybe while I'm home we can at least have something that resembles a friendship. If there's one thing we still have in common, it's Ronnie, and I'm sure we can both agree that she deserves to have the best wedding day possible, even if it is with some loser we both hate and despise," I ramble, clearly struggling to redeem myself.

"So, we're still going to let her marry him? We're not going to try and parent-trap her or something to try and stop the wedding?" he asks, the workings of a smile slowly forming on his face, thankfully seeming to ignore my big-ass rant about how stupid I'd been at his own wedding.

Perhaps I should feel annoyed, considering I'd just poured my heart out to him for the second time. However, I'd much rather let it go and avoid delving into what would likely be an awkward and uncomfortable conversation.

"Oh, believe me, I've learned my lesson. I'm never going to try and stop another wedding again."

"Yeah, I guess that's smart. Knowing Ronnie, she'd be stubborn and be like me and marry him anyway. Plus, weirdly enough, somehow I think she actually loves the guy."

I shake my head. "I don't get it. He doesn't even seem like her type."

"I dunno," he starts, shrugging his shoulders, "I could see her being with someone a bit more serious, someone that balances her out a bit."

I tilt my head and let out an annoyed puff of air. "There's balance, and then there's someone that squashes who you are and changes your personality completely. It's like he's molding her into some weird little Stepford wife, and I hate it. It's as if he's stripping away all of her best and most unique qualities."

"So you've picked up on that too?" he asks, glancing over quickly before looking back at the road ahead.

"It's pretty hard to miss. I mean, I know it's such a little thing, especially since hair grows back, but even going as far as to change her looks just drives me insane. She's easily one of the most beautiful women in the entire world and he somehow decided that wasn't enough and needed to change that about her too," I huff, folding my arms.

"So what do we do? Should we say something?"

"I don't think so. Like I said, I've more than learned my lesson about that. Obviously, I don't want her to have to learn the same lesson as you, but isn't this her choice to make? I mean, she supports me in my relationship with Max, and don't worry," I assure him, since I'm well aware of the fact that he never liked my boyfriend either, "I get that we're toxic, but her saying that isn't going to change my mind. My feelings are my own and if it takes getting my heart broken by him over and over again, then that's how it has to be. I'm the one that has to figure that out."

"Speaking of Max..." he trails off, seeming to consider whether or not this is a topic he wants to broach. "Are you really thinking about getting back with him when you leave?"

I shrug one shoulder and turn to look out the window. "I don't know. It's complicated."

"It just seems..." he hesitates. "I don't know. I just don't get the two of you together. Well, I mean, I get it to a certain extent since you both seem to be free spirits and have some similar passions, but if all you do is fight and break up, why stay with him? Why put yourself through that?"

"Like I said, it's complicated. Sure, we fight, but we have our good moments too. Plus, he keeps things exciting, and well, you know me, I've always needed a little bit of excitement in my life. I don't do well with monotony."

"There's a big difference between monotony and something that's functional and healthy. Please tell me that you know that?" he begs, doing his best to sound playful, but it's obvious he's concerned. I can't say I blame him either, if he or Ronnie kept dating someone who constantly cheated on them, I'd definitely have something to say about it too.

"What about you and Jenny?" I ask, turning the tables onto him.

His eyebrows knit together. "What about us?"

"I don't know. What happened? Why did things end?"

I ultimately know it's not my business, but clearly I've always had an issue with boundaries. Plus, the last time I saw the two of them was when they were having their first dance together, lovingly gazing into each other's eyes, clearly madly in love.

"I don't know if I can blame it on any one thing. I just...I don't think we were right for each other. Yes, we loved and cared about one another, but all the passion was gone. Instead of enjoying each other's company, it was like we were just tolerating each other, and that's not a life I want to live. I don't want to just tolerate the person I'm with. I don't want to settle. There needs to be passion and excitement, and recently, or not so recently, all of that was missing, and I know she felt that too."

"So was it you who ended things then?" I ask, knowing that I'm crossing a line, or at least walking dangerously close to one, but it's something I desperately need to know.

"I brought it up first, but in the end, it was something she agreed with too. We both knew that things weren't working."

"So, Ronnie had mentioned this being a separation, does that mean that there's a possibility for any sort of reconciliation?" I ask, holding my breath. It shouldn't matter. This no longer affects me, but I'm overcome with an overwhelming need to know where he stands, even if it's about something I'm no longer entitled to.

When I did what I did at his wedding and cut off contact afterward, I gave up all the rights I once had as a friend to know the intimate details of his life, but now, being in such close proximity, I'm feeling all mixed up. So many of the amazing memories we shared together have come flooding back these past few days, giving the illusion that we could possibly have what we once had, but I get that it's nothing but a pipe dream—he owes me nothing, and rightfully so.

"I wouldn't say there's no chance of that happening, but I'm pretty sure we're both on the same page. Last time we spoke, she requested more space and seemed to want and need this separation more than I did."

I'm not entirely sure what answer I was looking for, but the mere idea of a reconciliation between him and Jenny is like a dagger to my heart, reopening the wound I'd so desperately hoped was healed. I should want him to be happy, even if that means he lives happily ever after with someone else, but the thought of it feels like too massive of an undertaking. I'm not that strong, and clearly, I'm not that good of a person. Perhaps it was for the best that I left and cut off contact, since I have to imagine he's been much better off without having selfish little ol' me around.

"I'm sorry," I apologize again, not sure what exactly I'm saying sorry for, but even so, this time, it actually feels genuine.

"Don't worry about it. It's not your fault," he says, his voice fading into silence as I do the same, the air growing heavy between us.

Luckily, the drive from Pete's place isn't too far from my brothers. Then again, when you're in Evergreen Grove, nothing is too far away.

"Thanks for the ride," I say, unbuckling my seatbelt as he pulls into the parking lot.

"You want me to walk you up?" he asks, slowing the car down as he seems to debate with himself about whether he should park or if he should just pull up in front of the stairs.

"I can thankfully walk myself up tonight," I laugh, brushing a long strand of hair behind my ear before reaching for the handle once he's come to a complete stop. "So, I'll see you tomorrow then?"

He nods. "You'll see me tomorrow."

I know I shouldn't care either way, especially after our intense conversation about his heartbreak and my potential reconciliation with my ex. However, a fire kindles low in my stomach at the thought of seeing him again, and so soon.

I'm only supposed to be here for a few weeks, and while I had initially hoped that our paths would rarely cross and we'd only have to be in each other's company for the bare minimum, I exasperatingly catch myself longing for more.

"Good." I smile one last time as I maneuver myself up and out of the seat. With a final wave, I shut the door and walk toward the stairs, closing my eyes and wrinkling my nose.

Despite all the giddy butterflies floating around in my stomach, this isn't healthy. I'd been so convinced that I'd overcome my silly, childish crush on my best friend long ago, but now I'm starting to realize that some habits are impossible to shake. He's an addiction that I'm not sure I'll ever get past. Maybe I'm a lot more like my father than I'd care to admit.

8

BLAIR

"OKAY, WOW!" I EXCLAIM, completely taken aback as my mouth falls open in awe. My best friend is drop-dead gorgeous. There's no denying that, but there's a certain significance that comes along with seeing your best friend in her wedding dress for the first time—it's a moment I know I'll never forget.

"So you like it then?" Ronnie asks, her hands in the pockets of the dress as she swishes the skirt back and forth.

"Of course I like it," I promise, tilting my head to the side as I do my best to capture every detail. Would this be the dress I'd pick out for her or assume she'd pick? No. Although it doesn't give off Ronnie vibes, I can still appreciate the dress for its elegant beauty.

When I think about Ronnie, her style has always stood out as completely distinct and one-of-a-kind. While this particular gown embodies the ideal wedding dress with its A-line shape and elegant off-the-shoulder design, it lacks any additional flair. There are no unique features, or frills or thrills that differentiate it from any other wedding dress.

"But you feel like it's missing that certain je ne sais quoi, don't you?" she asks, practically reading my mind. Then again, I've never been all that good at hiding my thoughts.

"I wouldn't necessarily say that." I shrug, biting my lower lip as my eyes drift down the dress. "I mean, there isn't much going on, but maybe that's the beauty of it. It makes you, as the bride, the main attraction. Seriously, you're truly the most beautiful bride I have ever seen in my life." Wanting to reassure her, I step forward and reach out for her hands as she takes them out of her pockets and places them in my own.

"Thanks, Blair. I appreciate that," she says, her face relaxing into a smile as I give her hands a small squeeze.

"Holy shit!" Ford's voice rings out only moments after the bell above the front door rings. "You look amazing," he adds, his face lighting up in pure adoration.

"That's what I was just telling her," I say, releasing her hands as Ronnie once again turns around to take in her appearance through the large mirror.

"Now it's your turn," Ronnie says as our eyes meet through the reflection. "We just need to pray that the measurements you sent me were correct, because we don't have enough time to order a new one," she says, voicing her nerves. I understand her anxiety. I'm sure I'd be a hot mess too if I was less than two weeks away from my wedding.

Plus, if this is her version of being a bridezilla, I'd say I've gotten off pretty easy.

"Don't worry. I not only double-checked the measurements, but I triple-checked them. I get how important this is," I promise her. Not only did I not want to be the person responsible for messing up an important part of her wedding, but I also didn't want to have to witness Ronnie lose it. Despite her typically easygoing nature, there have been a couple of instances where I've seen her lose her temper, and I definitely don't want to be the one responsible for reawakening that sleeping monster.

"It's just back here, dear," Karen, the elderly dress shop owner tells me as she places a hand on the back of my shoulder and leads me toward one of the two dressing rooms.

Since this is the only formal dress shop in all of Evergreen Grove, it's, of course, not my first time here. It's where everyone from town comes for any fancy occasion, and where I got every homecoming and prom dress.

I'd already seen pictures online of the dress that Ronnie had chosen for her bridesmaids and had specifically ordered for this event. While the dresses here in the store aren't necessarily bad, the selection can, at times, be small and dated.

While there's that running joke of brides picking the ugliest dresses for their wedding party, if only to make themselves stand out more, the second I see the dress on the hanger, a soft gasp leaves my lips. It's gorgeous, and it's hard not to reach out as my hand moves over the soft dusty-blue silk. It's perfect. At least something from this wedding shows that Ronnie's put her mark on it.

"Just let me know if you need any help. I'll be right out here," Karen assures before closing the fabric curtain to give me some privacy.

Eager, yet filled with a slight hint of anxiety that I had somehow taken my measurements wrong, I quickly undress and step into the silky fabric. Like Ronnie's, it also has an A-line shape with sleeves that fall perfectly off the shoulder, but instead of leaving them completely bare, there are thin straps for added support. Even more stunning is the boning in the corset, which cinches in my waist in the most flattering and perfect way. There's also a fun slit in the skirt. Thankfully, I shaved this morning, so no mishaps there—not that I have anyone to truly impress. Other than Ronnie, it doesn't matter what anyone thinks, not even Ford.

"Okay, Karen. I think I could use a zip-up," I holler. While it seems to fit just right, the true test is whether it will zip or not.

"Oh, wow. Ronnie has some great taste, doesn't she?" Karen coos as she opens the curtain just enough to let herself slip inside. "You look so beautiful, dear," she further compliments as she tugs at the zipper. Thank God, it zips.

"Thanks, Karen."

I smile, taking in the view as I move from side to side, admiring the way the dress hugs my body and fits like a glove. There is also no denying that it shows off the ladies perfectly. At this point, the only thing that needs to be adjusted is the length, but given my height, and pretty much every dress I've ever tried on, that checks out.

"You guys need to see this," Karen insists, her excitement evident as she slips out first, and I follow.

I'm not sure why I'm so nervous, especially around these two of all people, but the awkwardness persists as I scrunch my nose and bite my bottom lip. I've honestly never been one to love a ton of attention. "What do you think?" I ask, my gaze finding Ronnie first, seeking her approval above all others.

"Wow!" she squeals with uncontainable excitement and clasps her hands together underneath her chin, "it's perfect."

Wanting Ford's opinion next, I swivel my head in his direction, finding him comfortably seated on the small couch positioned in front of the grand mirror and modeling stand. I don't want to read too much into things, but his body language tells me he approves as he goes from leaning back to sitting up straight, his mouth slightly ajar.

I don't want to overthink this, but I can't ignore the way his eyes meticulously examine every inch of the dress, lingering on the slit that shows off my leg before finally locking his gaze with mine once more.

"Well?" I prod, not sure why I need to hear it, but I do.

"It's...wow. That's all I can say. Wow," he stammers, his mouth still open, before shaking his head as we finally break eye contact and both turn toward Ronnie.

A sly grin crosses her features, accompanied by a knowing nod—I swear, if she says anything.

Luckily, before anyone can say another word, Karen quickly ushers me onto the small stand, wasting no time in starting her task as she skillfully sticks pins into the bottom of the dress.

Unfortunately, it's hard not to hyper-fixate on things, as the image of the way Ford looked at me consumes my thoughts. I know that I'm likely blowing this out of proportion, especially since he's going through a fucking divorce. Of course, he's not sitting here pining after me, especially not after the way I ghosted him these past few years.

It's time to face reality and realize that any chance of us happening is over and done with. Plus, I refuse to repeat the same mistake I made in high school and focus all my attention on one person, and the wrong person at that. Sure, Jenny may be leaving the picture, but I'm confident he has no interest in picking up something that never really even had time to begin in the first place.

Sure, after he and Jenny broke up the night of our high school graduation, Ford and I may have shared a fleeting kiss. But when Jenny showed up the next day as we set off for our big graduation trip, instead of choosing to spend his time with me, he and Jenny were practically inseparable, and by the end, like always, the two of them were back together.

The last thing I need to get mixed up in again is him and his drama. He is free to say that everything is over and done with in that relationship, but I know better. He'll never likely fully be over Jenny, and I'm not looking to be some consolation prize until he can get back with her. I refuse to play that role a second time.

As Karen finishes the final touches, Ronnie excuses herself to get undressed, with Karen following shortly after to help her.

As I look up in the mirror and catch Ford's eyes through the reflection, there's an inexplicable energy in the air. Then again, maybe it's just the dress making it hard to breathe. It certainly isn't helping, though, that his eyes remain fixated on mine, almost as if he's refusing to look away first.

"You're free to undress now too, dear," Karen calls from behind the curtain, causing me to jump in surprise.

"Okay, thanks," I reply, trying not to look back at Ford, especially since I'm sure my cheeks are now flushed with color.

Needing distance, I waste no time moving down from the small pedestal before disappearing behind the curtain. I exhale a long, overdue breath, allowing my head to drop forward as it leans against the mirror's cool surface. *Pull yourself together, woman!*

As I try to reach behind me, it doesn't take long to realize that before I can start undressing, I need someone to unzip the back. "Shit," I softly curse. I open the curtain and glance back and forth, only to realize that Ford is the only one around, as Karen still seems to be assisting Ronnie.

Ford's eyebrows furrow. "Everything okay?"

"Oh, uh yeah. I just need some help getting out of this thing," I say, pointing toward the back of my dress with my thumb.

It's now his turn to look around nervously before his gaze lands back on me as he seems to come to the same conclusion. "I guess I could help."

It shouldn't be a big deal, just a simple act of unzipping, since it's not like I'm asking him to completely undress me. Yet, there's an unexplained feeling of intimacy that accompanies this action. Is this really the best idea? I can pretend all I want I'm over him, but deep down, I know that I've only ever been lying to myself.

"Really?" I ask, my voice betraying my outward demeanor as it falters and goes up an octave. "Okay, yeah. Sure." I give in with a casual shrug trying to play it cool, even if the shaking in my voice says otherwise. This doesn't have to be a big deal, especially if I don't make it one.

Standing back, I hold up the curtain for him as he stands and makes his way over. While these rooms are large enough for two people, I can't help but notice our closeness as he shuts the curtain and positions himself behind me, and the air around us charges with electricity all over again.

Luckily, he doesn't seem to be fazed as he wordlessly unzips my dress, but my body begins to ripple and pulse with desire as his hand slows down. Instead of rushing and getting over with it, he takes his sweet time undoing the top, creating a painfully unhurried and intimate atmosphere as my eyes meet his darkening, hungry gaze in the mirror.

What is it with us and a mirror that seems to be so damn intense?

The dress starts to fall, causing the nice push-up effect that it'd had with my cleavage to lessen as I lift one hand to keep it up and prevent him from getting an indecent view. With our eyes still fixed on one another, his gaze alone practically undoes me; a shiver runs down my spine, causing goosebumps to rise along my arms as a blend of anticipation and longing take hold, and my body hums with need.

The desire to prolong this experience overwhelms me, causing my body to react involuntarily as my backside falls flush against him. He somehow manages to move in even closer, as something hard presses into my back.

He holds my stare, his hand moving even more achingly slow as the zipper finally descends to the very bottom, only inches above my ass. Given that I've never been one to fully think things through, I hadn't thought about the fact that I'd need to wear a strapless bra, so instead, I'd decided it best to just go without for the day's fitting and had tossed it into the small pile of clothing near our feet.

I'm left with no regrets as my back is now completely bare to him, and I can't help but savor the sensation as his hand moves upward, his fingers tracing a soft line along my spine, sending tingles and warmth throughout my entire body. I finally break eye contact and close my eyes, embracing this perfect moment as I rest my head against his chest.

Once his fingers reach my shoulder, his other hand joins in as my eyes slowly flutter open. I need to watch as his large palms trace a scorching line of heat in their path, brushing the thin straps down my shoulders, bringing my top dangerously close to exposing my breasts to him; I've never craved anything more.

Not only do I want him to see me in a state of undress, I ache for him to touch me there, and so many other places that I've craved for so long. He seems to be thinking the same thing as his hands move forward and over my collarbones.

"Everything okay in there?" Karen interrupts.

Startled, Ford jerks his hands away from my body as if he's been singed by a hot stove.

"*Shit*," I inwardly curse, exhaling the breath that I've been holding. "Yes, I'm good. I'll be out in a minute," I assure her, meeting Ford's eyes once more, but instead of holding my gaze, he immediately looks away and down at his shoes.

"I'm uh, going to... uh, I'll just be out there," he rambles, pointing toward the lobby before excusing himself.

What. The. Hell. Just. Happened?

A part of me has always fantasized about and yearned for a moment like this, but I never actually believed it could happen. Even worse, it's not like I can tell Ronnie about this.

This week and the next are about her; not me and my silly drama. While it may have felt so right in the moment, and while a huge part of me is disappointed that it hadn't gone any further when it was just getting good, the overwhelming emotion I feel now is relief.

I can't allow myself to go there, and as I slip out of the dress and into my plain black T-shirt and boyfriend jeans, I make myself a firm promise to never let a moment like that happen again, especially not with Ford Hastings.

9

FORD

I HADN'T EXPECTED MUCH this afternoon after I finally mustered the courage to send the text during my prep period, asking Blair to meet me for coffee after work. Honestly, I partially assumed it would be a repeat of the past two years where she's ghosted me on every single call or text.

Clearly, I'd panicked for nothing, but can you really blame me for worrying, especially after yesterday? It'd be pretty easy to assume I'd somehow ruined our friendship all over again. It feels like my specialty these days.

She doesn't trust me, and I get it. Given the circumstances in high school, it always felt like we were caught in a never-ending cycle of bad timing and uncertain feelings. Whenever she was single, Jenny and I were together, and whenever we had one of our occasional break-ups, Blair was taken.

The final nail in the coffin seemed to be when Jenny showed up on our senior trip to the Rocky Mountain Meltdown Music Festival just after Blair and I had finally shared our first kiss. I'd desperately wanted to confess my feelings and tell her it was her I wanted, but she distanced herself and devoted most of her attention to Max, whom she met the first day of the music festival.

Meanwhile, Jenny was constantly by my side, trying to win me back. Eventually, I gave in. If Blair wanted somebody else, I wasn't going to stop her. Making something happen shouldn't be that hard, or so I naively let myself believe. I was tired of fighting for something she didn't seem to want. It was painfully exhausting, and something I could no longer do to myself, or to Blair. It wasn't fair to put pressure on her when I was so sure she was no longer *the one.*

There was even a part of me that'd wanted to run away with Blair after her confession on my wedding day. I wanted to give myself permission to be with the woman I'd always wanted and been in love with, but I just hadn't been brave enough to do it. Not only could I not do that to Jenny, our friends, and family, but it also didn't feel fair to Blair. She shouldn't have had to be the woman who asked a guy to choose her. The man who truly deserved her would always make her his first priority, and given how long I'd waited, that no longer felt like me. I wasn't worthy of being with someone as perfect as Blair.

When she'd arrived back in town the other day, and I'd found out she and Max had broken up, a part of me selfishly wanted this to be our moment, but I also don't want anyone, especially Blair, to get the wrong idea.

I'm sure people would assume she's just the rebound woman, or say it's too soon and that I'm not ready to move on, and maybe I wouldn't be for anybody else, but this is Blair. She's the person I've secretly been in love with since the sixth grade.

Even worse, I feel like a creep who took advantage of her in the dressing room. In the moment, sure, it felt like she was just as into it as I was, but I don't want her thinking that's all I want from her, because that couldn't be further from the truth. With Blair Bennett, I want everything.

Either way, I felt a rush of relief when she immediately replied, agreeing to meet. Getting together in person gives me the chance to apologize, but there's an even more important and pressing reason we need to meet—Ronnie.

Walking inside The Steamy Bean, I'm not surprised that Blair isn't here. While we joked about Blair always being late at the barbecue the other night, it tends to ring true.

Approaching the counter, I order my typical black Americano and their signature pecan muffin.

"Is that everything?" Buddy, the barista, and the owner's son, asks.

I hesitate. I know Blair's usual order, and while it was unchanged throughout our teenage years and into adulthood on her occasional trip home, I get that it's been two years. There's always a chance she's changed and might want something different now.

After yesterday, do I really want to cause any waves or overstep? Then again, it's a fucking cup of coffee. Is it really that big of a deal?

"No, I'll also get an iced caramel macchiato and throw in one of those white chocolate chip raspberry muffins." If she doesn't want it, that's fine, but at least I'll have made the effort.

"Jenny trying something new?" Buddy asks as my stomach sinks. Of course, he's used to me ordering Jenny something, too, especially since this is my go-to stop after work. However, since our separation, I've only been picking up my order, but I can't imagine he'd be all that surprised if I started doing it again.

While I know there have been some rumors about Jenny and me, the gossip train strangely hasn't seemed to reach The Steamy Bean, something I'm more than grateful for, but I'm pretty sure that won't last long after today.

"No, this drink is for an old friend," I explain as he nods in response, thankfully not seeming to read too much into it.

"Gotcha, well just give me a few minutes and I'll call out your order."

I thank him just as the door opens. I don't even have to turn my head to know it's Blair. My body seems to sense it and know all on its own.

"Hey." She smiles, greeting me with a small wave. "Have you ordered yet?"

"Yep. I got you something too. He just started, so if you don't still drink iced caramel macchiatos, we might be able to stop him before he gets to it," I suggest, glancing toward Buddy, who thankfully seems to have only started on mine.

Her lips curve into a gradual smile. "A caramel macchiato is perfect. Did you also order the..."

"The white chocolate chip raspberry muffin? Of course."

Some things may have changed, but luckily, the fact that The Steamy Bean still has the best homemade muffins luckily hasn't, and I already knew she'd be dying to eat as many as she can during her stay in town.

"I must say, I'm impressed," she compliments, her smile widening. Honestly, though, how could I forget? I remember everything about her and our time together—literally everything.

"Well, if I'm going to ask someone to coffee, you'd best believe I'm going to do it right."

"Good, because I actually haven't made it here yet, if you can believe it, and I've been *dying* for one of those muffins."

I feign shock as my mouth hangs open. "Wow! Does this mean you're no longer a coffee addict?" While in any other town it's possible she could've been getting her coffee from elsewhere, in a small town like Evergreen Grove, this is the only place to go.

"Actually, for Christmas this year I got Miles one of those fancy espresso machines, and while it was still in the box when I got here, I've since set it up for him and have been treating myself," she explains with an almost embarrassed laugh and a shrug. "That man's got no sophistication or class. He still drinks from one of those old-school coffee pots."

"Ford," the barista calls as we both turn to look his way. "Your drinks and muffins are ready," he says, pushing the drinks and the bag toward us.

"Thanks, Buddy. You're the best." Grabbing the bag and my drink, I motion with my head for her to join me over at one of the small tables by the window.

"Just as perfect as I remember," she hums after taking a sip as she sits across from me, a huge smile plastered on her face. "What I can't figure out is how you can drink it plain like that, especially when you can have it taste like pure heaven and bliss," she adds, holding up her cup, where inside is a tan liquid with swirls of white cream forming intricate patterns.

"Not all of us can handle our caffeine parading as pure sugar." I chuckle. "Plus, you know me, I've always enjoyed my coffee like my soul..."

"Black," we say in unison as she rolls her eyes. Having heard that joke one too many times, she just shakes her head while bringing her drink to her lips once more.

"Still haven't stopped with the dad jokes, I see."

"I remember there being a time when you once laughed and found them funny."

"Exactly. *Once*. I mean, come on, how many times have you told that same exact joke?" she asks, raising an eyebrow as if to further make her point.

"Alright, fine. Maybe I need some new material," I concede, lifting my own cup as I take a drink, the warm, heavenly liquid hitting the spot.

"I have to ask. What do your students think of your cheesy jokes?" she asks, but continues before I can answer, "Let me guess, they eat you alive?" A mischievous grin lights up her features, and while that smile comes entirely at my expense, I can't fault her for it. I'm hopelessly bewitched and would still do nearly anything to witness it.

"I'll have you know they love my jokes."

She raises a skeptical brow. "Really?" she asks, clearly not buying what I'm selling.

"Okay, so maybe they give me some crap about it, but they're a lot like you. They like to pretend they hate them, while secretly wanting more."

She laughs, her head tipping back. "There's a lot to love about you, Ford Hastings, but your cheesy jokes definitely aren't one of them."

"As long as you love me, that's all that matters," I say with a small chuckle.

It isn't until she blinks a few times that I realize exactly where this conversation has gone—exactly where it shouldn't have. This shouldn't be a strange occurrence, especially considering that when Blair, Ronnie, and I were young, we would frequently express our love for one another.

However, as we grew older, these declarations became increasingly rare. In fact, the last time Blair told me she loved me was the day of my wedding, if my memory serves me correctly, and I have no doubt that it does. I mean, how exactly could one forget? I distinctly recall her declaration as she claimed that this wasn't just some fleeting, silly, and childish type of love, but that she was head over heels for me in a deep, unwavering, once-in-a-lifetime type of way.

"Anyway," I say, clearing my throat as I do my best to shrug off the palpable tension that's since surrounded us, "I'm sure you're wondering why I asked you to meet with me today."

"I mean, maybe a little, but why does it suddenly sound so ominous?" she asks, doing her best to smile, even if it doesn't quite reach her eyes. "You're not planning to off me, are you?"

"No, it's nothing like that," I laugh. "I just figured we should talk about what we're doing for Ronnie's bachelorette party. I know that's mainly your job as the maid of honor, and that you and Ronnie have always talked about the fun things you wanted to do when the time came, but since I haven't heard of anything being set in stone yet, I figured once it is, I can relay the message to the other bridesmaids."

It's possible that I'm overstepping, but that shouldn't come as a shock to anyone considering my Type A personality. I've always been the one to push both Blair and Ronnie when it was needed. I also feel like it makes the most sense for me to be the one in contact with the other bridesmaids, given that they both work at the school with Ronnie and me.

"Oh, yes, that's perfect," she says, setting her drink on the table as she claps her hands and links her fingers together. "I did actually have some ideas, so I'm glad you brought it up."

As she enthusiastically lists her ideas, I swiftly retrieve a notebook from my laptop bag, ready to document everything. It's honestly a little bit comforting how easily we seem to slide back into our old roles, almost like slipping into a familiar pair of shoes. I even do my best to keep my mouth shut as she animatedly rattles off some pretty racy ideas, leaving me blushing in my seat.

Nevertheless, I won't veto anything in Blair's plan. It's clear that despite the distance and even with my closer proximity to Ronnie these past ten years, they still have a strong connection and know without a shadow of a doubt what the other would want.

We're so engrossed in our plans that I pay little attention to the small bell above the door as it rings, signaling a newcomer. It isn't until a shadow looms over our table that I realize someone's joined us.

Lifting my pen, I turn and see my ex, or soon to be, I suppose. I don't even know. It's still a bit complicated.

As always, she looks great. While Blair and I appear as opposites in many ways, Jenny and I share several similarities. While Blair is much shorter than I am, Jenny is only a few inches shorter with matching brown hair and brown eyes. Her best and most unique feature by far is her long, curly hair, which is currently pulled halfway up.

She's stunning, which was easily what attracted me to her all those years ago, but if there's one thing I've learned from my years married to Jenny, there needs to be way more than physical attraction to make a relationship work.

I swallow. "Jenny. Hey," I say, glancing over at Blair, whose round blue eyes are as wide as saucers. I want to tell her she has nothing to worry about, since I never told Jenny about Blair's wedding day confession, but her nerves are likely warranted.

Despite my past frustration and countless efforts to foster a friendship between the two women, there remains an undeniable awkwardness between them, even after all these years.

"Jenny, wow. You look…" Blair starts, lifting a hand in the air as she struggles for words and I do my best not to wince. This little reunion is every bit as awkward as I could've imagined. "Great," she finally manages.

Jenny's lips twist, her eyes scrutinizing Blair as she looks her over. "You look great too," she offers, and given the icy tone, I have to wonder if Blair was right all those years ago when she constantly complained to me about my girlfriend being incredibly patronizing and passive-aggressive.

As a teenage boy, I suppose it was easy for me to bury my head in the sand, especially when I had such strong feelings for both of them. Plus, it wasn't just Blair who voiced her complaints; Jenny had been plenty vocal about her dislike for Blair as well.

With time, and as I grew up and let myself see things as they truly were, I became increasingly aware of Jenny's negative attributes. Despite my efforts to push away my worries and fears, the constant arguments during the last year of our marriage made it increasingly difficult to recognize the qualities of Jenny that I'd once fallen for.

"We were just planning Ronnie's bachelorette party," I explain, nodding toward the paper in front of me. I know I shouldn't care, and have no reason to feel guilty, but considering many of those arguments had involved Blair, even though I hadn't spoken to her since our wedding, I oddly feel like a child caught with my hand in the cookie jar.

"I see," she says, still using that same condescending tone that absolutely drives me nuts. "Well, I *definitely* don't want to interrupt this *important* conversation, so I guess I'll leave you two to it."

"It was good to see you, Jenny," Blair says, her smile forced, and her body tense.

"Sure," she says with a less than amused scoff, before turning toward the counter.

Blair lets out a loud breath. "Well, that went...well?"

"Yeah, sorry about that," I apologize.

"It's not your fault," she brushes me off with a wave before reaching for her drink and taking a long sip.

"I don't know about that. She is my ex, after all. I feel like that provides me with some sort of responsibility here."

"Well, in your defense, you did try your hardest to make us friends and get us to like each other, and I'm sure if I'd really wanted to, I could have tried a little harder...and I mean," she continues, leaning in close to whisper the rest, "I did try to steal her groom on her wedding day. I'm pretty sure she has every reason in the world to dislike me."

"If it makes you feel any better. I never told her."

She blinks. "Oh."

"I didn't think I should. I knew you already had a hard time with her, and while I didn't see us having too many more get-togethers after all of that, I just didn't want to somehow make things even worse," I ramble, doing my best to explain. But how can I? It's obvious that I never handled any of this correctly.

Maybe I should've been more open and upfront with Jenny, but that didn't seem like a healthy situation for anyone. I also knew I needed to forget it for my own sanity. There was no way I could have a healthy and happy relationship with my new wife when all I could think about was the girl I'd grown up in love with.

"No, I'm glad. I was so embarrassed. I still can't believe I let myself do something so irresponsible and unfair. I never should've put you in that kind of position," she says, reaching out to place her hand on top of mine.

I look down as the warmth immediately spreads, but she seems to think better of it and quickly removes her hand.

"Blair, I..." I begin, but she shakes her head as she pushes out of her seat, the scraping metal of her chair drawing the attention of everyone else in the shop, including Jenny.

"I forgot. I'm supposed to be meeting Ronnie soon. I need to go, but I'll uh, text you later with the final details?" she rambles, as I stupidly nod in agreement. "Thanks again for the coffee and the muffin."

I attempt a smile. "Anytime," I call, but her body language speaks volumes as she swiftly disposes of her trash in the nearest receptacle before the ringing of the bell marks her hasty departure.

I try not to take it personally. I know she's telling the truth, especially since Ronnie mentioned meeting with Blair during lunch today in the teachers' lounge. Nevertheless, it's clear that I was venturing into uncomfortable territory, and she sought to put as much distance between herself and me as possible. I'm starting to sense a pattern with us. Yesterday it was me running away, and now, apparently, it's her turn.

I want to believe this is a good thing, but as my eyes shift toward the counter, I catch Jenny giving me a knowing look that screams "I told you so." Nothing like your ex seeing you get flustered by the woman that she not only hates, but has always been convinced was the reason for the downfall of your relationship, and the worst part is, I'm starting to think maybe she was right. Hell, I *know* she was. How was I ever expected to have a strong marriage when I was so clearly married to the wrong woman?

While I've tried to lie to myself and think otherwise, it's become glaringly obvious. It's always been Blair, but after all this time and her eagerness to escape my presence, how can we ever possibly move past this?

10

BLAIR

I'M PRETTY SURE I'VE never run out of a place faster than I ran out of The Steamy Bean. All I've ever wanted to do is prove to the people of Evergreen Grove that I'm not the chaotic individual they expect me to be. Unfortunately, I'm probably just reinforcing their preconceived notions, as I've been nothing but a hot mess since my return.

The second Jenny walked into the room, all I could think about was what a horrible piece-of-shit human I am. I mean, who in their right mind has the audacity to walk into someone else's wedding only to try and steal their groom?

Sure, Jenny and I have never gotten along and are the epitome of oil and water, but nothing gave me that right. It shouldn't matter that I've always felt like Ford could do better, and maybe I was right, given the current state of their relationship, but actually telling someone not to marry another person and begging them to be with me instead was certainly an all-time low.

It's a relief to know Jenny isn't aware of just how far I crossed the line. If anything, she probably would've gotten off on it. She's always made it obvious that she knew of my feelings for

Ford, and I'm sure she would've relished just how much she'd truly won me over despite my pathetic attempts.

The only thing that made me feel better about things was that I never saw it as a competition or considered Ford a prize to be won. I'd genuinely been in love with him, and a part of me acknowledges that maybe I always will be. He's my person. He's the one that people always talk about—that first love that leaves an indelible mark on your heart. It's pathetic, I know, especially since we never actually dated, but with us, that never seemed to matter. We were each other's people, and I'm pretty sure everyone who saw us knew it.

At least I hadn't been lying when I'd said I was meeting Ronnie, since we really do have plans. Tomorrow I'm supposed to be shooting her bridal portraits, and in an effort to get her picture-perfect and wedding-ready, the two of us decided that today is the day we'd pamper ourselves with manicures and pedicures. Although, I *may* have overemphasized the urgency, since I still have twenty minutes until we're supposed to meet.

Maybe if this town were bigger than the set of Sesame Street and I had to do more than walk one measly block to get to the local salon, I'd have needed the full twenty minutes, but not here.

My stomach lets out a gentle growl, serving as an unfortunate reminder of my silliness as I'd made the unfortunate decision to not only leave, but also toss the rest of my barely eaten muffin into the trash. I'd gotten so caught up in the excitement of planning the perfect bachelorette party that I'd barely eaten anything. Then, upon Jenny's arrival, my mind went completely blank, and I impulsively discarded everything, desperate for air and an escape from the one person I've always struggled to be near. One could call it hatred, but if I'm being honest, an even bigger part of me realizes that it's nothing but pure jealousy.

In any other town, I'd likely be able to find somewhere else to grab a small snack, but here in Evergreen, my choices are limited. Needing something to tide me over, I reach into my bag as I walk toward the salon and pull out an old green apple Jolly Rancher. If there is one thing you can count on from me, it's that I'll always have some kind of hard candy within grabbing distance. It isn't much, but at least it should hold me over until after our nails are done and we go out for dinner.

Pulling up in front of Heritage Hair and Nails, I'm once again reminded that absolutely nothing has changed. The place is a time capsule, and that includes Peggy, whom I spot through the glass, sitting at the front desk, completely engrossed as she flips through a celebrity gossip magazine.

Opening the door, I'm hit with the oddly familiar scent of nail polish remover mixed with a fruity floral fragrance. As expected, this place remains unchanged, featuring two stations for haircuts, two stations for pedicures, and a single spot for manicures.

Peggy's face instantly lights up with joy as I raise an awkward hand in greeting.

"Is that really Blair Bennett in the flesh?" she asks in a high-pitched squeal.

"The one and only," I say, lifting my shoulders, and before I can register what's happening, her magazine is tossed aside, and I'm being pulled into a warm, cheery hug.

Given that this is the only salon in Evergreen Grove, it's where everyone gets their haircuts, and any other beauty regimens taken care of.

"I was hoping I'd see you, given that our little Veronica is all grown up and marrying that handsome West boy."

"Crazy, right?" I ask. It shouldn't be surprising, especially considering Ford and many of my other high school classmates have been married for quite some time now, but the idea still hasn't sunk in that we're old enough to do the same.

"So, when are you planning on settling down?" Peggy prods, hand on her hip, popping it out and tilting her head to the side, all but demanding an answer.

"Not any time soon. I mean, first I'd need to find myself a good man, and unfortunately, those are pretty hard to come by these days."

Peggy starts with a serious nod, but her expression soon turns mischievous. It may have been years since we last saw each other, but I unfortunately know that look, especially when it comes from the number one culprit of town gossip. Then again, can you really blame the woman for knowing all the town secrets? Once she gets you in that magical chair of hers, you start pouring your heart out without even realizing it.

"You know, I've heard that Ford and Jenny Hastings are supposedly getting a divorce. You used to have a thing for him, right? He was always such a nice boy," Peggy spills in a hushed tone, even if it is only the two of us here. As much as my heart secretly enjoys hearing about this particular news once again, I also ache for Ford, knowing that he's unfortunately become the next big story among the town gossipers.

Having grown up as Bill Bennett's daughter, I was always a favorite topic, and I can say from firsthand experience just how tiring and exhausting that can be.

"I think I may have heard something about that," I say, not wanting to confirm or deny. "But Ford is just a friend. Always has been."

"That's a shame. He's such a cutie," she gushes, and honestly, she's not wrong. In fact, I hate how much I've been thinking about that since returning, and even more so after yesterday's dressing room fiasco. A part of me has always been drawn to him, an irresistible allure that I've desperately tried to ignore. However, I've come to realize that, like with most things, that's much easier said than done.

Thankfully, I'm saved from having to comment as the bell chimes above the door, signaling the arrival of my best friend.

"Ronnie!" I exclaim, bounding toward her and wrapping my arms around her neck as we hug and sway back and forth.

"Happy to see you too," Ronnie chuckles before finally pulling out of my embrace. "Actually, I'm kind of surprised," she continues as she pulls out her phone and checks the time. "You're early. I thought we were running on BST."

I roll my eyes. "Ha ha," I say, doing my best to sound un-amused, even if I still find Ronnie and Ford's Blair Standard Time joke kind of funny.

"Seriously though? What's gives?" she asks, eyes narrowing as she gives me a thorough once-over. "I thought you and Ford were having a super-secret meeting today."

"Clearly not that secret if you knew all about it." Of course he'd spill. Then again, he's always been the weak link in this friendship, and was the one Ronnie and I went to when we needed information.

"Really, though? What's up? Something must have happened."

"Nothing." I shrug, doing my best to keep some secrets to myself, but unsurprisingly, she sees right through me.

"Blair," she presses, tilting her head as she folds her arms and taps her foot impatiently.

"Fine. Jenny showed up, and I bolted a little earlier than planned," I explain, figuring it best to just get it over with. This lady is relentless when she wants to be and would've gotten it out of me at some point. "Can we just get our nails done?"

"Yes, but you know I'm going to need more details, right?"

Despite my attempts to ignore her, I grab her hand and lead her toward Peggy at the front desk, who is innocently trying to look as though she hadn't just eavesdropped on our entire conversation.

"Two pedicures and manicures, please." I smile as Peggy willingly obliges before excusing herself to fill the water in the tubs for the pedicures.

I lower my voice. "So, I know you want more details, and I'll give them to you, but can we not do it here? You know Peggy is listening in, right? The last thing I need is for the entire town to know that things are still weird there."

She sighs. "Fine, but I expect full details at dinner tonight," she threatens, pointing a finger in my direction.

"Pinky promise," I assure her as I reach out my hand and we interlock pinkies.

"Alright, ladies. I'm ready for you." Peggy smiles, waving us back as we set our purses down on the small table next to the pedicure chairs.

Settling into my seat, I relish the soothing warmth of the water and bubbles against my skin, feeling the tension gradually melt away from my body. I'm still stressed about the whole Jenny and Ford situation, but as Peggy gets to work and I listen to Ronnie rattle off more wedding details, I remember exactly what and who I'm here for.

Ronnie is my number one priority and I'm done letting Ford consume my thoughts. A decade ago, I set out to rid myself of any trace of my infatuation for my friend, and today, I remind myself that this goal is not only attainable, but crucial.

Ford Hastings, you are officially being sidelined. Out with Ford, and in with Ronnie. She makes for a far less complicated kind of love, anyway.

11

BLAIR

"**Y**OU REMEMBER THAT PINKY promise you made earlier, right?" Ronnie asks, wasting no time as our plates
are set down in front of us.

I groan. "Now? Really?"

Peggy was in an exceptionally talkative mood tonight, multitasking as she worked on both my nails and Ronnie's, making
me regret even more that I'd been stupid enough to trash my
perfectly delicious muffin. I'd been half convinced I'd either die
or at least pass out from hunger the longer our appointment
went on, and as my Jolly Ranchers ran out, but luckily we made
it to the Starlight Diner just in time.

When it comes to diner food, there are likely better places
out there. Being out on the road with Max and his band, we'd
stopped at many diners that served food late at night after their
concerts. However, there would always be something special
about the Starlight.

"Well, I guess I could wait until you've finished inhaling that
grilled cheese," she laughs, and she's not wrong; I'm already
on my third bite. My hunger could be clouding my judgment,

but the taste of this extra gooey grilled cheese and freshly made tomato soup is even better than I remember.

Despite being caked in grease from the grill and cheese drippings, this sandwich is hands down the best grilled cheese I've ever had. I'm not usually much of a tomato soup person, but this house-made bowl is fresh and incredibly creamy.

"I don't even know what you're expecting to hear." I shrug before tearing off a piece of my sandwich and dip it into the soup. "Ford and I were talking and Jenny came in. Things got awkward, and I bailed before she could burn a hole in me with that weirdly intense gaze of hers."

She lets out a small laugh as she dips a fry into her hefty pile of ketchup. "Well, you could go into more detail about why she was glaring. You'd think she'd finally be past all that weird stuff from high school by now. Plus, it's not like Ford ever told her about that kiss you guys shared on graduation night."

A soft whine leaves my lips as I set my sandwich back on the plate. "I don't know. She's never liked me, and it's not like I can blame her. I *was* crushing on Ford. It wasn't just something made up in her head."

"Yeah, but that's ancient history, right? You and Ford haven't even seen each other since the wedding. What's there still to hate?"

I want to believe that this is all some innocent line of questioning, but I can't help it as I involuntarily wrinkle my nose and chew on my lower lip. Ford may have told me he'd never told Jenny about my confession, but what about Ronnie?

It's always been hard to keep secrets in our friend group, and as I sit, nervously attempting to hide my guilt, it's clear she suspects something is up as her eyes widen.

"Wait, what am I missing?" she presses.

I cave. "Alright, well maybe there is more to the story of why I cut myself off from talking to Ford. I may have confessed my real feelings for him only moments before he walked down the aisle, and I may have also begged him to pick me and not marry Jenny."

The fry that had been on its way to Ronnie's mouth hangs suspended in midair, her lips frozen in surprise. "Wait, what?" she finally manages.

I cover my face and shake my head. "Ugh, I know. I'm the worst."

"I might have to agree, but only because you didn't tell me," she cries, lifting off her seat as she moves to swat my arm from across the table. "I knew there had to be more to why you were always making excuses and refusing to come home. I mean, I knew you were heartbroken after you truly had to give Ford up, but wow," she utters, her mouth still open in awe.

"He told me he never told her, but still. I might not have ever been Jenny's biggest fan, and while I feel somewhat validated in the fact that I was right about them not being a good fit, I've also always felt so guilty at the same time. I mean, who does that?"

No matter how hard I try, the memory of that moment continues to haunt me, still filling me with shame as my cheeks redden.

"Someone who wasn't ready to let go, and I get it," Ronnie comforts me, as this time she reaches out and places her hand on top of mine. "Everyone in this town knew there was something real between the two of you, and if I'm being honest, I truly always thought it would be you two walking down the aisle together that day. So no, it wasn't your best move, but I also understand the reasoning behind it."

"Well, I'm glad you do, because I'm still trying to figure out what on earth possessed me to think that was even remotely acceptable."

"Hey, love makes us all do crazy and irrational things from time to time. While you may be Evergreen Grove's favorite badass bitch, even you're not immune."

"Crazy and irrational make sense, what I did was absolutely insane," I counter, pulling back my hand as I move to tear off a piece of my sandwich to dip in my soup.

"Maybe a little," she agrees with a soft laugh. "But not as insane as you running off and following some boy on tour and never moving back home."

"Hey, at least that one worked out in my favor," I say before dropping the perfect gooey and cheesy bite into my mouth.

"Did it?" she counters, as I fight both the urge to groan and roll my eyes.

"Maybe not in the romantic sense, but I've gotten to travel the world and improve my skills as a photographer, so it's not a total bust, right?"

Sure, it was hard to be away from my family and friends, but I'll never regret the experiences that came from my impulsive decisions. Even more, there's no way I would've gained the skills I now possess if I'd stayed. I'd fallen in love with photography when I'd taken some classes in high school, but even that was the bare minimum.

"But aren't you lonely? I know you and Max have your little thing going on, but aren't you ready to find your actual forever person? I'm sorry, and I know you guys have your *fun,* but we both know you'll never actually end up as Mrs. Fuckboy Rockstar."

"You make it sound so easy," I say, using my spoon to spin lazy circles in the red soup, while also doing my best to avoid her gaze. Unfortunately, I know she's right. Max fulfills some of my needs, but not the ones that count.

"What if it was?"

I finally glance up, raising an eyebrow. "But it's not. Maybe it was easy for you to find your person, but the rest of us aren't so lucky."

"Well, it's certainly a lot easier when you're not shutting yourself off from love and doing everything you can to run away and ignore what's right in front of you."

"And what *is* right in front of me, huh?" I challenge.

Ronnie tilts her head downward, incredulously. "Come on, Blair. Don't make me say what we both already know."

"Sorry, Ron, but I think I need you to spell it out for me." Okay, so maybe I know exactly what she's saying, but like usual, it's something that's way too scary to say aloud and I'm definitely not going to be the first one to say it.

"Ford."

I let out a loud sigh. "I can't go there again. You know I can't. Besides, these next couple of weeks are about you and your love life, not mine," I say, doing everything I can to do exactly what she accused me of—running from this.

"Quit making excuses. We're both allowed to be happy and think about our love lives this week. Even more, there's nothing that would make me happier than for the two of you to finally figure your shit out."

"There's nothing to figure out," I lie. "We had our chance ten years ago, and he chose her time and time again. I won't go there. I can't."

Ronnie's face flickers with concern, or perhaps it's just pity. Either way, I can't stand it. Like she said, I've always prided myself on being some 'badass bitch' who can brush things off, and while so much of that is an act, I despise the idea of people seeing past the mask.

"In his defense, I don't think you can really count his wedding day against him. That was sort of last minute, and if anything, I think if he could go back in time and change things, he would."

I interrupt before she can say anything else. "We can't change the past. What happened, happened. He chose her. End of story."

"But you can fix your future, and what if you're supposed to be together? What if he's your soulmate? You can't just give up on that," she says, her voice full of passion, which for her makes sense. She's always been someone who likes to look for the silver lining, even when she probably shouldn't. She's also someone who believes in fairytales and happily-ever-afters, but for someone like me, those don't exist; I just can't pretend or hope anymore, it's too exhausting.

I sigh. "It's not that easy. I just—I think if we were ever truly supposed to be together, then it would have happened years ago. Maybe this is all a big sign that we were never supposed to be anything."

"I don't believe that. Even now, I still see the way he looks at you, and even with that intense poker face of yours, I know you love him too," she insists, pointing an accusatory french fry in my direction.

"Can we just not talk about this?" I plead. Yes. I still have feelings for Ford, but this isn't what I came home to do. "I want to focus on you, and that's all I want to think about from now until your wedding day," I add, needing her to let this go.

"Fine, we can change the subject, but I want to make sure you know that you're allowed to change your mind about this. If you need to focus on you and your love life, there truly could be nothing that would make me happier. Besides, isn't it often said that weddings are the perfect setting for finding love?" she asks with a playful wink and shimmy of her shoulders.

It's clear that she's not as willing to move on from this as she made it seem, but I can't help but smile and let out a small laugh as I shake my head. "I'm pretty sure what they say is that a wedding is a great place to find a hookup. Isn't there usually a joke about the maid of honor and best man sleeping together?"

"Well, considering Pete's best man is his married older brother, I unfortunately have to inform you that's out of the question."

I wrinkle my nose. "Noted."

"He does have a few cute friends though, even if none are actually as good-looking as Ford."

My mouth flattens as I give her a deadpan stare. "Ronnie!"

"Fine, I'll drop it—for now."

"You better," I warn, and for good measure, I reach across the table and steal one of her fries.

I'm uncertain if it was the attack on her fries or what, but luckily the topic shifts, even if Ford remains on my mind. I may be ready to move on from him, but my mind and heart seem to have completely different ideas.

12

FORD

DESPITE MY BEST EFFORTS to distract myself, all I can do is think about Blair. Unfortunately, every conversation and interaction replays in my mind like a broken record. I enjoy my job, but I don't usually eagerly anticipate going into work each day. However, these past few days have been an exception—I've found myself genuinely excited. At least when I'm teaching, I have something else to focus my brain power on. I swear, if my brain goes back to that dressing room one more time...

The chemistry in that small space was undeniable, and I know she felt it too. She wanted me to touch her, just as badly as my hands wanted to sink lower and discover the way her soft skin felt beneath my fingertips, but given our long history, it's not exactly the easiest topic to broach. I was so tempted to bring it up during our bachelorette meeting at the coffee shop, but we both knew that moment needed to be about Ronnie. Then, the second Jenny walked in, any chance of us talking about anything serious went completely out the window.

There's no way I can do it now, either, since once again, the theme of this afternoon is Ronnie. When the two of them had asked me to come lend a hand with Ronnie's bridal photoshoot, there's no way I could've said no.

Jenny used to claim that it was because I was spineless and wasn't capable of saying no to either of my best friends, but that couldn't be further from the truth. Even beyond my feelings for Blair, and my desperate need to be with her every second she's in town, I genuinely enjoy being around them.

There's a reason our friendship has stood the test of time, or at least it has with Ronnie. They are two people who just get me, and I get them. It's that simple.

Sure, I'm doing a bit of the grunt work since I was asked to pick up the flowers from the florist, and now I'm the one carrying the props, holding the light reflector, and managing any other extra equipment, but I wouldn't have it any other way.

This may be Blair's big gift to Ronnie as her personal wedding present, but it's also fun to watch, especially since they're both killing it.

As Ronnie gracefully poses in her gown, adorned with perfectly styled hair and flawless makeup, it's even more exciting to witness Blair so blissfully in charge and thriving in what is so obviously her element.

We'd all known that Blair possessed a talent for capturing the perfect picture and uncovering beauty in even the most ordinary objects, but it's clear why she's now a highly sought-after photographer. She knows exactly what she's doing, and isn't afraid to get a little dirty in order to get the perfect shot, especially as she lays down on her stomach in the dirt and grass to get the perfect angle.

Ronnie wanted a nature-inspired look, so we opted to go a little outside of town. Luckily, we'd stumbled upon the perfect spot with tall, towering trees, wildflowers, and the striking backdrop of the Rocky Mountains.

"Alright, I need to see that one," Ronnie requests, lifting her gown as she makes her way over to Blair, who brushes herself off after standing.

"Just remember, I haven't done any editing yet," she warns before holding out the camera with the small screen for our friend to look at.

"Oh my God! It's amazing," she squeals excitedly, dancing from side to side.

"Of course it is. You're literally the most beautiful model I could've ever asked for," Blair scoffs as I take a step forward to look as well.

Blair isn't wrong. Ronnie looks stunning, but it's more than that. The shot is truly magical. In the photo, Ronnie's face is beautifully framed and illuminated by the sunlight as it shines through the trees. A one-of-a-kind shot, and I'm positive it's something only Blair could capture.

"It's stunning," I agree. "You're both absolutely crushing it," I assure them, giving Blair a meaningful glance so she knows just how much I mean it and that it's not just lip service.

"The only problem now is that my actual wedding photos are going to look so amateurish in comparison," Ronnie whines, her lips forming a small pout.

"Hey now, I offered to shoot your wedding, too, but you shot that down real quick," Blair reminds her.

"Only because I need you by my side more than I need perfect pictures. In fact, the pictures wouldn't be perfect unless you're standing right next to me in each and every one," she counters, as Blair rolls her eyes.

"I second this," I chime in. "Because Ronnie had also mentioned that if you weren't her maid of honor, I'd have to fill in and be the man of honor, and that's way too much pressure for a guy like me."

"Oh, whatever, you would have done just fine," Blair dismisses as she looks back down at her camera.

"He is the most put-together one out of all of us, even after all these years," Ronnie agrees with a small shrug. "I think you'd do a much better job than you give yourself credit for."

"I may keep you all on task, but you've both always been the ones with the best ideas, especially when it comes to weddings. I'm hopeless. Believe me, just ask Jenny."

There had been plenty of times during our own wedding planning that Jenny had asked for my advice or opinions on everything from dresses to flowers to seating plans, and never once had I been able to provide any useful feedback, or so she claimed.

"Psh, Jenny is divorcing the greatest man I know. Her opinions are less than valid here," Ronnie huffs.

"Well, you two were never her biggest fans in the first place, so I don't know if your opinions count here, either."

"And obviously for good reason," Blair mutters under her breath, but seemingly not quiet enough, since it's clear by the look on Ronnie's face that we both overheard it.

"And on that note..." Ronnie says, playfully wincing as she takes a few steps back, once again lifting her dress to keep it from dragging on the dirty ground. "I'm going to go back to the car and touch up my makeup before we take the next couple of shots."

Nodding our heads, Blair and I stand in awkward silence, the tension thickening as we watch her retreat toward the car.

"Sorry about that," Blair finally says, but instead of looking at me, she keeps herself busy by studying and flipping through the pictures she's already taken on her camera.

"No, it's fine. I get it. You have every reason to dislike Jenny. If it wasn't already made clear the other day at the coffee shop, she isn't exactly your biggest fan either. If anything, I never should have kept trying to force the two of you to have some sort of friendship."

"Well, if it makes you feel better, for your sake, I really did try, but clearly I've never been all that good at keeping my feelings to myself."

I let out a small chuckle. "Well, there were often times that you had me questioning myself, wondering if our feelings were mutual growing up, but when it came to how you felt about my girlfriend, yeah, that was always pretty obvious."

"Hey." She frowns, though the corners of her lips are quirking up into a grin as she reaches out and gives me a light shove. "You could've at least lied to make me feel better."

"I could, but lying about my own thoughts and feelings is likely what got us into some of this mess," I joke, even if there is some truth to it.

We both would've been saved from a lot of heartbreak if either of us had been brave enough to confess our feelings before it was too fucking late.

"In your defense, the two of us not sharing our feelings was probably for the best." She shrugs as my eyebrows furrow. "Maybe that's the whole reason we were ever able to be friends for as long as we were. For all we know, we might never have worked and ruined everything either way, but destroyed it all even earlier."

"Or maybe we would've been the ones getting married and you wouldn't have ever left Evergreen Grove and I wouldn't be on my way to getting divorced," I say, deciding I'm no longer in the mood to hold back. Clearly, that never benefited us before, so what's the point in continuing this ridiculous charade?

She frowns, tilting her head to the side as she seems to contemplate my words. "Unfortunately, I did leave, and you did get married to someone else, and that's just the way it is. For my sanity, I can't live in a world of what-ifs. I have to believe that it was all for the best and that this is how it was always meant to be. Plus, what would I even be doing if I stayed here? Teaching Photography at the local high school like you and Ronnie?"

My brow knits together, not sure if I should feel insulted or not. "What's wrong with teaching at the high school?"

"I didn't mean it like that," she sighs, reaching out to place a hand on my arm. Suddenly, it's like I'm back in high school, hyper-aware of the intense heat that nothing more than a simple touch from her hand brings. "I just feel like I need more than that. Repeating the same lesson again and again would've caused me to lose my mind, even more than I already had before leaving. I also don't feel like it ever would've given me the opportunity to really explore my creative freedom."

"No, I get it. Your talent has always surpassed what this town could provide, but we could've figured something out. It isn't like you'd have much competition. Didn't Ronnie say that she had to reach out to someone from a few towns over just to find someone with enough talent to cover her wedding?" I point out. Evergreen Grove isn't devoid of people who can take decent photographs, but there isn't anyone that could truly offer anything close to what Blair is capable of.

"I still think she should've just let me do it," she huffs, wrinkling her nose.

"No way. Like she said; we need you in the pictures too."

"I don't know why. I'm not worth looking at. Believe me, there's a reason I prefer to be behind the camera rather than in front of it."

I loudly scoff. "Stop it. You're gorgeous, and you're most definitely someone that people want to look at. I think you're forgetting that I saw you the other day in that dress and know how good you looked in it," I say, doing my best not to think about how close I came to almost seeing her without it too. "While Ronnie is going to be the main attraction and look amazing while doing it, it's going to be hard not to look your way as well, and I'm sure others are going to feel the same."

There's a chance I'm biased since I've always found it hard not to look Blair's way. From the first day of school, when I'd just moved in and saw her across the classroom, I'd felt something and knew that she was different—someone that I needed to get to know. At just eleven years old, I'd been smitten, and from that day on, I've found myself completely mesmerized and enthralled by her.

Looking at the ground, she shakes her head. "You're ridiculous." She blushes as I reach into my back pocket and slip out my cell phone. After quickly unlocking the screen, I point the camera toward her, and snap a picture.

Hearing the small click, Blair looks up, eyes wide with shock. "What're you doing?"

"I'm showing you just how beautiful you look on camera."

"And you really think that's going to work?" she asks, popping out her hip as she places her free hand on top of it.

With that, I take another picture as her mouth drops open, causing me to snap another, capturing the moment perfectly. Despite the annoyed look on her face, a laugh escapes her lips as she takes a few steps closer while lifting her hand to block the view of the camera. I take a few steps back myself and continue to snap picture after picture while carefully dodging all her attempts to reach for my phone.

"Stop," she begs, but it's accompanied by another beautiful giggle as I take yet another shot before she finally manages to yank the phone from my hand. "You know I'm deleting these immediately, right?"

"You better not," I warn, moving to stand next to her as she pulls up the pictures. As predicted, she looks perfect, even if she doesn't look all that convinced.

"And why not? I mean, look at this one; it's blurry," she protests, stopping at one of the pictures where her hand is held out in front of her. Sure, she has a point, but there's something uniquely beautiful about it as well, especially since you can see just how in the moment she is. If anything, it's nice to see a genuine smile on her face again, especially after going so long without having it to brighten up my life and my world.

"Hey, I never claimed to be the professional photographer here, but that's not the point. The point is, you look great in every single one, even the ones that are blurry or out of focus."

"Fine, keep them if you want." She shrugs, shoving the phone back into my hands. "It's your phone storage that's going to suffer."

"That's what the cloud is for," I answer with a smug smile.

"What's the cloud for?" Ronnie asks, appearing behind us.

"Nothing important," Blair answers first. "Plus, we need to hurry. We don't want to miss this light. It's almost golden hour, and I'm not about to miss it due to Ford's ridiculous shenanigans."

Ronnie looks at me with a questioning brow, but I lift one shoulder in a shrug. "Go on, we can't have you missing this golden hour," I say, dismissing them with a wave of my hand.

Ronnie bites down on her lip, making it clear she wants to press the issue. She's always been the noisiest one out of the group, but she ultimately decides not to miss out on the perfect moment and picture as she lifts her dress once more and scurries after Blair toward the tree line.

I'm unsure if I truly convinced Blair, but as she glances back over her shoulder one last time, smiling and shaking her head in a way that sends warmth throughout my body, it no longer matters. As usual, it's always a win in my book when I get to see her smile like that, especially when it's a smile that's exclusively meant for me.

13

FORD

BLAIR WAS RIGHT—I SHOULD'VE deleted those pictures of her from my phone. Not because of storage concerns, but because I constantly find myself looking back at them like some obsessed stalker. Even after only a few days without seeing her, my body still reacts to nothing more than the mere thought of her. It's pathetic. Hell, *I'm* pathetic.

I'd been hopeful a few days apart would bring clarity and remind me of all the reasons why we shouldn't be together, but now I can't help but question if she's wrong about us. Even after all these years, she's still on my mind more than she should be, and there has to be a logical explanation as to why that is. It's either that, or I'm nothing more than a pathetic loser who can't stop dwelling on the past and the woman I let slip through my fingers. I'd much prefer it to be the first option, since at least then I'd have the option to fix things and make it right.

Despite everything, though, I'm reminding myself once again that today isn't the day to dwell on this, especially since this is another significant day for our other best friend. I'm not invited to the actual bridal shower—even though I'm part of the wedding party—it turns out Pete's family is incredibly traditional and requested that today be women-only. I can't say I mind that I've never been invited to a bridal shower, including my soon-to-be ex-wife's; I'm perfectly fine with keeping that tradition alive.

Ronnie and Blair didn't let my lack of invitation stop them from asking for my help though. Knowing that they'd need someone to assist with the heavy lifting, they enlisted me to set up the tables and chairs under a large white tent that's been placed in the spacious backyard of Pete and Ronnie's soon-to-be-home.

Luckily, the temperature outside is still pretty mild, given that it's mid-spring here in Colorado, but I still feel beads of sweat forming on my forehead as I pause to catch my breath and lift the bottom of my shirt to wipe it away. I don't know what they were thinking when they asked me, of all people, to help with this particular job. There are much bigger and likely more capable men who can handle all this lifting, but I'm doing my best to remain useful.

"Showing off those abs are we? Blair asks, amusement lacing her tone as she stops at a nearby table that I'd just set up so she can add the finishing details. The women have gone all-out with today's event, with each table getting a light blue tablecloth with a blue-and-white flower centerpiece adorned with greenery and candles.

"Does it count if I don't actually have any of those?" I chuckle, well aware of the fact that I don't have anything to show off in that department. I wouldn't say I'm overly thin, but I also don't exactly have anything to brag about either, with little to no muscles in sight. If anything, if one were to say something about my stomach, they'd likely say it was flat as a pancake.

"I didn't think it looked too bad." She shrugs, adjusting the light blue tablecloth so that it falls perfectly flat.

I can't stand the goofy grin that pops up, but it's impossible not to smile at her compliment. I've always been a pushover for any nice sentiment she sends in my direction, and I'll happily embrace any praise she'll willingly give me, even if she likely didn't mean much by it. I'm basically her own personal obsessed golden retriever, but isn't that seen as a good thing these days?

"So you were checking me out, huh?"

She scoffs. "Don't let it get to your head. You're the only guy here, and I'm about to spend the day surrounded by women. It's not like I have a lot of options."

"Oh, it's already gone to my head," I playfully warn, as I move to unfold another chair and set it near the current table I've been working on. Although, I'm not kidding here. In fact, I'll likely be obsessing over the compliment all day. "It's not every day that a guy gets checked out, especially when you're usually known around town as the nerdy science teacher."

"You really think that's how people see you?" she asks, stopping what she's doing as she turns to look at me and plants her hands on her hips.

"It's not?" I ask, my skeptical expression mirroring my words.

She rolls her eyes. "No, believe me. I hear all the gossip, and even being here less than a week, I've already heard people talking about how the good-looking Ford Hastings is newly single and ready to mingle."

My face drops. Perhaps I should be happy about the fact that people are supposedly complimenting my appearance, especially since I've never really seen myself that way. Yet, all I can focus on is how more people than I realized are aware of my separation from Jenny.

It's possible she's been the one going around talking about it, and I wouldn't blame her if she needed the support, but it's oddly depressing to think about the entire town knowing of my failings as a husband, especially since even Blair, who's no longer a local, is aware of it. It's been real for a while now, but this somehow adds an extra layer of finality to things.

"Oh, Ford," she starts, clearly reading the emotions on my face as she hurries over and places her hand on my shoulder before gently caressing the top of my back. "I'm sorry. I shouldn't have said anything. I know this is a weird and sensitive subject."

"No, it's fine. It's not even the fact that Jenny and I are separated," I sigh. "If anything, maybe I should be relieved. The more time we spend apart, the more I realize just how necessary this separation is. Jenny and I are done," I add with a definitive nod. "At least we don't have to worry about making some official announcement and catching everyone off guard with it."

"Well, unfortunately, or maybe fortunately, in your situation, Peggy is the one that told me, which likely means everyone in the town really does already know."

"Oh God," I half-laugh with no trace of amusement. "So everyone does know, huh?"

"Probably." She nods, her hand falling to her side as I immediately feel the absence of her touch, realizing just how much I needed it.

"I guess at this point we just need to go about making things official. We have the paperwork drawn out, but I don't think either of us has been ready to make the final move."

"What's specifically been the thing that's held you back?" she asks, returning to the table as she picks at the centerpiece to fluff out the flowers, making sure everything sits just right.

"I'm not sure," I muse, also trying to distract myself from the serious conversation at hand as I set up another chair. "I guess I just hate feeling like I'm giving up on something. It doesn't help that it was something I chose despite...well," I hesitate before continuing, "despite you giving me another option and going through with it anyway. Part of me worries that I never truly gave it my all because I was never able to fully let go of the idea of you, or rather, the idea of us."

She stops messing with the floral arrangement as she turns to look at me. "What?"

"Is it really that much of a surprise?" I ask, genuinely curious, as I freeze and glance her way. "You have to know that even though we never dated and even with me still marrying Jenny, that didn't suddenly mean that everything I ever felt for you went out the window. You were a huge part of my life and while maybe that day marked the end of things for you, I could never get myself to stop caring, even when I probably should have. That wasn't fair to any of us, especially not Jenny."

"It didn't end there for me either," she softly confesses, her luminous blue eyes revealing the weight of our shared guilt.

Despite the honesty in what she said, there's no comfort to be found in this revelation, especially since it only makes me feel worse about how much time was wasted, not just for us, but for everyone involved. "But like I said the other day, I think it was for the best. It had to be, right? We never would've worked."

My frown deepens as a line forms between my brows. "What makes you so sure of that?"

"I was the daughter of the town drunk who now spends her life traveling around the world with a bunch of rowdy musicians. You're the son of the good ol' town sheriff and everyone loves and adores you, and rightfully so, especially since now, on top of all that, you're the goofy and lovable science teacher. What about the two of us being so different makes you think we could ever work?"

"Why couldn't we?" I press, setting the chair that I've been holding aside as I take a step toward her. "We've been friends since the sixth grade, or at least we were until two years ago, and we were always close and made it work."

"There's a huge difference between being nothing more than platonic friends and being two people who can work in a long-term relationship, especially in a town like Evergreen Grove. If you don't think I heard the gossip about how I was such a bad influence on you and Ronnie and how people didn't know how you put up with me and my family, then you're clearly mistaken."

I do everything in my power not to roll my eyes because I get why she feels this way. In a town like Evergreen, where gossip spreads like wildfire, Bill Bennett's notorious reputation ensured that Blair and Miles were frequently the subject of conversation. It didn't take much for people to make snap judgments about Blair and Miles, but for those who were close to them, we all knew those assumptions couldn't be further from the truth.

Even now, Miles, who has a great job and runs his own successful business, continues to spark rumors. Given that he tends to be standoffish and aloof, sticking mostly to himself people see that and assume he somehow thinks he's better than everyone. I've even heard that some people think he's untrustworthy or that he's partaking in shady business dealings.

Yes, most people are sane and go to him for all their automotive needs since he's easily the best in the business, but a select few still decide to go to the next town over just to avoid dealing with him.

It didn't help that, no matter who was behind the crazy scheme growing up, Blair always took the blame for being the bad influence, even when most of the time it had been Ronnie's idea. Blair had always tried to brush it off or pretend like it didn't bother her, and sometimes she even played into it, but I could always sense the vulnerability beneath her brave facade. She was always so good at pretending like she didn't care, and while she played that role well, Ronnie and I always knew better.

"If you think for one second that I care what they think—"

She interrupts. "It doesn't matter what *you* think. *I* care what they think, Ford. I don't want you getting lumped into things with me. And sure," she continues, throwing her hands into the air, "maybe two years ago I did try to break the two of you up, but even with us having not spoken for two years until now, I'm sure if we were to get together, everyone would still find a way to blame me. I would be the one who ruined and broke up your marriage. I'd be the one responsible. It's me. It's always been me. I've *always* been the problem."

I want to tell her that I get it, or that I don't care what anyone thinks, but as she rightfully pointed out, she does. A loud, frustrated breath escapes my lips as I shake my head and rack my brain for a way to convince her that, despite everything, it can all be okay. Unfortunately, the doubt slowly starts to creep in. Is she maybe right about this?

The air grows heavy with an uncomfortable silence, amplifying the sound of our breathing, but soon, a voice breaks through the quiet. "We forgot the ice. How could I forget the ice?" Ronnie panics as she rushes toward us.

"It's fine, Ronnie," Blair assures her, turning to give Ronnie her full and undivided attention. I should be grateful for the interruption, but there's a nagging feeling that I once again screwed everything up and let another precious opportunity slip through my fingers.

"We got this, right Ford?" Blair asks, interrupting my thoughts as she brings me back to the present.

"Uh, yeah. Of course." I robotically nod, saying what I assume is the right answer.

"You go hop into the shower, take a much-needed break, and don't stress. As soon as Ford finishes with the chairs, he'll get the ice, and I'll finish up here. Everything is going to be perfect. I promise, alright?" Blair soothes, placing her hands on Ronnie's shoulders.

Ronnie lets out a long breath, the tension visibly leaving her body, as she nods her head slowly.

"Now go. We got this," Blair says, taking matters into her own hands as she spins Ronnie back toward the door and gives her a light, encouraging shove in that direction. "I mean it. I don't want to see you until right before the shower."

"Yeah, yeah," Ronnie calls back to us, but thankfully she manages a smile, one of the first I've seen from her all day, which, knowing Ronnie, says something. The woman usually exudes pure sunshine, rainbows, and butterflies.

After watching her follow directions, I wait until the back door is shut, before I turn to face Blair again.

"Blair, I should..." I begin, but she holds up a hand to stop me.

"No more. Not today. Please," she sighs, closing her eyes. "Let's just get this done like we promised."

I pinch my lips together in a straight line before agreeing with a quick nod. "Okay, yeah. Sure."

Selfishly, I want to continue right where we left off, but Blair's right. Ronnie's apparent stress makes it clear just how important this event is to her, and I'm determined not to add to that, even if it means taking on all the stress myself. Like usual, I'm going to prioritize Ronnie, and Blair's peace of mind.

"Thank you," she says, her voice quiet before heading back toward the house. I have to assume she's going to grab more of the centerpieces, but it also feels like an obvious attempt to achieve as much distance from me as she possibly can.

Then again, distance is likely the best thing for both of us, especially as I think over our conversation. Blair's mere presence is driving my senses absolutely crazy, so maybe it's best I wasn't invited to today's event, especially given how on edge the two of them seem to be.

Then again, how crazy could a bridal shower get? I'm sure they're overreacting. Isn't today supposed to be a fun and relaxing event to celebrate the bride? Either way, I'm not about to question any of it as I do as I'm told and get back to work.

While I get that I might be making things more difficult for Blair, I'm fully committed to going above and beyond to ensure that this day is nothing short of perfection for both of my best friends.

14

BLAIR

KEEPING MY PROMISE AS Ronnie's maid of honor, I survey the impressive results of my and Ford's handiwork and smile at what we've put together in such a short amount of time. Not only does the decor fit the theme perfectly, but the tent is alive with laughter and chatter, as everyone seems to be thoroughly enjoying themselves.

Most importantly, Ronnie looks beyond gorgeous in her stunning white wrap dress. Today, I finally see a glimpse of her true and uninhibited self, even if there still seems to be something hidden behind that smile of hers. When you know someone as well and for as long as Ronnie and I have, you can always tell when something is real, genuine, or forced, and while she looks happy, something still feels—off.

I can't make sense of why she's placing such high expectations on herself, especially considering today is supposed to be all about her. Everyone here, and in town, absolutely adores Ronnie, and this place is packed to the absolute brim.

I can't even say that I'm surprised that everyone who was invited said yes and showed up. Ronnie's dad has been the mayor since we were children. He is so loved and adored, it hadn't taken much for the town to fall in love with his wife and daughter as well, along with their bright and bubbly personalities. It could definitely be said that Ronnie got her charming and charismatic personality from her parents, and while I gave them ample reason to dislike me growing up, they took me in and treated me like a second daughter.

Her parents are just two amazing people and is likely why everyone always seemed so ready to forgive Ronnie for all the crazy shenanigans we put this town through, and why so many people tolerated me as well. If I was Ronnie-approved, then there must be something redeemable or slightly likable about me.

"May I steal the bride-to-be?" I ask, linking my arm through Ronnie's. I've been watching as she converses with a few of her teacher friends, and while she's appeared to be less nervous than earlier, it's still undeniably obvious that something is bugging her. As her maid of honor, I'm obligated to figure out what in the hell is going on so I can fix it as soon as possible. This is her special day and there's no way I will let it be less than perfect.

"I guess we'll let you steal her away," a middle-aged woman agrees with a playful wink as I send her a grateful smile.

"Thank you." I nod before leading Ronnie away from the small crowd.

"Is everything okay?" she asks, her face maintaining a calm facade, yet the slight tremor in her voice gives away the underlying panic that's washing over her.

"I should ask you the same thing. You seem...distracted." The last thing I want is to insult her or make her feel even more on edge, but clearly, something is going on, and I'm not backing off until I get to the bottom of it.

"I just need everything to go perfectly today."

"And it will, and it is," I promise, giving her arm a small squeeze as I lead her toward the refreshments.

This is the area I feel most proud of, as the nearby table is filled with charcuterie boards lined with cheese, fruit, and meat, along with some platters of mini caprese skewers. However, the true stars of the show are the desserts that have been made to match the blue and white theme of the wedding: macaroons, cupcakes, Rice Krispie treats, and cake pops.

However, we walk straight past the food as I lead her toward the bar.

"Two Rosy Ronnie Refreshers, please," I order as Pam, the resident bartender from Timberline Tavern, gets to work.

Living so far away, as the maid of honor, I haven't felt like I've gotten to help or support as much as I'd like. Wanting to surprise her with something unique and different, I took a chance with a signature cocktail in her honor. I'd worked with Pam to create a drink made with elderflower liqueur—giving off light floral notes—with a splash of cranberry and lime for tartness, which, to me, just fits my best friend so perfectly. She's easily one of the most stunning and beautiful people that you'll ever meet, but there's way more to her than that, as she constantly leaves you wondering and guessing what she'll do or say next.

"Sorry I'm being so weird," Ronnie apologizes as the two drinks are placed in front of us. "It's just that Pete's mom is here, and so are other members of his family from out of town. I've always felt like I'm not good enough for her or her son, and the last thing I want is for the rest of his family to think so, too."

My mouth drops open. "What? You? Not good enough for Pete?" I ask, stunned into silence as I shake my head. "If anyone is not good enough for someone, it's Pete not being good enough for you."

"You only say that because you're my best friend and you have to."

"No, I say it because I'm your best friend and know you better than anyone else, which means if anybody knows how amazing you are, it's me. You're one of a kind, and literally the most interesting and unique person I've ever met. If somebody doesn't agree or see that, then they're wrong. If anything, his family will see that today and any other time they get to be around you. There's no way they won't see how absolutely amazing you are."

She sighs before lifting her glass and taking a large gulp of her signature drink. "I hope you're right, I just can't seem to shake these nerves."

"Well, I'm obviously here with you, so if you need your wingwoman to pump you up while you go and talk with them, I'm down."

"Really?" she asks, her face lighting up with hope.

"Of course," I scoff, dismissing her worries with a small wave. I'd do anything for Ronnie, especially if it's something as easy as boosting her up. Pretty sure that's the easiest job I could ever have. "For all we know, you won't even need me, since they're likely going to fall in love with you the moment you start talking."

"Well, I'm not so sure that's true, but I do think you coming with me will help. If anything, your presence will probably calm me down and prevent me from acting like a complete weirdo."

"I really don't think you have anything to worry about, but like I said, I'll be there the entire time."

She sends me a grateful smile before lifting her glass to her lips once more, likely for some much-needed liquid courage. "Alright. Let's do this and get it out of the way so I can finally relax and actually enjoy the rest of my bridal shower."

I take an amused sip of my own drink before nodding as she leads me toward Mrs. West and the rest of Pete's family, who've all congregated at a table by themselves.

"Hey, everyone," Ronnie greets them in an exaggeratedly friendly tone. She's definitely putting on a show and going all out, and I can't say I don't understand it. I'd want my future in-laws to like me too. It's one of the many reasons why I'd be terrified to settle down with anybody in Evergreen Grove. Most everyone already has their opinions when it comes to the Bennett family, and I'm sure they'd be less than pleased to watch their son walk me through their front door. "I wanted to introduce you all to my best friend and maid of honor, Blair."

Everyone greets me with friendly enough nods and smiles, but when I look at Mrs. West, her expression shows obvious displeasure. It suddenly clicks why Ronnie was so worried.

"Hi." I wave back before being introduced to Pete's Grandma Selma, Aunt Wendy, and two cousins, Leslie and Anna.

"I remember you," Mrs. West acknowledges, her voice lacking any warmth. "You were the girl who seemed to always leave a trail of destruction and mischief wherever you went. Hopefully we don't have to worry about any of that during the wedding?"

"Oh, you don't need to worry about that. I was a stupid kid back then. I'd also never do anything to mess with Ronnie's special day." I warmly smile as I follow Ronnie's lead and do my best to remain sweet and cordial, despite feeling anything but.

"Ronnie?" Grandma Selma asks.

"Oh, that's my nickname," Ronnie explains with an awkward laugh.

Mrs. West shakes her head as she wrinkles her nose. "Oh no. That's a horrible name for a young woman. I hope you never plan to go by that in public. How would that look for Pete and his political career?"

"It's mostly just a childhood nickname that my close friends call me," Ronnie explains further as my brows furrow. Growing up, Ronnie had despised the name Veronica and had insisted that everyone call her Ronnie.

"Good, it's atrocious. If I were you, I'd insist that everyone stop calling me that immediately, especially if you expect to be taken seriously," Mrs. West adds with a slight shudder.

"I think it's a perfect nickname. It's different and unique, just like our Ronnie here." I place a hand on her shoulder. "And I don't think it sounds unprofessional at all. If anything, I think having a nickname makes her more relatable and likable to the masses. Plus, everyone in town already loves Ronnie as she is, no need to change anything about her, including her nickname."

Perhaps no one speaks back to Mrs. West, because she looks utterly astonished that I would even think about contradicting her advice. "Well, *dear,* given who your parents are, I'm not surprised that you'd be into a nickname like that. Furthermore, it makes your advice less than credible, so I would have to hope that Veronica would have a better sense of who to listen to here."

"You don't need to worry, Mrs. West. I grew up with a family in politics. I know exactly what would be expected of me, and in the circles where it's needed, I can be more than professional," Ronnie once again chimes in, clearly trying to keep the peace.

I purse my lips tightly, exerting all my self-control to refrain from unleashing my anger on this woman. If these weren't Ronnie's future in-laws and this day weren't so important, I'd definitely speak my mind, but today isn't about me, and that's what I keep reminding myself of. Instead, I lift my glass to my mouth and take a drink.

Mrs. West seems to take notice as she looks me up and down with even more disdain and disapproval. "Let me guess. You were the one who picked out the drink for this afternoon's event?"

I lift an eyebrow. "Yes. And they seem to be a big hit."

"Don't you think it's a little tacky?" she presses, lifting a brow of her own.

"Aren't bridal showers in general a bit tacky?" I challenge.

"No. Most events that I've attended have been classy and elegant. This one, on the other hand..." she trails off, letting her eyes glance around the backyard.

"Is perfect," I cut in before she can say anything else and make this even harder on Ronnie. "Everyone is having an amazing time, and like I said, the drinks have been a hit. Just look around, everyone is enjoying them," I reiterate, especially as I look at Ronnie, who appears to be on the verge of tears.

"Enjoying them or not, alcoholic beverages at an afternoon event are completely inappropriate, and it honestly makes me question your judgment, Veronica," Mrs. West admonishes.

"I think it's kind of fun. They're just drinks, Auntie," Pete's cousin, Anna, chimes in.

"Fun or not, this event is not the time or place for day drinking. It's utterly tasteless," Mrs. West says, indicating that there's no changing her mind on the matter.

"I'm sorry you think so, but either way, I hope you can at least try to have a good time. Ronnie here has lots of people who absolutely adore her and are dying to chat with her today, so I hope you'll excuse us," I say in an overly sweet tone as I grab Ronnie's hand and lead her away before anyone can say anything else. I know I probably shouldn't have used the dreaded nickname that Mrs. West so obviously hates, but I've always found it impossible not to fight back when someone pushes me first.

"Ronnie," I start once we've made some distance and I've led her away from the small mass of guests. "I'm so sorry. The last thing I wanted to do was make things even worse or harder on you."

"No," she begins, shaking her head, "you said what I've always wanted to say, but have always been too scared. Nothing I do ever seems to be good enough, and I don't know what else I can do to make her like me."

"I would say just be yourself and she's bound to love you, but for a woman like that, I don't think there's any chance of winning," I huff, looking back over my shoulder at the woman who still seems to be looking at everyone as though they are beneath her. She is clearly one of those overbearing mother-in-law's who thinks she knows best, but when it comes to Ronnie, she knows absolutely nothing.

"It's just so hard, especially when she's someone who's so close and important to Pete." She frowns, still pushing back the tears.

"I know, I'm sorry." I place a hand on her arm. "Just don't change yourself for her, or anybody. You're amazing and perfect just the way you are, and I have to imagine anyone that she deems to be good enough is a boring old snob, and that could never be you. You've always been someone who was made to stick out and be different. Please don't ever conform to being someone that she, of all people, wants you to be."

In many ways, finally meeting Mrs. West and after having spent a night with Ronnie and Pete, so many of the little changes I've noticed in my best friend are starting to make a lot more sense, and I can't say I like it. In fact, I absolutely hate it.

A smile slowly starts to form on her features. "Thanks, Blair bear."

"I mean it. Don't let these people change you, alright?"

"I promise," she assures me with a small nod.

"Now," I say, dropping my hand before once again linking my arm through hers, "we're going to spend the rest of this shower having fun and partying with the people who we know love you, alright? No more stressing about the monster-in-law."

"Alright," she agrees, as I lead her toward the rest of the bridesmaids, determined to make her forget all about that nasty run-in, while also doing the same for myself.

I can't exactly tell Ronnie to forget about what Mrs. West said when, unfortunately, my mind can't help but remember the way she also called me out for my past and for my parents. While I'd held onto the hope that my old reputation would fade away with time, it's becoming increasingly clear that some people are still unwilling to move on and forget.

Then again, how exactly can I blame them when I'm still just as stuck in the past as they are, not only with my own worries about my reputation, but with Ford's as well. If anything, I've been reminded more than ever that despite wishing to move forward and forget about who you once were, it's always going to matter, and the last thing I want to do is bring Ford down with me.

15

FORD

WHEN BLAIR CALLS, I answer. Okay, so maybe she didn't technically call, but she did send a text asking if I could give her a ride tonight.

After a few hiccups at the shower, the girls were insistent on letting loose and having a much-needed night out. Eventually, they settled on heading to the Timberline Tavern, where we can not only enjoy drinks but also take part in their weekly trivia night.

It's also been decided that tonight is the perfect opportunity for Pete to get to know everyone better, especially in a "more relaxed and casual setting" as Ronnie put it. I'm pretty sure a small barbecue is the epitome of casual and relaxed, but as usual, if Ronnie suggests something, we all go along with it.

Plus, I understand Ronnie's reasoning, but honestly, I don't want to get to know him better. I know him well enough, and I'm fully convinced the more I get to know him, the opposite will happen, and I'll only grow to despise him even more. He's shown his true colors, and as they say, when someone shows you who they truly are, believe them. I want to have faith that there's some underlying goodness in this guy, otherwise, Ronnie wouldn't have chosen him, but so far I've yet to see any evidence of that.

The problem is, I understand what it's like to have a significant other that my friends don't approve of, and navigating a situation like that can not only be emotionally draining, but incredibly isolating as well.

While my friends have valid reasons to dislike and disapprove of Jenny, it's worth mentioning that she isn't entirely without redeeming qualities. It is, after all, those attributes that made me fall in love with her in the first place, and I fully believe that, to some extent, a part of me always will, even after everything. We just weren't meant to be, and as tough as this road has been, I don't want Ronnie to have to endure that too.

Despite my reservations, I'm committed to trying my hardest tonight to be nice, and I'm assuming the same for Blair. Supposedly, Ronnie had volunteered to pick Blair up, but she'd gone and said I was taking her, so here I am doing my usual Ford thing—getting dragged into the middle—all because I've never been able to say no to her.

Then again, I don't want to. I'll happily say yes to her a million times over if it means I'm the one responsible for making her smile or making her life easier.

As I pull into the parking lot, I debate whether to take the easy route and send her a text or be a gentleman and make my way to the front door. I go with the latter, even though I find myself second-guessing that decision as I walk the steps up toward the door and knock. After everything she said the day before, the last thing I want is to make her feel weird or like I'm trying to turn this night into something it's not.

Shaking my head, I do my best to rinse my brain of those thoughts. This is simply a night of four friends getting together and enjoying each other's company, despite the mix of two guys and two girls, one of whom is an actual couple. The last thing I want to worry about is how this could look to the judgmental people of Evergreen Grove, who always seem to have something to say. Hell, even *I'm* overthinking this and reading into things, so why wouldn't they?

Raising my hand, I give the door a firm knock and don't wait long before her brother swings it open. "Uh, hey, Miles," I say, lifting my hand in an awkward greeting.

Using his head, he gestures for me to come inside, his face devoid of any true emotion, somehow making me feel even more anxious. I'd consider asking who shit in his Wheaties this morning, but given that this is a typical Miles Bennett greeting, I don't even have to wonder. Hell, that was pretty friendly for this guy. Plus, I kind of enjoy my face the way it is, and I'm definitely not looking to get it pummeled or rearranged tonight.

"So, I take it Blair is still getting ready?" I ask, already knowing the answer. Blair is forever caught in her own timeline—it's her world and we're all just living in it. Even after purposely arriving ten minutes later than planned, it's really not much of a surprise that I'm left waiting.

"I'm sure she'll be out soon." He coolly shrugs as he walks into the kitchen. The smell of something delicious wafting in the air lets me know he's likely working on dinner, so I place my hands in my pockets and nervously sway back and forth.

"So, what are you up to tonight?" I ask, attempting to make conversation.

Miles looks up from where he's standing behind the counter with a raised brow. "You know you can take a seat, right? You don't just have to stand there."

"Oh, uh, yeah. I'm fine here," I ramble. You'd think as a grown man, I wouldn't still be intimidated by Miles Bennett, but there's just something about him that always puts me on edge. I know I shouldn't judge, but his intense gaze constantly makes me feel like I'm one wrong word away from getting punched in the face.

"Whatever you say." He shrugs, dismissing my question without a second thought, his focus shifting back to the task of cutting up what looks to be a random assortment of vegetables.

I'm relieved that I don't have to endure the awkward silence for long as Blair emerges, her hair styled in a high ponytail. She's wearing a black lacy corset top, distressed jeans, and her trademark leather jacket draped over her shoulders. Spotting me, her big, beautiful, round eyes widen in surprise.

"Miles," she admonishes. "You didn't tell me Ford was here."

"And if I had, would that have made you get ready any quicker?" he inquires, his gaze never leaving the vegetables in front of him as he continues chopping.

She rolls her eyes as she walks toward where I'm standing and grabs a pair of ankle-length black boots. "Probably not," she honestly replies. "But that's still the polite thing to do. Hell, Ford here looks like he's about to shit his pants. You still giving him a hard time?"

So much for hoping that I don't look as awkward and nervous as I feel. Then again, the sweaty palms and forehead are likely a huge giveaway. Plus, does he really have to be holding a knife right now?

"Me? Give any of your friends a hard time?" he scoffs, finally looking up. "*Never*. Plus, he's the one friend of yours I *actually do like*."

I shouldn't care, especially since I have no reason to impress Miles, but it feels strangely exhilarating to know that the town grump, who doesn't seem to like anybody, doesn't mind me.

"Wow," Blair says. "That's *impressive*, he doesn't tend to like anybody. I'd take that as a *huge compliment* if I were you."

"I honestly do," I admit with a small chuckle as I reach to push my glasses up the bridge of my nose. However, as I look toward Miles, who is as stony-faced as ever, it's hard for that smile not to falter, at least a little bit.

"Don't get too excited. Plus, *like* might be a bit of an exaggeration. What I should've said is he's the one friend of yours I can tolerate," Miles offers instead.

"Honestly? I'll still take it," I chuckle. I've probably bought into the whole Bennett gossip thing a little more than I should, since, while Miles has never actually gotten physical with anybody, he really does give off that '*don't mess with me*' with attitude. Although he looks like the type of guy who's likely been in a lot of fights, I've never actually heard of any going down, and I assume that's because people know not to mess with him.

"Maybe you'd actually find certain people more likable if you actually spent some time around my friends, or really anyone for that matter," Blair offers, her hands landing on her hips, boots and all.

"I have friends," he challenges.

"No, you have colleagues and people who work for you. There's a difference," Blair shoots back.

"That's not true. I go out all the time. I'm just not one to go out for stupid shit like the Timberline Trivia Showdown."

"Yeah, that's because it's a good time, and as far as I can tell, you're still allergic to anything remotely fun," Blair doubles down.

"Fine," he says, throwing his hands up, knife and all. "You win."

I look between the two of them. "You win what? What'd I miss?"

"I'll come. Blair has been hounding me all day about going out with you guys. Just know I'm going to be miserable the entire time."

Blair props her boots beneath her armpit before happily clapping her hands together. "Good. Plus, you've been constantly hounding me about our lack of quality time while I'm home, and now we have the opportunity to spend an entire night together."

Miles sets the knife down with a shake of his head. "Yeah, with you and the rest of the three stooges, and whoever else is crazy enough to marry Veronica Prescott. You're already making me regret this, you know?" he says, turning off the stove before exiting the kitchen area while wiping his hands on his sweatpants.

"We're the three stooges, huh?" I ask with mild amusement, even though Miles is sending an annoyed glance my way. "Which one am I?"

"Oh, you're Larry, without a doubt," Blair decides right away with a definitive nod, which I suppose fits. Larry did have a tendency to go along with the crazy plans of the other two, and it seems I've yet to outgrow that part of myself.

"While you two ding-dongs figure that out, I'm going to hurry and change," Miles says, excusing himself.

With her boots back in hand, Blair finally moves to the couch and takes a seat as I follow closely behind, feeling a bit more comfortable with Miles out of the room.

I also do my best not to let my eyes roam over her body, since damn, she looks amazing tonight, but then again, what else is new? I've never failed to be impressed not only by her beauty, but also her unique personal style. In a place like Evergreen Grove, where being different draws extra attention, she's never been afraid to be her true self and stand out.

"You look really good," I can't help but blurt.

She looks up at me, grinning. "You don't look so bad yourself," she says, her eyes scanning me from top to bottom.

I do the same and shift my gaze downward. I'm wearing a pair of jeans and a plain white T-shirt with a red and black flannel thrown over the top—nothing even remotely special. "Sorry, but I've got nothing on you," I argue.

"That's debatable," she challenges, holding out a hand so I can help her stand up now that her boots are securely in place.

"I'm more than willing to debate this with you, since, like usual, I'll win," I joke, letting her hand fall into mine as my fingers wrap around hers and pull her up and into me.

Like the day in the dressing room, a warm silence envelopes the two of us, but instead of acting like a sane person, I find myself utterly transfixed by her, and instead of letting go of her hand, we hold on.

"Ford," she softly whispers, her lips drawing my gaze.

I battle against the overwhelming impulse to lean in and kiss her, summoning every ounce of self-restraint I possess. As much as I want to take advantage of the moment, deep down I know that this isn't how it's supposed to happen.

"Alright, I'm ready," Miles's deep voice says, breaking the magic as I drop Blair's hand and take a large step back. If I'm going to kiss Blair again, I need the moment to be right, and it certainly isn't going to be in her brother's apartment with him in the next room.

"Perfect. So are we," Blair says, her calm reply making me question my instincts, as if the almost-kiss never happened. Did I just make that all up in my head?

Maybe I misinterpreted the moment, and she hadn't been feeling the same powerful pull that I was. Thank God I hadn't followed my instincts and leaned in to kiss her. She had just told me yesterday that she didn't think we could work, and maybe I need to start taking her word on that a bit more seriously.

Even though I know she's only here because of Ronnie and her wedding, I can't deny that every feeling I've ever had for her has come flooding back. Sure, the timing might finally work in my favor, but it may be time to face the facts: I waited too damn long, and Blair got sick of waiting.

16

BLAIR

I KNOW I DIDN'T just make that up in my head. Ford had wanted to kiss me, and if Miles hadn't walked out at that exact moment, it probably would've happened. The opportunity was right there. All I had to do was lean in half an inch closer, and our lips would've connected.

The worst and most embarrassing part is, I'd wanted it to happen. Unfortunately, given our shared history, it's impossible for us to simply have a few random kisses or a casual hookup and expect things to return to normal. Then again, what even *is* normal when it comes to us? If I thought I was confused back then, it's a thousand times more confusing now.

I'd avoided things happening between us for so long because of the possibility of jeopardizing our friendship, but I'm no longer sure what exactly I'm trying to preserve anymore. Sure, we're slowly finding our footing once again, and I'm not completely oblivious—I get that the feelings are mutual, especially since I've come to realize that my own feelings never went away. It's no longer possible to lie to myself about it anymore, but seriously, what kind of future could we realistically have?

It's not like we can avoid the elephant in the room either. Ford is going through a divorce, and even if he wants to play it off like he's ready to move on, how can I believe he's truly ready? I know Ford well enough to understand I wouldn't be some random rebound to get him through the initial pain, but there's no denying this would be a little fast, even with our shared history.

It doesn't help that I already know how everyone in town would see it—I'd once again be the villain in this particular story. The preconceived judgments were easy enough to blow off in high school, and mostly, I didn't mind taking the heat, but now that we're grown adults and Ford's reputation as a well-liked and respected teacher is on the line, I'm no longer comfortable bringing him down with me. I refuse to do that to him.

Fortunately, I managed to persuade Miles to join us tonight, intentionally placing him between Ford and me as we sat at the table. I can't say Ford seems to be the biggest fan of this arrangement; he was not only silent on the drive over, but he's currently sitting up straight with his arms folded. There's always been something about my brother that puts him on edge. While I usually find it mildly amusing, it's hard not to feel at least a *little* bit guilty about it.

I deserve to feel bad, and I truly do, but what I really need right now is space. Even the slightest touch sends electric sparks through my body, making it increasingly difficult to keep my thoughts in check whenever he's around. He's my friend, or at least I think he is, and I'm determined to keep it that way.

"Okay, team, we need to pick it up. Second place is not an option," Ronnie motivates with a loud clap. She's always been the most competitive among us, so honestly, I'm not the least bit surprised.

"Come on now," Ford says, trying to be the voice of reason. "We're not doing too bad. We're only two points behind."

"And whose fault is that?" she asks, casting a few accusatory glances our way before fixing her gaze on me.

"Ugh, I'm sorry," I pout, since I was the one who answered our last question incorrectly. Unfortunately, my wrong answer allowed the team in first to gain an extra two points, solidifying their lead.

"In Blair's defense, none of us knew the answer either," Ford chimes in, and I toss him a grateful glance.

"Well, then next time, if you aren't sure, don't ring the bell," Ronnie suggests, once again shooting a playful glare in my direction.

"Alright, I think it's time you rein it in. It's just a game, and you're starting to sound a little desperate, and it's getting embarrassing," Pete warns his fiancé as he places a hand on her arm and pulls her back into her seat. "People are looking."

"It's fine, Pete. We know Ronnie. This is just who she is," I say, doing my best to wave it all off with a laugh, even if I don't actually find his reaction all that funny. In fact, if anyone is embarrassing themselves, it's him.

"Well, it's a little much, don't you think, babe?" he asks, turning his attention to his fiancé, clearly trying to get her on his side with this one.

"Maybe a little," she agrees, glancing down at the table like a child who's just been scolded by a parent. "I'll try to relax a little. Like you said, it's just a game."

"A game we're going to win. I'm with Veronica. We got this," Miles chimes in out of nowhere as he sets his beer down on the table.

Not only has my brother been sitting back without answering a single question, but he's barely said more than a few words the entire night. Looks like Ford and I aren't the only ones annoyed with Pete's constant badgering.

Given my brother's usual aversion to Ronnie, I'm somewhat taken aback, yet it oddly makes perfect sense. As Bennetts, we've had our fair share of being told what we should or shouldn't be, and even he can only take so much of someone doing that to someone else, even if that someone else happens to be Veronica Prescott.

"Alright, who's ready for the next question?" the announcer asks into the microphone from their spot behind the bar.

While most of the bar patrons erupt into whistles, cheers, and applause, Ronnie seems to have taken Pete's words to heart. Instead of being one of the loudest, she sits back and softly claps along.

"Alright, here is our next question: For two points, and like usual, the first team to ring in gets the chance to answer. What Italian luxury sports car manufacturer produces the models Gallardo, Huracán, and Aventador?"

Without hesitation, and almost as soon as the man finishes the question, Miles slams his hand down and rings our team's bell.

Without waiting to be called on, he answers. "Lamborghini."

"That's correct," the bartender says. "Two points for Team Bridal Brainiacs."

Our team immediately breaks out into applause as I slap my hand on Miles' back. "Wow, look at you coming in clutch. I knew we brought you for a reason."

"Well, it was about cars, and they're kind of my specialty." He casually shrugs before grabbing his beer and lifting it to his lips.

"Okay, maybe we really do got this!" I clap this time, figuring if Pete won't let Ronnie act that way, I'll have to fill in for her. "We're all tied up."

Unfortunately, as the game continues and the last questions are asked, it's clear Ronnie hasn't returned to her usual bubbly self. Her lack of enthusiasm doesn't hinder us, though; in fact, it motivates the rest of us to bring even more energy and win the entire trivia night challenge, if only to prove a point.

Ford reaches behind Miles as we exchange a triumphant high-five, and despite everything—not to mention this not being my brother's usual scene—even he can't help but sport a proud grin.

Thankfully, Ronnie seems to be returning to her normal self as we rise from our seats and share a hug. Maybe we can salvage some of the night, and my girl can finally have some fun. If anything, given the stress Pete's family put us through yesterday, this is more than needed. Hell, she deserves to let loose and be exactly who she is and wants to be.

"I think this deserves another round of drinks and maybe some more wings," I decide, figuring a celebration is more than warranted after the hard work we all put in—including Miles.

While I'm sure my brother would be happiest if we all went our separate ways and he made his way back home, I can't help but want to savor this moment and extend the night a little longer, especially as I watch Ronnie transform back into the woman I know and love. Plus, even with the lingering tension between Ford and me, I want to savor this rare opportunity to be with all my favorite people for as long as possible.

"Oh, and you know what else?" Ronnie chimes in, her face lighting up with that gorgeous smile of hers. "We should get some of those mini powdered donut things that you dip in the chocolate."

I nod vigorously, my mouth already watering. "Hell yeah we should."

"Are you sure about that, babe?" Pete's grating voice interrupts, causing my lips to press into a straight line as my hands ball into fists at my sides. I have a sinking feeling I know exactly where this is going, and the irrational urge to slam his face into the table grows by the second.

"Am I sure about what?" Ronnie asks, turning to look back at her fiancé over her shoulder, the tension between them palpable as the rest of us observe in silence, our expressions reflecting a shared sense of annoyance and frustration.

"Oh, come on, you know." He shrugs with a small laugh, as if this is the most hilarious conversation ever.

"Know what?" I press, fighting every instinct in my body to take a step toward him.

"We all know the stress of wedding planning has been a lot, so it's no surprise you've put on a few pounds these past few months, and I know you've been stressed about fitting into your wedding dress so..."

"I saw her in her wedding dress at her fitting the other day and she looked perfect," I snap. I couldn't honestly care less about how much my friend does or doesn't weigh, especially since she'd be able to rock it at any body size, but to have him comment this in front of a group of people, when she looks as stunning as she does, is a fucking joke—and not a funny one.

"I hope you aren't serious," Miles cuts in, stunning all of us. "Your fiancé is literally one of the hottest women in this bar right now, and you're worried about her eating some fucking donuts? You need to get a grip on reality, and fast. In fact, the next round of drinks, wings, and donuts is on me, and you better not say one fucking word to anyone about what they are or aren't eating."

Clearly unwilling to engage in further discussion, he abruptly pushes off his stool, the screeching sound of metal against the floor echoing before he heads to the bar to place our order, leaving us all in stunned silence.

"I need to go to the bathroom. I'll be right back," Ronnie finally says, her voice quivering.

"I'll go with you," I say, moving to stand as well.

She shakes her head and gestures for me to sit. "I'll be fine," she assures me. While I don't completely believe her, I nod in agreement, reaching out to give her hand a gentle squeeze as she walks away, reluctantly letting go only when our hands must finally separate.

"I'll be back," Pete says. While I'm tempted to tell him to go fuck himself and leave her alone, I decide not to insert myself into this one as he makes his way toward the bathroom as well. Plus, he owes her an apology, and that fucker better be on his way to give her one.

"Did I just make a mistake by not following?" I ask, my brows creasing in concern.

"No, I think it's probably best that they hash this out without an audience," Ford decides. "I can't imagine it was all that fun to have Pete talk to her like that in front of her best friends."

"That's the problem, though," I cut in. "If this is how he talks to her in front of her best friends, I don't even want to imagine the way he talks to her when it's just the two of them."

"I've wondered and worried about the same thing," he admits with a sigh.

"So what do we do?"

"What *can* we do? Are we supposed to tell her that we don't think she should go through with the wedding? I'm not sure if you remember, but I don't think that one worked out all that well for you the last time you tried it," he says, with a teasing undertone.

I shoot him a look, especially since now is *not* the time. "In my defense, last time was different. I had completely different motives for not wanting that wedding to happen."

"Well, who knows, maybe she'd actually be smart and listen to you. We both know I should have," he admits, letting out a large exhale, the full gravity and seriousness of this situation seeming to consume both of us.

"Can we be serious for a minute, though?" I ask. While I get where he's coming from, I also feel like this is an important conversation to have. "I was being selfish when I asked you not to marry Jenny, but with Ronnie and Pete, it just feels wrong. This isn't how it's supposed to be. He's not the guy she's supposed to marry. He's just so...icky."

"Icky?" Miles asks as he plops himself back down between Ford and me.

I try not to panic about what he might've overheard, especially since I've never opened up to him about my little love confession when Ford got married. Fortunately, he seems to move past that part.

"Yes, icky," I huff, sitting up straighter and sticking by my word choice.

"When it comes to that dipshit, I think it deserves something a little stronger than '*icky*.' Seriously, that guy is the biggest narcissistic asshole I've ever met in my entire life. What the hell is Veronica thinking?"

"Well, in her defense, you can't always help who you fall in love with," Ford says, coming to our friend's defense as our eyes meet. A peculiar warmth snakes through my body, but when he glances at my brother, I realize he's not referring to me; he's likely recalling the memory of falling for Jenny. "I also have to believe that he isn't always this bad. She couldn't be that naïve, right?"

"I would hope so," I sigh, dreading the idea of him getting even worse over time.

"Hey guys," Ronnie's cheery voice greets us just as the drinks and food are brought over to our table by our server. "Sorry about all that," she further apologizes.

There are red bags under her eyes that suggest she's been crying, and even though it does look like she's reapplied her makeup, I can't help but worry that she's only putting on a brave facade for our sake.

"No problem," Ford says, reverting to his usual people-pleaser self as he brushes it off, as everyone busies themselves with getting their fill of food and drinks.

"You okay?" I mouth, trying not to focus on the way that Pete has wrapped his grimy little arm around her shoulder. While I should be happy that things seem fine, I personally want him to be as far away from my best friend as possible.

She nods her head and does her best to send me an encouraging smile, but as her best friend, I can see right through it. However, I also know her well enough to know that now isn't the time to push. So much for a fun, celebratory night out with my favorite people.

17

FORD

I NEVER THOUGHT I'D reach a point in my life where I'd actually be grateful to be sitting in a car next to Miles Bennett, yet here we are. Then again, it's definitely better than the excruciating awkwardness at the Timberline tonight. It was obvious that Ronnie and Pete's over-the-top affection was clearly a desperate attempt to make us believe everything was fine, but given the tense atmosphere, it was obvious that none of us were buying it.

From the driver's seat, I glance in the rear-view mirror and catch a glimpse of Blair lost in thought, her gaze fixed out the window at the passing scenery, which given that we're in Evergreen, isn't anything special. Unfortunately, I have a pretty good idea what she's thinking about, since I'm doing the same as we all sit quietly and half-heartedly pretend to listen to the song playing on the radio.

"Thanks for being the designated driver tonight," Miles says, his voice cutting through the awkward silence as I pull into the parking lot of his apartment complex.

"No problem. I've never been a big drinker anyway, so it's not a big deal. It's kind of like my designated job anyway," I ramble.

While I'll have a drink or two every now and then, I still feel compelled to show Miles that I'm not some delinquent and that he should be glad his sister has someone like me. I hate that I'm still stuck in this perpetual cycle of needing to prove myself to him, but I just can't seem to stop.

"On that note," Miles says before clearing his throat, obviously eager to get out of my car as he swiftly unbuckles his seatbelt and opens the door just as quickly.

So much for my attempt at making a good impression. Then again, it's not like I was trying to prove to Miles that I'm some well-spoken Casanova—nobody could ever accuse me of being that.

Having been so absorbed in Miles, even I startle when he taps the back window to get Blair's attention. Looking through my mirror once more, she finally seems to come out of the trance she's been lost in.

My brows furrow. "You okay?"

"Oh," she starts, her eyes flickering with confusion as she blinks a few times before shaking her head to clear her thoughts as she brings herself back to reality. "Yeah, sorry. I think I just..." she trails off as Miles opens the car door.

"You coming?" he asks.

"Actually, I think I need a minute," she tells her brother before meeting my eyes in the mirror once more. "Do you mind hanging around for a few minutes?"

"Yeah, sure. Of course." I nod.

Miles seems to hesitate, concern etching his features, but he gives in with a firm nod. "See you in a few." He shuts the door and sends us off with a small wave before heading up the stairs toward his apartment.

Taking initiative, I quickly maneuver the car into a nearby parking stall, figuring it best not to linger in the middle of the lot. "So what's up? What's going on in that head of yours?"

"I don't even know. I'm just so worried, Ford," she says, her face etched with a seemingly permanent frown, the lines of concern somehow deepening. "When I came home, I expected everything to be one way, and I wanted to believe that everything that's happened, happened for a reason and that you were happy, and Ronnie was happy too. It didn't matter that it felt like I was being left behind and you two were progressing while I stayed the same. To me, if you both were happy and living the dream, then it was fine. Instead, it's been the opposite. You're going through a divorce or separation"—she casually waves as she spins her hand in a small circle—"or whatever it is, and then to find Ronnie marrying a guy who's taken away all the amazing and beautiful things that make her so special, it just...it sucks, and it hurts, and I hate this, and I feel so powerless to stop it."

"I hate it too," I assure her, my hand itching to reach out and offer comfort, but given our positions in the car, it isn't it all that easy. Unable to bear it any longer, I propel myself out of my seat and clumsily shuffle into the back, plopping down beside her as I hastily adjust my glasses and settle in.

In the past, I probably would've felt stupid for doing this or pushed myself into overthinking and not doing it, but as I watch her lips curve upward into a smile, I know I made the right decision. "So yeah, maybe we should think about having some kind of intervention with Ronnie to make sure she's happy, but if there's one thing I unfortunately had to learn on my own, it was that I had to make my own choices and mistakes to learn what I truly wanted."

"And did you actually find out?"

My brows pinch together in confusion. "What?"

"You said your mistakes led you to finding out what you really wanted, so did you do it? Do you finally know what you truly want?"

You. That's what I want to say, but given the current strange and disordered state of things with Ronnie, it almost doesn't feel right to say it just yet. "Maybe," I lie instead. "If anything, I now know what I don't want. It isn't like I have everything figured out, but it finally feels like I'm heading in the right direction."

"And you don't think we can help Ronnie figure this out before she makes too huge of a mistake too?"

"Well, I can't exactly say that you doing something similar on my actual wedding day helped me all that much."

She lets out a frustrated breath and rolls her eyes. "Yeah, well, clearly I waited too long and was too late. Maybe if we sit her down before the actual wedding day, we can stop it before it goes too far."

I hesitate. Would I have stopped the wedding from happening if Blair had told me earlier instead of waiting just minutes before I was supposed to walk down the aisle? "Maybe," I concede. "But do we really think Ronnie is the type of person to be talked out of something she has her mind set on? You two are practically the same person, and I highly doubt you could be talked out of anything, especially when you felt like it was the right thing for you."

"You're probably right," she agrees with another sigh. "But if there is one thing I've learned, it's that there's nothing worse than having regrets. While I still look at your wedding day as one of my most embarrassing and traumatizing moments, I'm glad I did it; otherwise I would've spent the last two years wondering 'what if?'"

"Well, unfortunately for me, I'm now the one living in that 'what if' scenario. I still wonder how different our lives would've been if I'd actually done what I'd really wanted to do that day and called off the wedding and ran off with you instead of walking down that aisle."

Her face goes pale as her eyes widen in surprise. "What you really wanted to do?" she repeats.

"Obviously. You had to have known that my feelings were mutual. I've always been in love with you, Blair," I say. Without thinking, my hand reaches out as I place it on top of her own, my fingers falling perfectly between hers, almost like a missing piece of a puzzle that's finally been solved. "It just felt like it was too late, and despite wanting to run, I couldn't do that to Jenny, not on her wedding day," I say, my voice softening into a regretful whisper.

Her eyes fall to our interlocked fingers as I brush my thumb against hers. "I loved you, too, and I want to say that I understand, but selfishly, I have to ask about me and my feelings. You say you couldn't do that to Jenny, but what about me? Was I not worthy of any consideration?" she asks, her eyes slowly rising until they meet mine.

"That's not fair and you know it," I challenge as I feel her pulling her fingers away from mine, but instead of letting her off the hook, I reach for her hand and grip it tightly. "You waited too long, Blair. I would've chosen you had you truly given me the chance, but you left me first. You left Evergreen Grove and followed Max all around the country. So I wasn't the only one that chose someone else. You did the same exact thing, and you did it first."

She pulls her hand away from mine more forcefully. "Are you serious?" she scoffs. "Because that's not how it went down and *you know it*," she echoes, repeating back the words I'd just used on her.

"What are you talking about?" I ask, my voice rising in frustration. Rewriting history is the last thing I'm going to let her do. "Of course, that's exactly how it went down. We kissed on graduation night, then we left on our graduation trip the next day to that music festival, and it was like you couldn't get away from me fast enough."

She stares at me as if I'm the biggest idiot in the world, and maybe I am, but I remember everything about that trip. Watching her fling herself at that musician right after I'd finally started to believe that I was on the verge of having the person I'd always wanted left me utterly confused and emotionally shattered.

She scoffs. "Yeah, because you kissed me, and I thought that was it. I was finally going to be your person, and then Jenny showed up, and it was like I was once again your second choice."

Now it's my turn to stare at her. "My second choice?" I ask, throwing my hands into the air. "Blair. You've *never* been the second choice. Yes. I'll be honest. I did love and care about Jenny, but she never held a candle to you. In fact, I think that's why she finally ended things. She has, unfortunately, *always* known where she stood. Even with you not talking to me these past few years, you were always the main source of all of our big fights."

I hate admitting this to her, since the last thing I want to do is blame my failed marriage on something Blair had no control over, but it's the truth. Despite how hard I tried to move past my feelings for my old friend, it was impossible, and Jenny, unfortunately, knew that too.

Her head shakes, mouth slightly agape, as she tries to process what I'm saying. "I can't do this. Not tonight," she says, moving to turn toward the door as she reaches for the handle.

I should let her go. I should let her walk away once and for all. That would be the smartest decision here, but when it comes to Blair Bennett, I could never be accused of being a smart man. Instead, I reach for her arm one more time, pulling her into me and pressing my demanding lips to hers.

I fully anticipate her resistance, but she completely surrenders into my embrace, her body melting into mine. I would've even understood if she wanted to slap me, but instead, her hand lands gently on my cheek as her lips greedily press against mine.

I lose myself in the smell and taste of her. Her presence has always been accompanied by a heavenly aroma of vanilla and honey, but it's nothing compared to the delicious taste of her lips. Sure, there is a slight hint of alcohol, but I can truthfully say that's not what's so intoxicating about her in this moment.

This isn't our first kiss, as we did share one back in our teenage years. However, that sweet and innocent kiss pales in comparison to the passion and fiery intensity of this moment.

No longer hesitant like before, I fully embrace the moment and draw her closer to me, yearning for her heat and her touch. She seems to feel the same way as she easily crawls into my lap, her knees straddling my thighs while my hands tightly grip her waist.

Despite being in the middle of a parking lot with the risk of being seen, the passionate collision of our lips consumes my full attention. My hands are also on a mission of their own: one slides lower, giving her ass a light squeeze, while the other slowly slides up her back before cupping the nape of her neck.

My tongue caresses her bottom lip, silently pleading for entry, and she eagerly welcomes me, deepening our kiss. Her hand moves from my cheek up and into my hair, giving it a light tug. I try not to smile into the kiss, but ultimately fail.

She's everything I've ever wanted, and this moment is a dream come true as I feel her body and hips grind into mine, where I've long since grown hard, as a soft panting moan escapes her lips. My eyes close, and I feel myself wanting to drift away.

I don't want to stop. In fact, it almost feels impossible, but as I'm hit with an overwhelming feeling to do the right thing, I bring my hands back to her waist and carefully peel my lips away from hers. Despite the strong desire to delve into these suppressed emotions and experiences that I've been craving for way too long, I recognize that now is not the opportune time.

Nor would it be appropriate for me to try in her current state. Not only has she been drinking tonight, but I know she's extra emotional with everything going on with Ronnie.

"Wait one second," I beg. *If I don't do this now, I'll never be able to stop.* "I'm not sure this is the best idea."

I'm not sure what she was expecting me to say, but that clearly isn't it, as her eyes go from glassy to dark in a matter of seconds and narrow. "You're the one who kissed me," she hisses.

"No, I know. I wanted to, and I still want to but I'm not sure..." I start as I reach a hand to adjust my glasses that had gone askew during the heat of the moment.

She interrupts. "Don't worry. I get it," she huffs, placing her hands on my chest as she pushes herself up and off me.

I reach for her once again, not willing to let her leave before we talk this out. "Blair, wait."

"Don't. Just don't," she says, lifting a hand to stop me as she reaches for the door and practically shoves it open.

"Blair. I don't think you get it." Now that the door is open, I probably shouldn't be speaking so loudly, especially since I sound so incredibly desperate, but by all definitions, I am. This can't be how this already shitty night ends. "This isn't about me not wanting you."

She waves me off as she steps out of the car and turns back to face me. "Oh, I get it. Believe me, I get it. If there's anyone out there who gets it, it's me."

"No, you don't," I argue. This was not how I wanted this night to end. "Clearly, you don't get it at all. I want to be with you, in every single way, but..."

"But nothing. There's a reason we've never worked in the past, and I momentarily let myself get distracted, thinking we could somehow work, but we can't. End of story!" she shouts before slamming the door in my face.

Maybe she's right. Maybe we can't work, but that is not what this is about, and it's also why I refuse to let her walk away from me all over again. I waste no time opening my own door and chase after her as she hurries toward the stairs at record speed. "Blair, please. Just let me explain."

"No, Ford. You need to stop," she says, thankfully halting as she turns to look down at me from the steps above.

I open my mouth to speak, but the door above opens and Miles' intimidating frame comes into view. "Everything okay out here?" he asks, a worried but protective glance moving back and forth between the two of us.

That guy could easily pummel me to death, but I'm willing to risk it. Clearly, I'm also not above begging. "Yes, or no...I don't know, but Blair, can we please talk about this? You have it all wrong."

Blair purses her lips as she looks at me for a few seconds before turning to look up at her brother. "No, I'm done with this conversation."

My shoulders sink as I watch her walk the rest of the way up the stairs. The one upside is that instead of looking at me like he wants to kill me, Miles at least looks vaguely conflicted as he wraps an arm around his sister's shoulder before leading her inside and shutting the door.

"Fuck!" I curse, my frustration at an all-time high as I lift my hands and place them behind my head and grab a fistful of hair in each hand. So much for trying to do the right thing. There's nothing I would've loved more than to keep going, but there was something that hadn't felt right. I love Blair way too much to ever put her in a position where I could somehow take advantage of her.

She deserves so much more from me than an emotional hookup in the back of my car. If we're ever going to cross that line, I need her to be sure. I refuse to be yet another mistake in her life.

Then again, I'm pretty sure I just blew whatever chance I had for anything real to ever happen between us. Even so, I'd do what I just did a thousand times over. Blair deserves so much more, even if I inadvertently hurt her in the process. I just have to hope that when things settle down, she'll give me a chance to explain myself.

18

BLAIR

NOT ONLY DO I get the pleasure of being turned down—again. I now have to be embarrassed about the fact that my big brother had to jump to my rescue and save me. While I should be grateful, I can't say I'm thrilled about Miles seeing me like this. I'm twenty-eight, for God's sake—one would think I'd finally be capable of taking care of myself by now.

"So, are you going to explain what that was all about?" Miles asks, clearly not in the mood to waste any time.

With a casual shrug, I shake his arm from my shoulder and make my way over to the couch. As I collapse onto the cushions, I let out a muffled '*oof*'. You'd think I'd have learned by now that this thing is anything but comfortable. "You really need a new couch," I complain, my features scrunching in annoyance.

"Nice try, but you're not changing the subject," he says, sitting down, and leaving the spot in the middle open. At least I can be grateful for some semblance of space, I suppose.

"Well, have you ever thought that I'd perhaps be more willing to open up if I wasn't sitting in pain? I'm pretty sure I just bruised my ass."

He rolls his eyes as his lips shift into an amused grin. "Well, considering you've been nothing but a pain in the ass my entire life, consider us even now."

"Ha, ha!" I say, my voice dripping with sarcasm and devoid of any amusement. "You know you love me."

"I do, which is exactly why I'm concerned about how I just saw you running away from Mr. Nice Guy Hastings. That guy couldn't hurt a fly, which is why I'm wondering what in the hell he could have done to have you doing everything in your power to get away from him so quickly."

I sigh, just as Bubba, my brother's overweight bulldog, pokes his head out of the main bedroom and slowly makes his way to join me on the couch. "He is a nice guy, and perhaps that's the problem." I shrug, looking down at the white and brown spotted bulldog as he cuddles in close, resting his head on my lap.

"Yeah, sorry, kid. I'm not exactly following. How is him being the nice guy a problem?" he asks, reaching over to give the dog's backside a few small and loving pats.

"We all know I'm the messed-up white trash girl, and despite trying to fit in with the mayor's daughter and the sheriff's son, I've never been able to shake my reputation. I've never been good enough for any of them."

His brows furrow. "Please don't tell me you're still feeding into that bullshit, and please don't tell me that Ford said any of that tonight, because if he did..."

I interrupt, since clearly I'm only making things worse. "No, he didn't, and he never would. It's me. I know where I stand, and I'm the one who messed things up—like usual."

"I'm lost," he says, shaking his head as he tries to keep up, but is clearly failing. "Just tell me what the hell happened tonight."

Covering my face with my palm, I release a small groan of frustration. This isn't exactly a conversation I want to be having with anyone, let alone my brother, but I also know he isn't about to let this go. Plus, I feel like I need to talk to someone about this, and since I don't want to worry Ronnie with my drama, this feels like my only option.

"He kissed me, and then I kissed him, and then he ended it. I mean, obviously, he regrets it, and I get it. I'm a mess, and I'm not sticking around, so what's the point?" I ask, throwing my hand up in the air, causing Bubba to jump as he lifts his head and tilts it up in confusion. "Even so, that doesn't mean it didn't hurt."

As Miles looks torn between confusion and annoyance, there's a small flicker of understanding that takes over as he slowly nods his head. "So you two finally did something about those feelings of yours after all these years, huh?"

Now it's my turn to be taken aback as I wrinkle my nose. "What?"

An annoyingly smug grin crosses his features. "You two were never fooling anybody. It was so obvious that you had feelings for each other. I'm just surprised it's taken you this long to do something about it."

My cheeks warm with color, but not for the reason he probably assumes, as I'm unfortunately reminded of the first time I tried to do something about it on Ford's wedding day. However, despite my willingness to open up about being kissed and ultimately rejected, I'm not yet ready to reveal the details of the most embarrassing thing I've ever done. I can't even imagine what his take on that would be, and honestly, I'd rather never know.

"Does it really even matter at this point?" I ask, doing my best to shrug him off as I run my fingers over Bubba's soft fur. "He ended things, and I'm leaving in just over a week. I'm just so tired of thinking about this, and I'm ready to let go and finally be done with this drama once and for all."

He lets out a small laugh as he drapes his arm over the back of the couch. "Fat chance of that. You know you're going to obsess over this all night."

I stick my tongue out at him before carefully removing Bubba's paws from my lap and stand up with a satisfied huff. "Little do you know. Because, if anything, I plan to have the best sleep of my entire life. I mean, we kissed, so what?" I shrug as I walk toward the guest room where all my stuff has strategically been thrown about the room. "Now I can move on and let this old and silly crush officially die out for good. Adios! Sayonara!" I call behind me as I lift a hand and wave before doing the same with the other.

"Good luck with that," Miles calls one last time before I shut the door behind me.

Closing my eyes, I lean my head against the door and groan. He's right—there's no way I'm going to be able to sleep tonight.

"Ugh," I groan, my muffled voice escaping into my pillow as I press it firmly against my face. Unlike the couch in the living room, the bed at Miles' place is like sinking into a soft and fluffy cloud, enveloping me in its comforting embrace, yet somehow, sleep still evades me.

Normally, when I go out and drink, I peacefully pass out, but this time, just as my annoying older brother predicted, I'm wide awake, tossing and turning. Reluctantly, I let out a huff of air as I fumble through the darkness to reach for my phone.

I squint against the intense brightness, my whining growing even louder as I check the time. It's two-fucking-thirty in the morning. I should go out and see if my brother has any mela-tonin or maybe even some Nyquil, because at this point, I'm desperate for sleep. Is it too much to ask for at least a few hours of peaceful rest so I can finally let go and escape this nightmare of an evening once and for all, even if it is only for a few measly hours?

I'm even more desperate since I'm supposed to be meeting Ronnie for breakfast tomorrow before helping her put together the wedding favors. I need my beauty sleep, especially since she'll definitely be able to tell something is wrong when I show up with dark circles under my eyes that are bigger than Mount Everest. God, what is wrong with me? Why can't I just be there for my best friend without making something about me?

I'm sure the blue light from my phone isn't going to help, and I really should go and look for something to put me to sleep, but instead of doing just that, my fingers scroll through my screen until I end up in my texts and pull up in my last communication with Ford. I immediately type "I'm sorry," but before I can hit send, I delete the message and type in something else.

> **Blair:** You awake?

Not wanting to overthink it, I hit send as a wave of panic washes over me. Of course, he's not awake. I'm the only idiot who's stupid enough to overthink everything.

The irresistible urge to hurl my phone across the room consumes me, but just as I'm about to give in, three bubbles materialize. So maybe I'm not the only one awake, tormenting myself over our disaster of an evening.

With a jolt, I sit up straight in bed, eyes widening in anticipation. I'm not even sure how I'm supposed to feel right now as my emotions shift between happiness, worry, and confusion. My gaze remains fixated on the three small bubbles, teasing me as they repeatedly disappear before suddenly resurfacing. Looks like I'm not the only one obsessing over what happened and how the hell we're going to talk this through.

Finally, his message appears.

> **Ford:** I'm so sorry, Blair.

> **Ford:** The last thing I'd ever want to do is hurt you. You have no idea how hard it was for me to pull away from that kiss. Don't think for even one second it was because I wanted to.

Getting confirmation that he didn't entirely want to end things brings some relief, but it doesn't change the fact that he ultimately did. Before I have the chance to reply, three more bubbles appear as he continues typing away. Lifting my hand, I nervously nibble on the edge of my thumbnail, a horrible habit, especially since I'd only just gotten a fresh manicure a few days ago.

> **Ford:** Ever since we kissed that first time, I've dreamed about what it would be like to kiss you again, and while it was mind-blowing and everything I'd ever imagined it would be, I also didn't want it to be something you'd regret. I also know you were drinking earlier, and I just panicked. I can't be the guy that takes advantage of you in a weak moment. If we kiss again, I need it to be when you are fully clear-headed and know without a shadow of a doubt that it's something you want.

My breath catches, and a flutter runs through me as I read his message. Okay, so maybe it's still slightly annoying that he ended things since that kiss was anything but a drunken mistake, but at least it shows he still cares. It also shows that he's still the same Ford I fell in love with when we were kids—his genuine kindness and unwavering protectiveness remain. He's always had a special knack for looking out for others, particularly me.

Before I can type out a reply, he once again beats me to it. "*Come on, Ford,*" I mumble to myself as I toss my head back in frustration.

> **Ford**: So what do you think? Do you think it's possible that I'll get a second chance?

I bite my bottom lip as it tugs up into a smile. Hell, we aren't even in the same room and the guy has me blushing.

Blair: That depends…

Ford: On what?

Blair: How much begging you plan to do for my forgiveness

Ford: Oh, so it's like that, huh? Plus, I was thinking the next time we kissed, it would be you who'd do the begging.

My mouth drops open in pure shock before a pleased, girlish giggle leaves my lips. Who knew my little Ford had it in him? But honestly, I kind of love it.

Blair: I don't know. Once again, I think that depends.

Ford: On what?

Blair: On whether you're capable of giving me something to beg for.

Ford: I think you underestimate me, Bennett. They don't call me Panty Dropper Hastings for nothing.

I laugh out loud, quickly lifting a hand to stifle the giggles. Just because I've been unable to sleep doesn't mean Miles has been cursed with the same problem. The last thing I need to do is wake him up with my flirty texts with the guy I'd been whining to him about only a few hours earlier.

> **Blair:** No one calls you that!

Ford: Maybe not yet, but I think you will be after the next time we're together

> **Blair:** In your dreams, Hastings!

Ford: Pretty sure it's you who is going to be seeing me in your dreams tonight.

I raise an eyebrow. Since when did he get so cocky? Not that I dislike it. If anything, I kind of like seeing this side of him, even if I've already been in love with the sweeter and softer side of him for years.

> **Blair:** Speaking of dreams, I should probably get some sleep. We're supposed to be meeting Ronnie tomorrow.

Ford: You're probably right. I'd say in that case I'll see you tomorrow, but we both know you'll be seeing me sooner than that.

I roll my eyes. Although, why do I have the feeling he's right?

> **Blair:** Goodnight, Ford

Ford: Goodnight, Blair bear

19

Ford

"THANK YOU SO MUCH for coming," my mom says, her hug tight and comforting, and like usual, she holds on for a few seconds longer than needed.

"Of course. Where else would I be?" I ask, even if a part of me is currently wishing that I could've gone to breakfast with Blair and Ronnie this morning. While I'd been invited by the ladies, I couldn't bring myself to ditch my mom and our weekly Sunday church date. As tempting as it is, spending more time with Blair will have to wait a few more hours. Given the thoughts I've been having about her after our text conversation, I can't help but think that this is exactly where I need to be.

Okay, maybe I'm not actually devoutly religious and don't necessarily view my explicit thoughts about Blair as morally impure. In fact, I have no intention of suppressing these fantasies—if anything, I'm hoping to make them a reality.

My attendance at church week after week is solely to ensure my mom's happiness—a result of my inherent need to be a perpetual people pleaser.

"So, I'm going to guess that I can't convince you to come over for some brunch?" she asks, attempting to sway me with a soft pout.

Apologetically, I give a slight shake of my head. "Not today. I'm supposed to be heading over to Ronnie's to help with some last-minute wedding stuff."

As if slightly inconvenienced, she lets out a huff, but her smile reveals her true, playful intent. While my dad, the town sheriff, was never fully supportive of my friendship with Ronnie and Blair, my mom has always held a soft spot for the two women. "In that case, I suppose I'll just have to see you soon," she says, leaning closer and giving me one last hug before we say goodbye and I make my way out the church doors.

Unlike my mom, I'm impatient to make my escape, relieved that this week I won't have to waste hours of my day listening to her gossip with the other churchgoers. There's something about this particular setting that's not only fascinated me, but driven me crazy at the same time.

Ever since I was a young kid, week after week I'd been surrounded by the constant chatter of the same women repeating the same gossip over and over again. While they'd sit there gossiping away, we kids, and occasionally their husbands, would exchange knowing glances, silently urging each other to step in and break up the conversation so we could finally go home and eat.

Walking out the door, I reach up and loosen my tie, feeling immediate relief, but it doesn't last long as I practically run straight into Jenny. It's really not a surprise to see her here; while we were married she joined me week after week. For appearance's sake, she even sat next to us for a few weeks to avoid the gossip and stares, but eventually, we bit the bullet and she moved to sit elsewhere. That week, it was especially impossible to avoid the stares, and even worse, it took even longer to get the women to leave.

Jenny quirks a brow. "Running off already?"

"Oh, uh yeah. I have some plans," I say, hating the way my cheeks seem to flush. I know it shouldn't matter, but a wave of guilt also washes over me as I recall the texts I sent Blair last night. Even though we've agreed that it's okay to see other people, that doesn't mean that I want my soon-to-be ex-wife to know about it.

She seems to see right through me as she knowingly nods her head. "Let me guess, those plans include Blair Bennett."

I nonchalantly shrug my shoulders, attempting to dismiss her judgmental tone. "Well, yeah, but Ronnie's going to be there, too. We're helping with wedding favors."

We may be separated, but that doesn't make it easy to shake the feeling that I'm somehow in the wrong here. Despite her obvious attempts to keep her distance, and the gossip about her dating other people, it seems that old habits are proving hard to break.

"Right, and I'm sure you're hating every minute of it," she says, rolling her eyes.

"Considering she's been one of my best friends since child-hood, I think it's understandable that I would be happy to see her. So no, I'm not hating it," I say, not hiding the defensiveness in my tone. I was never a fan of this attitude before, and now I'm even less inclined to appreciate it when I no longer have to put up with it.

"And I'm sure your silly little crush on her has nothing to do with it," she challenges, placing her hands on her hips as she tilts her head to the side.

"Even if it did, that'd be none of your business. Considering you've been nothing but vocal about needing this separation and divorce, I'm simply not in the mood to revisit the same argument that we've been going in circles about for years."

"And this is exactly the reason why I did. I'm tired of playing second best to the one you've always wanted."

I try my best to suppress the guilt, but it stubbornly persists. As much as I wish I could be the guy who could argue and say that she's wrong and I've only ever wanted her—she's right. As much as I loved Jenny and tried to be the husband she deserved, a part of me always longed for Blair.

My face falls. "Jenny—"

"No," she starts, raising a hand to stop me, "I'm no longer looking to hold you back from spending time with the one you really want to be with, so go."

I sigh, wishing I knew what to say, but unfortunately, I'm at a loss.

"Seriously, Ford, just leave already," she insists, and although I wish our parting could be more amicable, I recognize that I won't be the one who comes out on top. I'm pretty sure neither of us is truly winning here. A part of me knows this is probably a test, like so many others that she's subjected me to during our marriage, but I don't have it in me to keep fighting this same fight. Instead, I do as I'm told and make my way toward my car.

Arriving at Ronnie's parents' house, I wish I still felt as excited about seeing Blair and Ronnie as I did earlier. Regrettably, during the drive over, all I could focus on was what a letdown I've been to the people who counted on me and loved me the most. Not only did I let Jenny down, but Blair as well when I knowingly let the wrong woman walk down the aisle toward me.

The only consolation I have now about this afternoon is that we won't be working on today's project at Ronnie's future place with Pete. Dealing with Jenny has already soured my mood enough, and I'm certain it would only worsen if I were forced to spend even more time with that guy. Luckily, it seems like today will only be the three of us.

While heading toward the front door, I take out my phone and shoot Ronnie a text, letting her know I'm here. Luckily, she promptly responds, letting me know they are in the backyard and to let myself in.

While it's clear Pete has been trying to make his place the nicest in Evergreen Grove, the real honor has always gone to the Prescotts. With its expansive size and breathtaking beauty, the place boasts a giant and inviting porch along with an eye-catching red door and shutters, truly defining its unique character. He can try all he wants to outdo this place, but I'm pretty sure it'll be next to impossible.

Heading back down the front steps, I let myself through the side gate, the familiar scent of freshly bloomed flowers filling the air, reminding me once again, why it truly is the best in town. Ronnie's mom has more than outdone herself. The backyard is large and sprawling with a massive array of different colored flowers. That's not the only thing she's prided herself on growing, as she's also renowned for cultivating the most delicious fruit and vegetable garden in town, which she's constantly sharing with her neighbors and friends.

In the distance, a stunning red barn catches the eye, but the true beauty lies in the expansive, sparkling pond. It's hardly surprising that Ronnie has chosen this spot to get married next week.

"There's the golden boy. He finally made it," Ronnie cheers as she waves me over to the table where the two of them have set themselves up at, currently filled to the brim with tiny jam-filled jars, likely made from Mrs. Prescott's garden.

Yet, it's not the first thing that catches my eye; instead, my focus goes to the beautiful doe-eyed blonde sitting at the table. Today, she's opted for a more relaxed look, wearing an oversized band T-shirt and black biker shorts, her hair pulled up into a giant messy bun on the top of her head, with random strands falling to the sides.

While Blair might have been the catalyst for my fight with Jenny today, all those negative thoughts evaporate as soon as I see her. I can't concentrate on that, not when I can finally immerse myself in the intoxicating feeling that comes along just from being this close to her. My top priority, though, is not dwelling on our conversation from last night, as it would surely turn my face bright red as the two of them gave me shit for it.

I've known these two long enough to know exactly how that would go down.

"You know, you two heathens could easily have joined me today. In fact, I ran into your parents there," I say, doing my best to focus my attention on Ronnie, even if all I want to do is stare in Blair's direction.

"And risk ruining the reputation for being known as the town's resident bad girl that I've spent years and years building? No thanks," Blair tsks.

"Plus, not all of us enjoy being suck-ups. The second I turned thirteen and my parents let me, I stopped going and haven't looked back," Ronnie adds, her gaze downward as she skillfully wraps a blue ribbon around one of the jars.

"I'm not a suck-up," I defend, placing a hand over my heart as I walk closer. "I can't help that I enjoy seeing my mom happy."

"Sorry bud, that's quite honestly the definition of a suck-up," Ronnie says, finally glancing up.

"Fine. Call me whatever you want. I can take it," I say, lifting my hands in the air, as if beckoning for them to continue.

"Whatever you say, mama's boy," Blair happily obliges.

I chuckle and roll my eyes. "There are worse things I could be than a mama's boy."

"I don't know. Pete is also a pretty big mama's boy, and I have to say, it's probably one of my least favorite things about him," Ronnie admits as she reaches for another jar to work on.

"My least favorite thing is that he's a giant ass," Blair bluntly states as she grabs the jar that Ronnie had just been working on and attaches a small card to it that reads "*Spread the Love*".

With bated breath, I anticipate Ronnie's annoyed response, but fortunately, she doesn't appear to take it too personally. Instead, she reaches toward Blair and lightly smacks the blonde on the arm.

"Blair!"

"Hey," she begins, holding up her hands. "I'm just speaking the truth and saying what no one else will."

"He's not always an ass," Ronnie tries to defend. "Right, Ford?" she asks, looking over my way.

I hesitate as my eyes move between the two women, who clearly want me to take their side. "He's not always *not* an ass," I give in, feeling the need to have Blair's back here. If she's going to be honest and go there, then I need to as well.

"Okay, so maybe he can be an ass sometimes, but I promise he has his good qualities, too."

"Honestly, Ron? I'd love to see that side of him. I really would, especially since an amazing guy is exactly what you deserve, but every time I try to give him a chance, he only shows the opposite of what you've been claiming him to be."

Ronnie reaches out and places a hand on Blair's arm. "I appreciate you looking out for me. That means everything and I truly wouldn't expect anything less," she says before looking up at me, too. "From either of you. But seriously, neither of you need to worry. He's great and I love him, and that's what matters here. Okay?" she asks, in a tone that not only shows how serious she is, but also indicates that she's done with this conversation and doesn't want to discuss it any further.

"Okay," I say, while Blair nods her head too.

"Just —" Blair starts before pausing as she seems to process her thoughts. "Just know that if you ever change your mind or if you ever need to talk about him or anything, for that matter, you know you can always talk to us—always."

Ronnie scoffs. "Of course I know that. You two are my people, and even after I get married, I'm always going to need my two best friends."

"Same." Blair smiles, her gaze briefly connecting with Ronnie's before settling on me, conveying a subtle tinge of sorrow that, unfortunately, I understand all too well.

After I got married, she distanced herself from me, and although it was undeniably painful, I get why she found it necessary. If anything, distance was likely what I also needed while I tried to make my marriage work with Jenny. However, if there's anything that this last week has shown me, it's that I need Blair in my life, and it finally seems like we might both be on the same page about that.

20

BLAIR

I'VE OFFICIALLY BEEN BACK in Evergreen Grove for exactly one week, and that can only mean one thing—Margarita Monday! However, I'm overcome by an odd sense of excitement and sadness as I walk into SalsaLeedo Sal's. When I first arrived in town, I'd been stressed and counting down the days until I could fly home to Los Angeles. With the first week having flown by so quickly and only one week left before I have to say goodbye to Ronnie, Miles, and Ford all over again, I'm filled with an overwhelming sense of melancholy.

From my earliest memories, I'd always imagined what it would be like to escape this small town, so when it actually happened, it felt like a dream come true. Yes, it had been hard to leave Miles, Ronnie, and Ford, but it also felt needed. Distance seemed like the key to not only escaping my unfortunate reputation, but also my feelings for Ford.

The joke's *clearly* on me, since even with him choosing to get hitched to someone else, my feelings have refused to fade away. Even to this day, he still feels like the one person in my life that I can't function or live without.

Ugh, why did he have to go and ruin everything by kissing me? It would've been so much easier to leave all over again if I didn't have to remember the electrifying sensation of his lips pressed against mine. Then again, if history repeats itself, this will just be another one of those teasing one-offs where I think *this is finally it* before it gets taken away from me and my world comes crashing down all over again.

A little dramatic? Probably. But that's exactly how it felt to eighteen-year-old me ten years ago. So much so that I took a crazy offer from a complete stranger and his band to follow them around on tour.

One would think I've matured since then, but between the lingering glances and the electric sensation coursing through my body at even the slightest contact with Ford while we helped Ronnie with her wedding favors, all those vulnerable feelings came rushing back. The simple act of him passing me a jar, our fingers grazing for nothing more than a split second, sent a surge of tingling heat down my spine.

Then again, maybe this is nothing more than my body's physical reaction to not getting laid in far too long. Whenever Max and I got back together, things were always hot and heavy for the first few weeks, as we couldn't keep our hands off each other. While we may struggle in many aspects of our relationship, sex is not one of them. But as we each got busy, and he decided he'd rather go out, party, drink, and get high instead of spending quality time with me, it became way too easy to fall out of sync with each other, which is exactly what happened in the last few weeks leading up to our most recent break-up.

While weddings are often seen as prime opportunities for romantic encounters, the lack of suitable candidates in Ronnie's wedding party dampens any hopes of finding a worthy hookup partner.

Then again, while Ford and I haven't brought up the topic of those flirtatious texts on Saturday night, my thoughts have often circled back to them. Sure, it'd be nice to fuck him and get it out of my system, but part of me knows that being with Ford could never be like that. Given our history and shared feelings, I think we've both always known that if something were to happen, it'd be life-changing, and I'm guessing neither of us is truly ready for something that big happening right now.

Not only am I still trying to live my dream life away from Evergreen Grove, but he's going through a divorce. It's way too complicated, or at least that's what I keep telling myself, especially as the temptation to be near him only intensifies.

Walking into Sal's, I'm once again greeted by that same nostalgic scent of warm tortillas and tangy salsa. I've heard that it's never a good sign when you can smell the food so strongly when you enter a restaurant, but given how amazing Sal's is and the staple it is in the community, there's no way I could agree with that statement.

It's no surprise to see that Ronnie and Ford have already arrived and are both snacking on the chips and salsa as I approach. Unlike last time, though, when Ronnie and I arrived first and it had been Ford who'd been forced to choose who to sit next to, it's now my turn to make that choice.

Back in the day, I'd been faced with the same question many times about who to sit next to, especially given my chronic lateness, but today, there's an extra layer to all this that has me feeling oddly conflicted, almost as if this is some kind of test that I haven't studied for. While maybe it's not some life-changing decision, it does feel like what I decide will ultimately change the course of my life. *God, I really am dramatic today.*

I'm pretty sure I'm the only one overthinking this, as the right and sane answer is to choose the spot next to Ronnie. Then again, in this town, nobody would ever accuse me of being either of those things, so I go against my better judgment and slide in next to Ford, nudging his butt with mine, while also elbowing his arm. He immediately moves over, making more room on *our* side of the booth.

"Some things never change, I see," Ronnie teases before crunching down on a chip. "Late as always," she clarifies, even if I suspect the double meaning there.

"One of these days, I swear I'm going to arrive early and surprise the hell out of you," I declare, immediately reaching for a chip myself.

"I'll believe that only when I see it," Ford teases, and this time it's his turn to give my arm a playful nudge.

"Well, maybe it's for the best," I decide definitively as I dip my chip into the perfectly runny salsa. "If I changed, I wouldn't be the same old Blair that you both know and love, and then where would we be? I need at least a few people in this town to like me."

"Oh, be quiet," Ronnie scoffs, dismissing my comment with a wave of her hand. "Do you know how many people have asked me when you were coming back into town?"

I try not to roll my eyes. "Yeah, probably so they can hide their kids and hide their husbands since the big bad Blair is coming back to town to ruin everyone's lives."

"No, I mean it," Ronnie huffs, tilting her head downward. "So many people that I've talked to have been excited for you to come back. I also get so many people asking how you're doing and whenever I pull out my phone and show them all the amazing pictures you've taken on various tours, they're all so impressed."

"Yeah, they're all probably happy and impressed because I'm doing it in a whole different state, as far away from their precious little town as I can be."

She lets out a heavy sigh, her features pinched. "You're impossible. Tell her, Ford."

I tilt my head and angle it upward.

My stomach immediately erupts into a fit of butterflies. Who decided it was fair for him to be this damn beautiful? Maybe that isn't the way you're supposed to describe a man, but it's true. He may not have the chiseled jaw or sculpted body of a Greek god, but there's something undeniably perfect about him. It probably helps that the light misting of facial hair has grown, giving him a more edgy look, or at least as edgy as one can be when you totally look the part of a high school science teacher. Even his glasses sit on his face in a way that accentuates his features, as if they were always meant to be a part of his appearance.

His boyish grin just tops it all off. "You're impossible, Blair," he says, his eyes not leaving mine. The allure of his beautiful brown eyes, accentuated by subtle hints of gold, threaten to overwhelm me as I'm tempted to stare into them all night. But I choose to maintain my composure instead, returning his smile before diverting my attention to our friend seated across from us.

"Fine. I'm impossible, but you two are delusional, so there," I grin before sticking my tongue out at Ronnie.

Luckily, we don't have to keep going as our server comes to take our drink orders. Learning of the special, Ronnie and I quickly celebrate by exchanging high-fives. Peach has been, and will always be, my favorite flavor. We also put in our food order, which is much needed since I'm likely to eat the entire basket of chips if my tacos don't come out soon.

"Before the food comes, I'm going to make a quick phone call and freshen up in the bathroom. I'll be back in just a few," Ronnie says as she scoots out of the booth. "You two behave," she playfully warns, pointing a finger in our direction.

"Us? Never," I joke.

"Fine, Ford, you behave and keep an eye on our girl here. Apparently, everyone in town is concerned for their children and their husbands." She winks as I roll my eyes.

"I'll do what I can," Ford agrees before Ronnie makes her way toward the back of the restaurant.

"You guys may think I'm joking, but as *we*," I start, pointing my finger between the two of us, "both know, I have indeed tried to steal a husband before."

"Well, I'm hoping that was only a one-time thing, and only done because the husband you tried to steal was ridiculously handsome and good-looking."

"Eh." I shrug, a small grin slowly spreading across my face. "He was alright."

"Just alright?" he asks, his eyes going wide. "I don't know. For you to make such a big move, I have to assume he was more than just a little alright."

"Fine. He's maybe a *little* more than alright. A pretty good kisser too," I add, diverting my attention as I casually reach for another chip and dip it into the salsa, still doing my best to act casual and brush it off, like it's not actually him we're chatting about.

"A good kisser, huh? He sounds amazing," he says, sitting up straight, a gloating grin playing across his features.

"Well, too bad for him it was a one—or rather, maybe a two-time thing. It's completely over now," I say, looking back his way as I sink my teeth into the chip.

There are definitely much sexier foods to eat than a chip, but with the way his eyes drop to my lips and darken, it clearly doesn't matter to him.

"I don't know about that. I have a feeling," he says with a mischievous smile playing on his lips, "that there are going to be more than just a few kisses coming up in your future." His eyes moving back up to meet mine.

"And what makes you so sure?" I ask, my voice lowering.

"Because if this guy is smart, and by the way you've described him, I assume he has to be, he'd be an idiot to let things end there."

"I beg to differ. I think if he were smart, he'd end things now before they get too messy."

"Maybe he doesn't mind messy. Maybe..." he trails off, his gaze piercing into me, his hand subtly sliding under the table to rest on my thigh, "he's tired of living up to everyone's expectations. Maybe he's finally ready to give in to his feelings and be with the woman who's always made his life better and more exciting."

I feel the heat of his touch building on my leg as his thumb brushes slow, lazy circles, but I refuse to divert my gaze; my eyes remaining focused on his. "What if it's finally her turn to be the smart one, and it's her turn to protect him from making a big mistake?"

"How does she know it'd be a mistake? What if this is just something that's always been destined to happen, and it's time for them both to stop fighting against what's meant to be?"

I want to believe him. Part of me already does. No matter how hard I've tried, and despite the passage of time and physical distance, it's done little to alleviate my feelings for him. If anything, as I sit here, our bodies yearning to close off any and all distance, it's clear the feelings have only increased. Even now, sitting in this booth, it feels as though we're in our own little bubble, oblivious to the bustling Mexican restaurant surrounding us with its loud and lively chatter and mariachi music blasting through the speakers.

The bubble officially pops as a voice interrupts and Ford's hand immediately flies back into his lap. "Alright, here are the two peach margaritas, and one Dr Pepper," our server says, setting the drinks on the table.

Fully aware of just how close the two of us are, I scoot over until I'm practically falling off the edge of the bench. "Your food should be out any minute, but in the meantime, is there anything else I can get you?" he asks, his eyes moving between the two of us, clearly unaware of the tension that'd been building between Ford and me.

"No, I think we're good." Ford smiles, even if it is incredibly forced.

Needing the drink, I lift my margarita and take a long sip just as Ronnie comes back into view and slides into the booth, completely oblivious to everything that just transpired during her time away.

"So what did I miss?" she asks, reaching for her drink.

"Not much," Ford thankfully replies, and while his voice sounds steady, I can sense he too is a little off-kilter.

However, I can't let that be a problem, especially as Ronnie animatedly discusses her wedding plans and how she just got the good news that the necklace she'd ordered and had been waiting on had just arrived at her parents'.

While I may be internally conflicted about my feelings for the man sitting next to me, I remind myself that this week is not about that. It's about Ronnie, and even though a big part of me wants to open up to her and ask for her opinion, I can't do that. She deserves so much more than a self-centered maid of honor. I can give her at least one full day of my attention focused on nothing but her.

With that, I do my best to shut out all thoughts of Ford and instead gush with Ronnie about how perfect her wedding is going to be—even if I secretly, or not so secretly, may also be a little worried about that too.

21

FORD

I DON'T THINK I'VE ever sat through a dinner that dragged on quite like that one. Normally, I don't mind sitting there with my Dr Pepper, but the longer I sat, the more I found myself wishing that I'd gotten one of those margaritas. At least maybe I'd have something to take the edge off with.

Unlike me, Blair effortlessly flipped the switch, seemingly forgetting our earlier conversation. Even more confusing, was that while I know Blair still has some reservations about Ronnie's wedding, her attitude drastically changed as she suddenly seemed to be fully on board with the upcoming nuptials.

Then again, for all I know, I'm overthinking things, like usual, and she really is excited for Ronnie. Our friend made it pretty clear yesterday that she was happy and ready to get married to Pete and wasn't in the mood to hear us talking negatively about him. I have to assume that's precisely what that was all about, but as I pull up in front of Ronnie's apartment, I'm relieved that at least for now, all this possible pretending can stop.

"See you both tomorrow." Ronnie waves as she hops out of the backseat of my car.

"See you later," I holler, leaning forward to see her over Blair in the passenger seat.

"Love you, bestie." Blair waves as we watch Ronnie retreat toward her front door.

"Hey, Ford," Blair says, cutting through the silence as she looks my way once we've made sure our friend made it safely inside.

"Hmm?"

"Do you think we could hang out for a little bit before you drop me back off at my brother's?" she asks, looking up at me from beneath her lashes.

Despite her striking blue eyes—which she's learned to effortlessly enhance with makeup, it's her luscious red lips that I find myself irresistibly drawn to at this moment, especially as she lightly chews on the bottom left corner. She has to know what she's doing to me, because she's driving me absolutely feral right now.

I cough out a small lump in my throat and nod. "Uh, yeah. Of course," I agree, struggling to keep my voice steady and composed. I might have outgrown my teenage years and uncontrollable hormones, but she somehow has the power to make me feel exactly like I did all those years ago. "Is there anywhere you want to go or..." I trail off, waiting for her answer.

"Your place?" she innocently asks.

Calm down, Ford. Now is not the time to let my mind go to those dirty and illicit places, yet, it's the only place it seems to want to go.

"Yeah, of course. Sure thing." I nod, my heart racing beneath my facade of calmness.

Putting the car in drive, I make a right turn toward my place, and though in a town like Evergreen Grove, there's hardly any traffic, I still manage to get there in record time. Admittedly, I *may* have pushed the speed limit a little during my drive.

Then again, risking a speeding violation, or any ticket for that matter, isn't my smartest move. I doubt my father, the sheriff, would consider my excuse of bringing a woman back to my place as valid. *"Sorry Dad, but I was in a hurry to possibly get laid by my dream girl."*

After moving out of the two-bedroom house I rented with Jenny, I found a small studio apartment just above Bob's Quick and Tasty Pizza. It may have a permanent scent of garlic and pepperoni, and my students may have made some comments about how I sometimes come in smelling like a breadstick, but it's still managed to be the perfect transitional spot for me.

It may be small, with a tiny kitchen, bathroom, and living space that doubles as my bedroom, but it's cheap, and that's what matters. It feels slightly embarrassing to bring Blair back here, of all people, but as I pull into a spot behind the shop with stairs that lead up to my place, that doesn't seem to matter, as she unbuckles her belt to get out of the car.

I follow her lead, trailing a few steps behind. There's something about the cheetah-print skirt she's wearing that fits snugly yet also flows so gracefully until it reaches her mid-calf, that makes me unable to resist checking her out from behind. I promise, I'm not usually this guy, but I can't help but be captivated by the way she bewitchingly ascends the stairs, her hips swaying with each step, igniting a pulsating desire deep within as my eyes fall to her perfectly round ass.

As she glances over her shoulder, I know I've been caught; however, instead of calling me out, a mischievous grin spreads across her face before she strides toward the door and patiently waits for me to unlock it.

Honestly, in a town like Evergreen Grove, you don't even need to lock your door, but it's become a habit at this point.

Embarrassingly, I struggle to find the right key, my hands fumbling until I eventually locate it and slide it into the lock. Once I've quit making a fool of myself, I reach my arm forward, holding the door open and gesture for her to enter first.

"You just want to check out my ass again, huh?" she teases, seeming to stoke the already budding fire within.

A sound escapes my lips, something between a laugh and a cough, somehow adding to my already pathetic demeanor. "No. Me? Never," I say, trying to recover. I may have been projecting confidence before, especially in our text conversations where it was easy to be more daring, but in truth, I lack experience when it comes to women.

In high school, I spent way too much time pining over Blair while she dated guy after guy until Jenny came into the picture, and then after that, she was the only woman I'd ever been with physically.

I'm not even close to being in the mood to ponder who or how many other people Blair's been with, especially considering she's been with a literal rockstar. Obviously, I don't judge, and that sort of thing doesn't bother me. She's been free to be with whomever, but it does make me question if I could ever be enough for her.

Sure, I've seen her use self-deprecating humor, but in my eyes, she is the epitome of perfection, radiating pure angelic grace—even if there have been some in this town who've refused to see it. Regardless of the trouble she's found herself in, or her own self-doubt, I'll never perceive her as anything other than flawless. And hell, if she's the devil, I'll still gladly be her number one follower.

"Sure... she trails off, making herself comfortable as she walks further into my place, her eyes taking in every detail while her hands and fingers run across the wall as she walks.

I shut the door and lean back against it, folding my arms self-consciously as I watch in awe. "I know it's not much, and it probably smells like pizza in here, but it's mine and—"

She interrupts with a smile as she glances at me over her shoulder. "It's perfect, Ford. I love it. It's very you."

"Really?" I skeptically ask, and this time it's my turn to look around. Since I let Jenny keep most of our furniture, the majority of the items in here are secondhand from my parents' place. The only things currently adorning my walls are the items Jenny had reluctantly allowed in our old spare bedroom—Star Wars posters, a framed periodic table picture, and my favorite photo captured by Blair of a tour bus, which she'd once shared on her Instagram.

Although I lack a couch, my bed dominates the living space with its red and black plaid bed sheet and comforter. Normally, I'm not too concerned about my personal space, especially since I rarely entertain guests. But with my dream woman inside, I can't help but feel a bit self-conscious.

"Is it the most aesthetically pleasing room in the world?" she asks, a soft giggle leaving her lips as she walks toward my bed and takes a seat, kicking off her white tennis shoes, which land on the floor with a small thud. "No, but all the different pieces tell a story. It's very Ford Hastings, and since he is still one of my favorite people in the entire world, I love it."

Settling onto the bed, she leans back and supports herself with her hands, making herself at ease. I wish I could say the same, but unfortunately I'm completely on edge, willing myself to not screw this up. Even worse, I can't help but notice how my eyes are immediately drawn to the small glimpse of bare skin on her stomach that can be seen just under where her dark blue band T-shirt has been tied.

"So you love me, huh?" I ask, my mouth arching into a grin, determined to bring back the confidence I'd displayed earlier.

She laughs. "I don't know if I'd go that far, but yeah, probably something along those lines."

I keep my pace steady, arms still folded as I slowly inch toward her. "So, how come you wanted to hang out tonight? You're not still thinking that this," I say, unfolding my arms as I point between us, "would be a mistake?"

"I think it's a possibility, but I'm sick of fighting it. I'm tired of pretending and acting like this isn't real, and that there isn't something going on between us," she starts, giving a small shrug of her shoulder. "What about you? Are you still so sure this is a good idea?"

"I've never been more sure of anything in my entire life."

I believe it too. The longing to be close to her consumes me, my body yearning for her touch, and like her, I'm so damn tired of fighting what's obviously been in front of us for years. We were meant to be together, and it's time we finally start acting on it.

I take another step toward her, but she holds out her foot, stopping me before she sits up from her spot on my bed. "Before anything else happens, I can't have a repeat of the other night. If you're going to kiss me, Ford, I need you to really kiss me and mean it. Yes, I had a margarita tonight and I can't promise how I'll feel tomorrow, or even a few days from now, but I know what I'm saying, and I know what I'm asking of you. So no blaming it on anything else. If we do this, it's because we both want it. End of story."

I nod in agreement. "End of story."

Before she can say anything else, I swiftly close the gap, my body leaning toward hers, my arms gently framing her on the bed as our lips meet in a fervent, hungry kiss. In the past, my kisses were hesitant and more exploratory, but at this moment, all I crave is her lips on mine. She tastes like a subtle blend of peach and tequila, but it's the sweet essence of vanilla and honey that envelops me, reminding me once again that I'm finally doing what I've truly wanted to do for so damn long.

The sensation of Blair's hands on my chest amplifies the intensity of our kiss, her tongue sweeping against mine. Her desperation to be close mirrors my desire as she fists the front of my shirt, tugging me toward her with urgency.

Yearning to feel her pressed against me, my hands slide beneath her ass, effortlessly lifting her and pulling her toward me as she wraps her legs around my waist. With a quick and fluid motion, I flip over and settle on the bed, gently placing her on my lap. She wastes no time pressing her hips to meet mine as my body responds, instantly growing hard, pressing painfully into the fabric of my jeans.

Groaning into her lips, I feel the smile forming as a gentle gasp escapes her and I buck my hips to meet her movement. Dry humping on my bed feels almost juvenile, but in many ways, it feels like the right way to start, since despite our prominent feelings for each other back in the day, it was something we'd never experienced together, despite how badly I'd wanted it.

With her knees on either side of my thighs, her skirt rides up even higher, revealing the smoothness of her creamy thighs as my hands explore downward to caress them.

Eager to savor her taste, I reluctantly detach my lips from hers, only to pepper a path of kisses along her neck and jawline. She obligingly tilts her head, granting me more access. The primal part of me wants to linger in certain spots as I kiss, lick, suck, and nip lightly at her skin. However, I thankfully seem to possess some semblance of self-control as I acknowledge that marking her up only days before our best friend's wedding likely isn't the move to make.

Instead, I continue my mission as I reach her ear, giving it a gentle nibble. While my hands move up from her thighs, my fingertips brush against her smooth skin. Instead of encountering fabric, I realize that she isn't wearing any underwear and my fingertips grip her bare ass.

"Fuck, Blair," I moan into her ear at the discovery. A pleased giggle escapes her lips and she pulls back to look at me, her hands lingering on my shoulders.

"Surprise," she says with a mischievous wink, somehow amplifying my already deep fascination. Letting her hands fall from my shoulders, they descend gracefully, and she skillfully unbuttons my flannel shirt with swift, deliberate movements.

"You know, you kind of messed up my plans. How am I supposed to convince you that I really am the panty-dropper?" I tease, helping her along as she finishes with the buttons and I wiggle out of the sleeves while she pushes the shirt down my arms.

I can't help but notice the way her eyes confidently roam across my chest, and although I'm not muscular, her satisfaction is clear, and that's enough for me. "Honestly, Ford, you have nothing to prove to anyone, especially not me," she assures, leaning forward to once again press our lips together in a fiery kiss.

Consumed with an urgent need for physical closeness, I maneuver to keep our lips locked as I carefully remove her shirt, yearning for the sensation of our bare skin pressed together. As soon as the fabric is lifted over her head and tossed aside, our lips eagerly find each other again.

It doesn't last long, though, before our lips break apart, Blair asserting her dominance as she presses me down onto the bed with a firm hand on my chest. I fully expect her to crawl over me, but instead, she stands tall, looking down at me. A devious smirk dances on her lips as she reaches behind her, unclasping her bra before letting it fall softly onto the floor.

I can't control myself as my eyes reverently take in her body and her curves. In every aspect, she embodies flawless perfection. Despite my eagerness to reach out and touch her, she signals for me to hold off, prolonging the anticipation as she slowly lowers her skirt to the floor. My cock twitches in response. That body of hers is meant for worshiping, and I plan to be its most devout follower.

"Blair..." I say, my eyes making a slow trail up her body until they meet hers, my lips curling into a smile. "You're so fucking gorgeous."

"Now it's your turn," she says, her eyes filled with an intensity that sends shivers down my spine, as I find myself willing to do whatever she asks. I'm all hers.

22

BLAIR

I'M FULLY AWARE THAT I'm jeopardizing everything Ford and I have built by letting ourselves cross this line, but I'm powerless to stop it. I've wanted him for as long as I can remember, but it's so much more than that. What was once a simple want has now become an urgent need. I'm completely his for the taking, but most importantly, he's now mine as well.

The scorching air crackles with overwhelming heat, his intense gaze igniting an insatiable desire to have his body pressed into mine, never allowing any space to separate us ever again. Despite being in his lap just moments ago, it hadn't felt like enough, and I'm willing to do whatever is needed to make sure I never go without his touch ever again.

As his tongue wets his bottom lip and I place my hands on the bed to crawl back toward him, it's clear we're on the same page. His gaze stays fixed on me as I reach down. I unbutton his jeans and slowly unzip them, needing us to be on an even playing field. I've always been comfortable in my skin, never shy about being naked in front of someone else, but I desperately ache for him to be naked with me. I continue my work and tug the jeans down his legs, my smile only widening.

There's a part of me that has always recognized the uncertainty that Ford feels about himself, but I've never understood it. He's effortlessly captivating with his striking features that make him handsome in his very own unique way. He may not have the ruggedly handsome looks that many women tend to go for, but it's his softness and charm that have always captivated me and made me realize he's the one that I want—hell, the one that I need.

With a swift pull, I strip the jeans off his legs, and he willingly helps me along, seemingly appreciative of the newfound freedom from the constraints of the fabric.

However, instead of letting me completely free him, he once again takes control as he reaches for me, and before I can complain, I'm pinned beneath him as he holds my hands above my head by my wrists. "Let me just take a moment to appreciate this. I've waited too damn long for this moment," he explains, his nose running softly along my jawline, before pressing a kiss and trailing downward. He tastes and savors my skin as he moves toward my neck. From there he trails to my shoulder, before finally reaching my right breast.

Right away, my back arches into him, as he licks, nips, and sucks on my pebbled nipple, skillfully using his free hand that isn't holding himself up to massage the other. While my body is thankful for the feeling, the ache between my legs only grows stronger.

"Ford," I moan, my breath hitching as he leisurely switches sides. He gives the other breast and nipple equal love before his lips trail down my stomach, gradually moving lower toward my thighs, before gently nudging and parting my legs.

"Say please," he says, his voice taking on a deep and velvety quality that is completely new to me, yet so utterly enchanting. I've yet to experience this side of him, and so far, it's impossible not to be infatuated and crave more.

"Please," I plead, my voice filled with desperation. It's not like me to beg, but I've been waiting for this moment for years. I'm typically a pretty patient person, however, impatience consumes me while he deliberately takes his time, and savors the moment, planting soft kisses on the sensitive skin of my inner thighs, the thick stubble of his chin brushing against my body only adding to the experience.

"Good girl," he teases, just before his lips finally connect with my clit, causing my hips to practically jolt off the bed.

With anyone else, I might feel embarrassed by my body's responsiveness, but under his expert touch, I can't help but surrender to the pleasure. My moans grow louder with each lick and suck as he expertly uses his tongue to send me into oblivion. I want to use the excuse of not having been intimate in a while, but with it being Ford—*my* Ford—it's only natural that my body would react in this manner.

As if aware of my need and how close I am as I writhe beneath him, Ford's hand descends. His finger runs softly over my slick center, and a deep, husky groan leaves his lips as he pulls away from my throbbing clit. "Fuck, Blair," he says once again. "You're so damn wet and you taste so fucking good," he compliments, before he takes the small bud into his mouth once more and lets a finger sink inside me.

I gasp, my body welcoming and needing the touch. I lift my body to meet his movements, and one of my hands moves to grip his hair. He starts off slow and gentle at first, then adds another as he increases the intensity. His touch is exhilarating, but my body can only withstand so much as he moves his fingers rhythmically inside me while his mouth continues to suck at my most sensitive area. With each thrust, my body quivers and I feel myself teetering toward the edge. My free hand grasps the comforter, the other tugging on his brown curls, unable to contain my pleasure, as I let out a small scream, calling his name as my back arches and waves of ecstasy crash over me.

With relentless determination, Ford persists in his movements until it becomes evident that my body has reached the pinnacle of release. Finally he eases back and moves his lips up to mine, where I taste the salty and sweet flavor of myself on him.

My body is still doing its best to recover as my eyes slowly flutter open to see a smile that I imagine mirrors my own.

"Hi," he whispers. While his eyes had been dark before, now they're filled with nothing but light and softness as he lovingly gazes down at me.

"Hi." I smile back before leaning up to press my lips against his one more time. "Your turn now," I say, more than ready to repay the favor. He shakes his head as I raise an eyebrow.

"Next time. Right now, I just want to be inside you," he says, his words causing my confusion to transform into a knowing smile.

While I'd have no problem going down on him and repaying the favor, I can't argue with that. I may have tried to tell myself over and over throughout the years that there was no reason to think of my best friend like that; that sex would only complicate things, but that doesn't mean it wasn't something I'd fantasized about. Now, knowing it's reality, I'm completely on edge, fully ready to experience everything with him.

If the pleasure and satisfaction I'd felt from him going down on me was any indication of what to expect, I now know that having sex with him and feeling him inside me will far surpass every single expectation I could've ever imagined.

As our lips meet again, I run my fingers through the soft strands of hair at the nape of his neck, while my other hand gently rests on his chest before slowly making the descent downward. A girl can only wait so long, after all, and I move my hand beneath the fabric of his boxer-briefs, which honestly should've been discarded a long time ago.

Through our kiss, I can feel his breath hitch as my fingers wrap around his thick and heavy cock. "Fuck, Blair," he growls in appreciation, my pussy clenching in need once more.

I let my hand slowly move across his length, taking in the size. "Say please," I purr against his lips.

"Not a chance," he somehow manages, but before I can fight him on it, he pulls back, removing his glasses and setting them on the bedside table. He reaches into the drawer and pulls out a condom, a proud smile spreading across his face as he shows me what he's grabbed.

In a small town like Evergreen, I can't help but wonder who he'd need those for now that he's no longer with Jenny, but I forcefully suppress the thought. It doesn't matter who either of us has been with, because right now, we're with each other. We're with the one person we were always destined to be with in the first place. It might have taken us way too long to get here, but at least we made it through, and that's all I want to focus on.

As he removes his boxers and his cock springs free, I finally get a full view of him for the first time and give him an approving smile. In what feels like record speed, he's removed the wrapper and sheathed himself as he crawls back toward me, settling between my legs and nudging them apart with his knee.

"You're so beautiful, Blair," he whispers, saying my name as if it's a prayer, his eyes gazing down into mine intently, and I can tell he means it. I've heard that line countless times before, often in intimate moments with other men, where their eyes linger on my breasts or my ass. While I can understand the appeal in those moments, it holds a certain significance to hear those words from Ford, of all people.

"So are you." I smile up at him, placing a hand on his cheek as my thumb spins in soft, lazy circles.

With a surge of desire, I lift myself off the bed, my hand instinctively finding the back of his head, fingers entwining in his disheveled brown hair as our lips crash together once more.

With each passionate and hungry kiss, the heat between us only grows stronger. As my legs entwine around his back, he skillfully positions us before guiding himself inside me. As he enters, a quiet gasp escapes my lips as my body adjusts to accommodate him.

This is not one of those times where we can take it slow or savor the moment. Neither of us can hold back as the intensity overwhelms us. He drives himself deep inside me, and I respond by rolling my hips, eagerly meeting his every thrust.

The room fills with the sounds of our pants and moans, as he nestles and buries his head into my neck, placing the occasional kiss there as my fingers dig tightly into his shoulder blades. My body is completely consumed by him, yet even now, all I can do is crave more as I nudge his head so our lips can meet again.

"Fuck, Blair," he breathily growls once he manages to untangle his lips from mine and he continues to press himself inside of me. "You feel so fucking good and I can't even tell you how amazing and beautiful you look as you take me so perfectly."

His words only make me feel even more desperate for him as the passion engulfs me, igniting the same sensation within my body, and the overwhelming pleasure takes over. Unable to help myself, I cry out his name, my nails digging into his back, likely leaving fresh marks as my body arches and contracts against him.

Undeterred, he maintains his rhythm, pushing me to new levels of ecstasy as I'm hit with wave after wave of pleasure. Gradually, his body tenses up, and he lets out a groan as he comes along with me.

Pulling back slightly, his lips meet mine in a soft, lingering kiss before he gracefully rolls off. However, I'm not ready to lose that closeness. I press myself against him, feeling the warmth of his chest and beating heart, his protective arm enveloping me, as he places a tender kiss on my forehead.

Yes, we should clean up, and we will, but right now I need to savor this perfect moment with him for as long as possible.

"Holy shit," I say, my breathy giggle mingling with the pounding of my racing heart.

"Holy shit," he tiredly agrees, sounding equally amused.

I knew being with him would feel good, but I never could have predicted it would feel so electric and so damn right at the same time, like our bodies and souls truly were meant for each other.

"Ready for round two?" I ask. Despite his laughter and the playful shake of his head, I can tell that round two is inevitable, and there's a good chance for a round three as well. Hell, I'll take whatever I can get if it's anything like what we just experienced.

23

FORD

WAKING UP WITH BLAIR wrapped in my arms, her body pressed into mine, is easily one of those moments that will stay with me forever. Then again, maybe this could become routine, and each day will blend seamlessly into the next, as I lose track of these individual moments. A guy is allowed to dream, right?

Wanting to prolong the experience, I press my face into her neck, breathing in her signature scent of honey and vanilla that's still managed to linger on her skin despite our long night of lovemaking. There's nothing I want more than to stay wrapped up next to her in bed all day. Unfortunately, I still have to work for two more days this week before my pre-arranged days off for the wedding, so I know it's not possible. Somebody has to be responsible here, and since that's always been my job in this relationship, I decide to stick with it, at least for now.

I carefully untangle myself, not wanting to disturb her as she sleeps. I may have to go in for work today, but she deserves to sleep in for as long as she wants without feeling hurried or pressured to leave. I did keep her up pretty late last night, after all.

I grab my glasses and slide them on before reaching for my phone to check the time. Luckily, even after a long and eventful night, my innate ability to wake up early leaves me with sufficient time to shower and get ready. If I hurry, I may even have enough time for a quick detour for coffee and muffins to surprise Blair.

Looking down at her naked body covered by nothing but a thin red sheet, and her blonde hair splayed perfectly on the pillow like a beautiful golden halo, I'm so tempted to say '*fuck it*' and crawl back into bed, but I resist the urge and do my best to remain strong and stick to the plan.

Doing everything in record time, I take a shower and get dressed before quietly sneaking out to grab our treats.

As I order Blair's coffee this early in the morning, I can't help but notice the judgmental look Buddy gives me, but I choose to ignore it. They already know Jenny and I are separated, and we have nothing to feel weird about. If anything, I have to assume that nobody would or should be surprised that Blair and I are finally together. The signs were all there for anyone who really cared to pay attention, and in this town, I feel like everyone was watching and waiting. Hell, I wouldn't even be surprised if people were making and taking bets.

Back at my place, I cautiously insert the key into the lock, striving for complete silence. I gently prop open the door, relieved to find the blonde goddess still sound asleep, exactly as I left her.

Although I'm tempted to lean in and wake her with a gentle kiss, I decide it's best to let her continue sleeping undisturbed. Fortunately, as a teacher with a sticky note obsession, I whip out a small yellow pad and a pen and scribble her a note about the muffins and coffee, while also requesting a text when she wakes up.

However, the note proves useless as I hear the rustling of sheets and a faint moan. Blair's woken up all on her own as she stretches her arms above her head. With an amused smile, I watch as she takes a moment to register her surroundings, her eyes scanning the room.

From my spot in the kitchen, I lean forward on the counter. It takes only a few short moments before our eyes meet, and while a small part of me is terrified that she's going to look at me with regret in her eyes, it's the exact opposite as an enormous smile lights up her entire face.

"Morning." I smile back.

"Were you about to sneak off and leave me here all by myself?" she pouts, sitting up and pulling the sheet up with her as she keeps her chest completely covered, which is honestly for the best. I can't afford any more temptations; I'm already struggling with the desire to go to work as it is. The truth is, if she were to ask me to crawl back into bed with her, I'd do it in a heartbeat.

"Maybe, but does it help that I brought breakfast?" Pushing myself off the counter, I reach for the muffin and coffee, their delicious aroma wafting up as I hold them in front of me.

Her face lights up as her mouth drops open. "Ford," she coos, her tone full of admiration.

Moving around the counter, I deliver them to her in bed. Reaching out, she wiggles her fingers, as if to say "gimme."

"Here you go, princess," I tease, handing them both over.

"Princess?" she asks, wrinkling her nose. "I think I prefer Blair bear," she jokes before bringing the straw to her mouth as she takes a long, savoring sip.

"Really? You used to hate when I called you that," I chuckle.

Wanting to help her out even more, I reach into my dresser that doubles as a television stand and retrieve one of my plain T-shirts and a pair of boxer shorts.

"Maybe I didn't actually hate it as much as I pretended to," she says, casually shrugging while I set the clothes down in front of her.

"Just in case," I explain, as her eyes crinkle in joy.

Setting the muffin down on the bed, she uses her finger to beckon me to come in closer before tapping it against her lips.

Who am I to say no? Leaning down, I tenderly press my lips against hers, letting them linger there for as long as I can.

"Oh God," she curses.

I pull away quickly, raising a questioning brow.

"I haven't even brushed my teeth yet." She frowns, bringing her hand up to cover her mouth.

"You have to know I don't care about that. If anything, you taste like your coffee," I assure her as I move her hand away and once again lean down to press my lips against hers, as her hand softly cups the back of my neck.

"What could I have ever possibly done to deserve you?" she asks, finally pulling away.

"Believe me, I'm asking myself the same question," I assure her.

Growing up, I was always the socially awkward kid who struggled to connect with others, but everything changed when I moved to Evergreen Grove in fifth grade. Blair and Ronnie immediately embraced me, offering their friendship, and accepting me for exactly who I was. I can still remember that first day of school when some punk decided to make fun of me and my glasses, but Blair immediately came to my rescue. She confidently declared to everyone on the playground that she thought my glasses were cool and even asked if she could try them on. From that day on, not a single person made fun of me.

A lot of people have given me crap over the years for constantly going along with Blair and Ronnie's crazy plans, but I'd follow those women anywhere—I trust them with my life. Sure, there's a good chance I'd be following them straight into a jail cell, but that's a chance I've always been willing to take.

"Oh, hush. I'm not that great," she jokes, a smile playing at her lips as she lifts her coffee for another sip.

"I respectfully disagree," I say, the jarring sound of my phone alarm interrupting our moment from my pocket, reminding me I need to leave immediately if I plan to make it to work on time. "Unfortunately, that means I have to leave for school now, but you're more than welcome to stay here for as long as you want or need, or if you want to hurry and get dressed, I can take you home first."

She twists her lips as she takes a moment to think about it. "I think I may go back to sleep for a little longer," she decides. "I'll have Miles come and pick me up in a bit, or I'll just walk to his garage."

The mere thought of her brother picking her up and knowing what we did last night is terrifying, but I try to push those ridiculous thoughts aside. We're twenty-eight year old adults. We're free to sleep with whomever we want, and I plan to sleep with her whenever she'll allow.

"Alright, in that case, I'll see you later," I tell her, leaning down for one final kiss before sending her off with a wave. It should feel surreal to leave a naked Blair behind in my bed, but instead, it feels like the most natural thing in the world, as if this is how it was always meant to be.

24

BLAIR

J UST AS I TOLD Ford, I stayed in bed for a while, enjoying the
luxury of scrolling through my social media and indulging
in the scrumptious breakfast that Ford had surprised me with.
As much as I was tempted to go back to sleep, especially after our
long night of fun, the lingering scent of Ford in his bed made it
impossible to lull myself back into a sleepy state.

Once I finally managed to drag myself out of bed and slipped
into the T-shirt that carried even more of his familiar scent,
I couldn't resist indulging in a bit of snooping. Just call me
Sherlock Holmes.

In so many ways, he's still that silly and adorable Ford that
I've always known and loved. However, after not speaking for
over two years, there are parts of him I don't fully recognize
anymore.

For my sanity and well-being, I can't deny that I made the
correct choice to remove him from my life when he married
Jenny. However, now that there's a chance for him to be completely mine, I feel the need to rediscover every detail about Ford
Hastings that I can.

I can't say that my snooping helps me discover all that much, but as I spot the discarded note he'd started to write before I woke up, I decide to write him my own little message.

> *Ford-*
> *Thanks for breakfast! 10/10*
> *Yours truly, Blair bear*
> *P.S. Sex was an infinity/10. Will definitely try again :)*

Laughing to myself, I stick it on his fridge, choosing not to dwell on the fact that it's probably not all that funny and that my lack of sleep is finally catching up to me.

As I finish my snooping, I consider calling Miles for a ride, but given that he's likely already at work and at his garage for the day, I decide to just head over there. Although there are numerous things to complain about when it comes to Evergreen Grove, one of the few positives is the unrestricted ability to get anywhere you want on foot.

Before changing back into my walk-of-shame clothes from the night before, I snap a quick selfie of myself in Ford's shirt and send it his way before getting dressed.

Stopping in the doorway, I give his place one final glance, praying that this won't be my last night here. I know it was me holding us back, but after last night, there's no way I'm willing to let this be a one-and-done type of thing. He's officially done it—he won me over.

After a short ten-minute walk to Miles' place, it's clear he's less than pleased as I walk in wearing the same clothes from the night before.

"I'd ask if you had a good night, but honestly, I don't want to know," he says, doing his best not to look up from behind his desk as he sits at a computer, likely doing some of the admin work.

With a father who had a well-known reputation for being the town drunk, I can't help but feel a sense of pride in seeing my brother's success. He has shown everyone that we aren't the trash that so many people thought we'd turn out to be, and he not only get to works at a job he loves, he's fucking owns the place like the badass he is.

With his love for cars and exceptional problem-solving skills, he has always excelled at identifying and resolving issues quickly. While he does still enjoy doing the dirty work, he now has the luxury of delegating the physical labor to others whenever he needs to, while he handles the administrative stuff in the office.

"Would it make you feel any better if I let you know that I ended up at Ford's last night, and not with some random stranger or some other person that you probably hate from this town?" I ask, a teasing grin on my face as I take a seat on the hard metal chair across from his desk. Would it kill this guy to invest in some comfortable furniture?

"Maybe, but not by much," he admits, choosing not to look at me as he continues typing. "For the first time, I think I'd actually prefer it if you'd somehow ended up at Veronica's."

"Wow, are you finally having a change of heart about my best friend?" I tease, my mouth dropping open in excitement.

"I wouldn't go that far," he scoffs. "In this case, with you being my sister, it just feels like the lesser of the two evils."

"Oh, come on," I say, positioning my elbows on his desk as I lean forward. "Admit it. You love Ford."

"Love? That's a little much, but do I think he's a good guy who would treat you right?" he asks. "I do. As your older brother, that's all I've ever wanted for you. Even more, it's exactly what you deserve."

Miles has always been incredibly protective. Given his more than vocal disapproval of my relationship with Max, it's a nice change to hear how supportive he is about me and Ford. If anything, this only makes my feelings toward my best friend even stronger. It truly feels like everything is finally falling perfectly into place. Maybe I will finally get to experience that happily ever after that so many people talk and dream about.

"He is a pretty good guy, huh?" I muse, a content sigh escaping my lips.

"Speaking of the right guy..." he trails off as I raise a brow in his direction. "Veronica is really going to marry that jerk? Pete's been a tool since high school. I mean, I've always known she sucks at making good choices, but him, really? That's a new low, even for her."

"Right?" I ask, glad that once again, I'm not the only one who thinks so. "I'm going to forget the part where you shit on her for all of her other choices, but yeah, I just don't get what she sees in him."

"And as her best friend, you're just going to let her marry him?"

"Okay, first off, Mr. Judgy Pants," I say, sitting up straighter as I point a finger in his direction. "I don't think I have the moral high ground here since for the past ten years I've been in an on-and-off relationship with Max of all people, but I have said something, and she's made it perfectly clear that he's the one she wants and that she's not going to change her mind on it. I'm not really sure what else I can do or say at this point."

He shakes his head. "I just don't get it, especially after the way he treated her at trivia night. It's not like I know her all that well, but to let him control her like that is weird. I didn't take her for the type to let that kind of thing slide."

Considering how openly my brother has expressed his disapproval of my friendship with Ronnie, I'm somewhat taken aback by how much this is bothering him. However, I can't say he's wrong. When even he, who has always been critical of my best friend, can sense something is off, it speaks volumes about the situation.

"Tell me about it," I sigh once more. "But both Ford and I said our piece, and at this point, I think that's all we can do."

"I guess," he says, sounding just as frustrated as me.

"Speaking of Ronnie..." I trail off as he glances up, clearly aware that I'm about to ask for something. He knows me far too well. "I was thinking that if I perhaps bribe you by offering to pick us up some lunch, you could drive me to the school afterward when she gets off work? I'm supposed to help her finish up with some wedding stuff."

"Depends..."

I raise an eyebrow. "On what?"

"On what you're planning to get me for said lunch."

"Well, I haven't been to Simon's Deli since I've been home and I've been craving one of those huge club sandwiches of his, so maybe that?"

"I suppose I could be up for that kind of deal," he gives in, as a smile lights up my face.

"You drive a hard bargain, sir, but sandwiches it is!"

Bribing Miles with sandwiches had been a stroke of genius. Not only did it save me from the twenty-minute walk to the high school, but it also allowed me the opportunity to indulge in one of my beloved hometown favorites. I've traveled all over the country and even the world with various bands, but the tangy sweetness of the secret sauce in Simon's Deli sandwiches is unlike anything I've ever tasted. It probably helps that not only are all the ingredients fresh and locally sourced, but he makes the bread fresh in-house daily.

After agreeing to meet up with my brother for dinner and sending Ronnie a text that I've made it, she comes to meet me at the front of the school so she can walk me back to her classroom.

"Girl, spill whatever it is you've got on your mind," she commands.

My eyes widen. "What?" I ask, despite knowing full well that I can't keep anything from her. I might as well just give it up now. While I've maybe been a bit of a shitty friend by making it clear I don't like her fiancé, I've since tried to make it up to her by not drowning her in all my drama.

With her wedding only days away, the last thing I want to do is burden her with my problems. Then again, maybe for the first time, the whole me and Ford thing isn't feeling like so much of a problem anymore.

"Oh, don't even," she threatens. "It's written all over your face. Something is going on, so spill it. Now."

I wrinkle my nose and bite down on my bottom lip. "I slept with Ford."

She grabs hold of my arm and stops us in our tracks. "What? Are you serious?" she asks, linking her hands in front of her as she jumps up and down. "Fucking finally!" she all but shouts as she raises her hands and wiggles her fingers in excitement.

I quickly look around, but thankfully, no students or teachers seem to be lingering in the hallway. "Shhhh," I warn, lifting my finger to my lips, despite the full-fledged smile accompanying it.

"Okay, you can't expect me not to react. We've been waiting for this for like, what? Twelve years?"

"I'm glad that you're happy about this, too, but it's not like this changes everything. I live in Los Angeles and travel all over the world, and he lives here. There are still some things that need to be talked about and ironed out before we can truly get this excited about it," I try to explain as I link my arm through hers and try to rush her toward her classroom, just in case.

This is Evergreen Grove after all, where secrets never stay hidden for long. The last thing I need is for this to get around before any of it is truly worked out.

"You'll figure it out. There's no way that after all these years, when you finally catch the man of your dreams, you'd let something so silly and trivial stop you from taking what you fully deserve."

"I know you're right, and I don't want anything stupid or petty to get in the way, but it's also all so new. I don't want to jinx it," I explain, my smile dropping a little as she finally leads me into her classroom..

I've been in this room before since she's been a teacher at Evergreen Grove High for six years now, but it never ceases to blow me away how beautiful and colorful it is in here. Her artistic talent is not only evident in her own artwork that decorates the walls, but also in the impressive pieces created by the students that she's taught. Despite feeling like many of Ronnie's amazing qualities have been overshadowed by Pete, it's evident here that not everything has been changed or taken away.

"Well, I have faith that you'll figure it out," she says, walking toward her desk, where she does her best to straighten up a bit. "But I have to know...how was it?" she asks, wiggling her brows suggestively.

My mouth drops open in shock. Maybe I shouldn't be surprised that she would ask this, since we tend to tell each other everything and I've always been open about all my other sexual exploits, but now that it's Ford, it somehow feels different. It's a bit odd, but there's a part of me that feels a desire to safeguard it and keep so much of last night and that moment just for us.

"What?" she innocently asks as she looks up. "It may be Ford that we're talking about, but a girl needs to know these things."

"It was good." I smile, looking down at my shoes. "Really good, actually."

She rubs her hands together. "I knew it," she squeals before reaching for a sealed envelope on her desk. "And, it makes this make a little more sense," she says, bringing it over to me. "After lunch, he gave it to me and asked that I give it to you."

I'm sure I look pathetic with my lovesick grin as I look down at the letter, but I can't help it. Maybe it's sort of ridiculous since it almost feels like the bare minimum for him to bring me breakfast in bed and write a little note, but I'm honestly not used to this kind of treatment. I suppose what they say is true: if a guy wants to, he will.

"Well," she encourages, spinning her hand as if to beckon me to continue, "open it."

Doing as I'm told, I run my finger across the seal to break it before pulling out a small yellow sticky note.

> *Hey Blair bear,*
> *I was hoping you'd do me the honor of going out on an official date with me tomorrow night.*
> *Forever yours,*
> *Ford*
> *P.S. You look great in my shirt, but even better without it*

"Holy shit," Ronnie squeals next to me, making it completely obvious that she was reading over my shoulder. "He's got it bad."

I don't even know how to respond as my eyes trace over the words once more, that same silly grin lighting up my entire face.

"Well? You going to say yes?" she asks in a teasing sing-song voice.

"What do you think?" I ask, finally tearing my eyes away from his note.

"Well, I *think* we need to find you a hot-ass new outfit that will blow his silly little Ford brain to pieces."

"I thought today was about me helping you finish up your seating chart and centerpieces," I say, doing my best to not make this week or even today about me.

She brushes me off with a small wave as she reaches for my arm and yanks me toward the door. "This is way more important, and I'll get my mom and aunt to finish that up."

I pull back and stop in place. "Ronnie, I appreciate this, but the whole reason I came home in the first place was for you and your wedding. Not so Ford could take me on a date."

"And I love hearing you say that, but if things go well with you and Ford on this date, that could maybe mean I'll be seeing you more often. So once again, in my eyes, this is way more important, and you don't have to worry," she continues, dismissing my worries with another small wave. "One way or another, I'll get everything for my wedding done in time. I'm not worried about it, so you don't need to be either."

I can't help but give in as I move forward and give her a hug. "I love you, Ron."

"Love you too," she says, kissing the side of my head before reaching for my hand as she pulls back. "But enough of this mushy stuff. It's time to make sure this date goes perfectly. Our future lives depend on it."

25

FORD

THE WAIT TO SEE Blair after the other night's festivities felt like pure torture—a day and a half of pathetic longing, but I'm already addicted and I'm not afraid to admit it. Plus, it's been worth the wait. I've waited over ten years for this, so what's an extra day at this point?

As selfish as I want to be, I know that yesterday was about Blair helping and spending time with Ronnie as they worked out some last-minute wedding details. The least I could do was be patient, and thankfully, that patience has finally paid off.

I couldn't even say I minded picking her up at Miles' place. Witnessing her emerge, only slightly late this time, made every minute apart and any inconvenience worth it. She's every straight man's dream in a plain black top, a short black skirt speckled with white polka dots that hits just a few inches above her knees, and her iconic leather jacket and black Converse. She's always been skilled at doing her hair, and tonight is no different, as long beachy waves fall down her shoulders and a solitary braid adorns one side.

I still can't believe this is happening. Yes, we had sex, and mind-blowing sex at that, but it's so much more than that, and with her, it always has been. It's the fact that we're finally doing this and taking this much-needed and important step.

A part of me had expected her to pull away and had braced myself for her inevitably saying once again that we could never work. There's even been a part of me that has felt those same worries too, but I need this to happen—I have to see where this can go. If not, I don't think I could ever properly move forward in life.

Perhaps we'll only find out that our feelings are nothing more than just that, and we've somehow let our imaginations make this into some huge thing that it's not, but deep down, I know that's not true. I've always known that Blair is my soulmate, and I'm more than ready for this date to be what confirms it for both of us.

"Nonna's Trattoria, huh?" she asks as I pull into an empty parking stall.

"I considered driving out of Evergreen for this, but that just didn't feel right. If we're finally going to do this, it feels like I need to take you to a place where everyone here goes for their dinner and date nights."

In such a small town, the dining options are limited, but when people want something more upscale, this is the go-to place. Elsewhere, this restaurant would likely be seen as comparable to The Olive Garden, or perhaps even slightly lower, but in Evergreen, it's the epitome of fine dining.

"I guess it does feel a bit poetic," she agrees with a slight nod as she unfastens her belt with a soft click.

"Hold up," I say, quickly undoing my own before holding out a hand to keep her from getting out. "If we're going to do this, we're going to do it right."

As her eyebrows furrow, I waste no time in opening my door and swiftly making my way to her side to open hers before she gets the chance. "Are you serious?" she asks, shaking her head, but there's an amused lilt to her tone that lets me know she's enjoying herself.

"Of course I am," I say with a smile, extending my hand to help her out as she thankfully accepts and her palm falls into mine. "If you think for one second I'm not going to go out of my way to do everything right to impress the girl that I've had feelings for since I was a teenager, then you're insane."

Okay, so maybe I already have the girl and don't need to pull out all these weird and extra stops, but I can't help myself. I've dreamed about the day that I'd finally get to take Blair Bennett out on a date, and there's no way I'm not going to go all out to show her why I'm the only one for her. She deserves the world, and I fully plan on being the one who gives it to her.

"I don't know; if anyone is acting insane here, it's you, but luckily, I kind of like it. The bribery and flattery are kind of hot, so by all means, keep it up," she encourages as she flattens out her skirt and exits the vehicle.

"Oh, don't you worry; there's plenty more where this came from," I assure her with a wink before placing my hand on the small of her back to guide her inside.

Given our mutual desire to preserve our friendship, it was only logical to exercise caution and avoid crossing certain lines. We were far too aware of the possibility that it could ruin everything we've built, but since doing nothing left us in a place where we didn't even talk for two years, it only makes sense to give this a true shot. That's precisely why I plan on pulling out all the stops tonight, if only to show her just how right the two of us are for each other.

My mom went out of her way to make sure that her sons knew how to respect and take care of women. While I've always been taught the importance of opening the door for a lady, I meant what I said. I did my best to give Jenny everything she deserved when we were together. I planned extravagant dates, showered her with gifts, and always let her win every argument. So maybe there was some overcompensation on my part due to the guilt I felt for harboring feelings for my best friend. But now, with this date, I genuinely want and need everything to go perfectly. There's so much at stake, and I refuse to let something small mess it up.

Walking inside, part of me wonders if I've made a mistake by bringing her here. It may be one of the fancier establishments in Evergreen Grove, but part of me worries that I should have picked something nicer and classier out of town. The dark red booths and the fake candles on every table attempt to create an ambient atmosphere but, I can't help but wonder if this place seems a bit too cheesy when compared to some of the unique places that Blair's gotten to visit on her travels. However, as the hostess gives us a friendly greeting and welcomes Blair back into town, my concerns fade. The giant smile plastered on my date's face makes me feel secure in our choice, especially as the two of them do some quick catching up.

If anything, maybe the cheesiness is working to my benefit, especially since this is likely a huge blast from the past. While we'd each eaten here plenty of times on various dates, it was never on a date with each other. As she said, it seems fitting that this is finally where we get to have our long-awaited first date together.

I know I'm overthinking things as she slides into the booth we're led to, but instead of second-guessing myself, I confidently slide in next to her.

Not only does Blair seem a little surprised by my choice, but so does the hostess, as her eyes dart nervously between us. "So, uh, was it just the two of you tonight? Or did I misunderstand? Is Veronica joining you later?" she asks.

"Nope. It's just the two of us," I say, determined not to let her judgment affect our evening. Eager to move things along and diffuse any lingering awkwardness, I reach for the menus in her hand.

"Alright, well, your waitress will be with you soon," the hostess says a bit hesitantly before thankfully walking away.

"Well, I guess that's one way to just rip off the Band-Aid and let the whole town know we're on a date," she laughs awkwardly, accepting the menu before flipping it open.

"You're not second-guessing this, right?" I ask, my menu wide open, but my gaze firmly locked on her.

"No," she says, turning to meet my eyes. "If this is something we're going to try out, it's best that everyone knows anyway, right? Plus, it's not like I'm new to being the town's center of gossip. If anything, this just makes me feel more at home," she adds, a slight curl to her lips. Unfortunately, I know her too well to believe that smile is anywhere close to being genuine.

"Do you want to go somewhere else?" I ask, lowering my voice as I lean in close.

"No, it's fine," she says, brushing me off as she looks back down at her menu. "Plus, it's not like word isn't already going to get out. I'm pretty sure Lisa," she begins, nodding her head in the direction of the hostess, a girl we went to high school with, who had sat us down, "has already gone and spread the word to everyone else who works here."

Unfortunately, I'm pretty sure she's right. Lisa is no longer at the front of the restaurant, ready to welcome the incoming patrons; instead she is currently near the back, talking to some of the waitstaff. I could just be paranoid, and I hope I am, but knowing Evergreen's reputation, it's only logical to assume that we're the ones she's talking about.

"Let's just enjoy this. It's our first date. We deserve this," she reminds me as she places a hand on my arm, clearly picking up on my own nerves. Not only that, but she's absolutely right. I've waited too damn long for this date to take place to let something as trivial as gossip get in the way.

"So, what are you getting?" I finally ask, ready to take her mind off the weirdness so we can focus on what is important here—us.

"Are you serious?" she asks, laughing as I nod my head.

"Yeah, I kid you not. Every time I go into my classroom I have to look around carefully because they're constantly switching out the pictures around my room with pictures of Chuck Norris, Taylor Swift, or John Cena. I will say, I have left up a few because they're actually pretty funny," I chuckle as I swirl some of the leftover spaghetti on my plate around my fork.

"I could see it. You're definitely a secret Swiftie, huh?" she teases, poking my side.

"I see nothing wrong with that. The woman knows how to write an amazing song." I shrug before lifting the bite into my mouth.

"I feel like that checks out. Every time I talk to Ronnie she's always blasting one of her albums in the background and I'm sure she's forced you to listen to it, too."

"Oh, uh, yeah. It was all Ronnie," I playfully joke and nod, totally ready to let her take the blame, even if I do occasionally find myself listening to some of her songs on my own. "Truthfully, though, I don't totally mind her music, and Jenny was always super into her as well," I say, without much thought since, after all, Jenny has been a huge part of my life for so long. However, I'm filled with immediate regret, since while she recovers quickly, there's a distinct change in Blair's demeanor at the sound of my ex's name. "But it's the Chuck Norris pictures that are my favorite," I add, doing my best to change the subject. "Especially since they're usually accompanied by one of the many hilarious Chuck Norris jokes. Actually, one of my students told me a really good one the other day," I preface, setting my fork down as I turn my body to face her. "Did you know that Chuck Norris once kicked a horse in the chin? They now call it a giraffe."

She laughs, and it's hard not to find relief in that beautiful melodic sound. "That is a good one," she agrees. "Have you heard the one where Chuck Norris doesn't need a watch? He decides what time it is."

Her laughter is contagious as I laugh along with her. "I hadn't, but I like it. I'll have to tell it to my students. They'll love it."

"You know, it's actually kind of cute," she starts as I raise an eyebrow while reaching for my Dr Pepper. "It's clear you have a good relationship with your students and that they like and trust you enough to want to do all that."

"You know, it could always be the opposite and it could be because they have no respect for me," I offer, even if I don't actually believe that. I've always made it a point to connect with each and every student that comes into my classroom, and my effort has, thankfully, for the most part, been reciprocated.

"No, there is no way that could be true," she decides, and with little to no thought I lean forward to press my lips against hers for a quick kiss, but instead of pulling away, I can't help but linger, and she doesn't seem to mind as she kisses me back, her hand coming to rest gently against my chest.

"So, are we thinking we want dessert tonight?" I whisper against her lips, pulling back only enough so I can look at her angelic face.

"Oh, we'll definitely be having dessert tonight, but not here," she softly giggles before pressing her lips to mine once more.

"Ford Hastings," a stern voice says, killing the moment.

The last thing I want is to end my kiss with Blair, but at the sound of that unfortunately very familiar voice, I practically leap to the other side of the bench, leaving ample space between the two of us.

"Mary," I say, doing my best to control my racing heart. "Hey, how are you doing?"

"Oh, cut the shit, Ford. Is this seriously how you're going to act now?"

"Mary," I say, attempting to strike a fine balance between sternness and respect in my tone. While I can understand why Mary, Jenny's mom, is upset to witness this scene after our two-year marriage and the many years we'd dated before that, she has to realize that she can't address me in such a manner, especially in front of my date.

"Don't 'Mary' me," she huffs, clearly not planning to calm down. "Do you not get how disrespectful and embarrassing this is to Jenny?"

"Mrs. White," Blair cuts in. "I'm so sorry. The last thing we want to do is—"

The murderous glare that Mary sends her way stops her from saying more. "If you for one second think I want to hear anything from your whorish mouth, then you have another thing coming, missy."

"Whoa, I'm going to need you to stop right there," I say, stepping out of the booth as I stand between the two women. I don't expect things to get violent or anything, but I plan to put a stop to this immediately. There is no way I'm going to allow her, let alone anybody, to ever speak to Blair that way. Even more, this isn't the normal kind of behavior I'd expect from my former mother-in-law, and the last thing she needs is to say something that I know all of us will regret in the future. "Do you really think Jenny would want you out in public saying something like this?"

"No, she probably wouldn't," she says, her tone indignant. "But someone needs to stand up for my daughter after all you put her through. We talk, you know, and she," she continues, her gaze moving around me as she points a finger toward Blair "is the cause of all the problems in your marriage. If it weren't for her, you and Jenny would still be together. I know it."

Glancing back, it's disheartening to witness the transformation of the strong, confident woman I've always known shrink into a small, defeated figure, practically sinking into the corner of the booth.

"Mary, I need you to go," I command, not backing down. "But first, understand this: Jenny and I aren't together because we aren't right for each other. Whether you believe it or not, I do love and care for your daughter, and that is exactly why we needed to end things. She deserves to find the right person for her; the person who truly loves her, and it's only right that I deserve to find the same thing. End of story."

"And let me guess?" she asks, with a resentful huff. "She's the right person for you? The one that you're going to flaunt in front everyone's faces, not caring who you hurt in the process?" Mary seethes, her eyes once again shooting daggers in Blair's direction.

Yes. She is, but I'm not about to dignify her ridiculous question with a response, especially given the way she's acting—she doesn't deserve an actual answer. "We're done with this conversation," I say instead, as I nod for her to keep moving.

Mary looks like she wants to say more, but as I keep my composure, she shakes her head and gives Blair one final glare before turning to leave the restaurant.

"Blair," I say, instantly ready to apologize, but she just shakes her head with glassy, hooded eyes. I know her. So well, in fact, that I know she's about to cry, which is why I don't say more—at least not right now. I'll save it for when it's just the two of us and she's had some time to calm down after all of that.

"Let's just go, okay?" she pleads.

"Yeah, sure. Whatever you want." I nod before looking around, where I unfortunately find the attention of practically everyone in the room, even if they're all trying to act like they weren't just listening to the entire thing. The only positive is that our waitress rushes over to give us our check.

So much for the perfect date.

26

FORD

AFTER DROPPING BLAIR OFF at her brother's, it's hard to suppress the surge of anger coursing through my veins. Had my actions hurt Jenny? I know for a fact they did. It couldn't have been easy to be married to someone when you knew you were always their second choice, but it's not like I hadn't tried.

I'd done what I thought was best when I'd turned down Blair's request on my wedding day. I'd also done what I thought was my best in being there for Jenny by choosing her and committing to our marriage, but just because I'd put in the effort, didn't mean our union was meant to last. In fact, it was likely always doomed to fail from the start. She was never my person, and it's time that everyone accept and realize that I was never hers as well. There's someone out there for her; it's just not me.

So no, maybe it wasn't fair to Jenny, but the way her mother acted tonight was nowhere near being fair to Blair either. She's not the one who deserves to be yelled at or scrutinized for any of her actions—it's me. It was Blair, after all, who'd taken the bold step to cut off contact with me for these past few years. If anyone should've done that, it probably should've been the one in a serious and committed relationship.

Did I like being confronted at the restaurant with many of the town residents gawking? No, but I can take it. In many ways, I'm pretty sure I deserved it, but Blair should never have been dragged into it, or made to feel like she'd done anything wrong.

After paying the bill, I tried to get things back on track by suggesting going out for ice cream or seeing a movie, but it was obvious the confrontation had completely shut her down.

Even after suggesting we go to my place to be alone with no prying eyes, she asked me to just take her back to her brother's. As much as I wanted to push and keep her from pulling away, I gave in and did what she asked. Thankfully, she at least let me walk her to her door. However, instead of a long kiss goodnight, she ended things with a friendly hug and a gentle kiss on my cheek.

Still lingering in the parking lot of Miles's apartment, I slam my palms into the steering wheel, letting out a loud frustrated growl. We can come back from this, I know we can, but it's not out of the realm of possibility for Blair to use this as a sign. She's done it once before, so what's to stop her from leaving me and Evergreen Grove all over again? Hell, maybe next time it will be for good if she never looks back, especially now that she's tried this thing with me and somehow convinces herself that she's always been right and that we truly aren't meant to be.

With a determined nod, I know what I need to do. It's time I prove to Blair just how serious I am about her—about us. Okay, maybe I'm delusional, but more importantly, I'm desperate and willing to give just about anything a shot if it keeps Blair from leaving me a second time.

Slipping my keys into the ignition, I start the car and pull out of the lot. There's no chance in hell I'm giving Blair up without a fight. She's worth fighting for. Hell, she's worth dying for. Thankfully, I don't think I'll need to take it that far, but for her, I'd do it. For Blair Bennett, I'd do anything.

After knocking twice with no answer, I let out a frustrated breath as I note the light glowing through the window, peeking out from behind the closed curtains. Not ready to give up, I lift my hand to knock again. She's got to be home. She was always incredibly conscious about money and wasting resources and always freaked out if I left a light on in a room I wasn't occupying. However, as my hand hovers in the air, ready to knock once more, the door unexpectedly opens, revealing Jenny's bewildered yet irritated face.

Since we've both committed to our separation, we rarely talk anymore, and I never show up at our old place, especially without talking to her first, but the look she's sending my way isn't about to make me second-guess myself. I came here for a reason, and I'm not leaving before I do what I came here to do.

"Let me guess: you're here to defend Blair's honor after your run-in with my mom at the restaurant?" she asks, a hand landing on her hip.

I'm really not all that surprised to hear that the news has already made its way to Jenny, and knowing this town, there's even the possibility that it wasn't even Mary who filled Jenny in on the details.

"Yes—or no, not really," I say, shaking my head as I try to control my racing thoughts. "Just... we need to talk."

"Well," she starts, stepping back as she ushers me to come in, "then let's talk."

"So, who told you?" I ask, stepping inside, feeling oddly hesitant.

In the past, this place was home, and while it still has some of the same furniture, it also feels like she's done her best to wipe away all traces of the fact that I once lived here, too, including removing the giant wedding photo of us that had once been hung above the fireplace mantel. While living in the studio above the pizza place doesn't always feel all that homey, it definitely feels more like home than this place.

"Jessica and Brandy were at the restaurant and witnessed the whole thing and sent me a text," she explains as I nod my head in understanding. Jessica and Brandy both work with Ronnie and me at the school, but since they work in the English department with Jenny, they've always been much closer to her, and have made it pretty obvious in the staff room that they are and will always be Team Jenny. Not that I mind. Sure, Jessica and Brandy are great women, but I like knowing that Jenny has a solid friend group to support her during this time. "And don't worry, I called my mom and told her off. She really shouldn't have done that and I'm sorry, even if it did ruin your *date*."

She sounds sincere in her apology, but it's also obvious that there's still some lingering hurt and resentment as she says the word "date," which I get. I'm fully aware that my being with

Blair is a reminder that she's always been right about the two of us, and there really is no defending myself there.

"I appreciate that," I tell her. "And I hope you know I never wanted to hurt you in all of this."

"I know you didn't," Jenny says, walking further into the living room as I follow. She makes a beeline for the kitchen, where she grabs two glasses from the cupboard. While I can't be totally surprised, even she seems to understand that this is going to be a serious conversation as she reaches for a bottle of wine and pours us each a glass. "But just because you didn't mean to hurt me, doesn't mean you didn't break my heart, and that you didn't leave a destructive trail in the process."

"I know I did, and I'm so sorry, Jenny," I attempt to apologize as she walks back around the counter and hands me the drink. "I know I hurt you, and I get that I made far too many mistakes in our marriage to count, but I think that's exactly why it's time for both of us to move on. You deserve someone amazing. Someone so much better than me. I was a shitty husband, and you didn't deserve that."

She holds out her glass as if to toast to my sentiment. "To someone better," she says right before taking a large swig of her drink.

My face falls into a frown, not sure I want to drink to that. "I hope you know that's not how I see it. I'm not choosing or moving onto Blair because she's better than you or because you weren't enough. I don't want this to come out wrong, but I want us to be honest with each other, too. I'm moving on and choosing to be with Blair because she's the one for me, and you deserve to find the one that's right for you, too."

Jenny glances away, twisting her mouth to the side before taking another drink from her glass. "I can't say that I'm ready to see you move on, especially with Blair Bennett, but I do want you to be happy, so if it has to be with her, then you need to do it."

Although I don't technically need her permission, it feels like a huge weight has been lifted from my shoulders. "I'm glad, because that's actually kind of why I'm here," I admit, looking down at my feet as my free hand scratches at the back of my neck. "I think it's time. We need to sign those papers and make this official," I say, bravely doing my best to finally look up and meet her eyes.

She nods her head knowingly, even if there's a clear sign of sadness written across her face. "I kind of had a feeling that was what this was all about, and I think you're right. I think we've been holding onto this thing that we both, deep down, knew was never right."

I solemnly nod my head, wishing I could say that she's wrong, but I can't. Even though I knew we were truly over and that there was no going back after our decision to separate, I've still had a hard time biting the bullet and ending things once and for all.

"So, what about Monday?" she asks, and for the first time, the traces of a smile slowly spread across my face.

"Really?" I ask, surprised at just how easy this is, and how soon we can move things forward. I really had come in tonight expecting a huge fight, especially after hearing from her mom just how much they all truly disliked Blair.

"Why not?" She shrugs before taking another sip. "We both know this has been over for a long time now. I'm tired of holding on and fighting for something that never felt quite right. Let's just make it official and meet with our lawyers on Monday after everything is finished with the wedding."

"You're really okay with this?" I ask, feeling the need to ensure she truly means it. As much as I'm ready to move on and be divorced, I also don't want to bully or push her into something she isn't ready for. Yes, I came in tonight with the idea of moving things forward, but I also don't want to break her heart any more than I already have.

"Yes. It's time we both get to move on, and I don't think either of us can get there if we keep dragging our feet. Let's just do this already. Let's officially get divorced." She nods, holding out her drink for another toast, and this time I clink my glass against hers.

"Let's get a divorce."

27

Blair

MILES HAS ALWAYS ENJOYED playing the nosy and concerned big brother, but it's a relief that, despite arriving at his apartment much earlier than expected, if at all, he chose not to ask any questions. There was probably no need for it, since I'm sure the answer was written all over my face. I'm just glad that I somehow managed to hold in the tears that have been threatening to fall ever since our run-in with Mary White.

Ford and I gave it a shot, and clearly we weren't meant to last. I don't even know how I let myself believe that the two of us could ever work in real life. Sure, dreaming about what could happen between us has always been fun, but that's all it ever was—an unrealistic fantasy.

I'm pretty sure I let Ronnie get a little too much in my head, and I should've known better. I'm not like her. I'm not the Disney princess who ends up with Prince Charming. I may have the tragic backstory, but that's about all I have going for me, and Ford deserves so much better than that.

I truly don't know what I was thinking by even agreeing to go on a date with him. I've always known I was never meant to fit in here, and since this is the place where Ford fits in best, how I thought we could work is beyond me. The last thing I'd ever want to do is bring his reputation down with mine.

Walking into the guest room, I shut the door behind me and head straight for my skincare supplies, more than ready to cleanse my face and erase any and all traces of tonight's date. I let myself listen to Ronnie as she hyped me up, and I went all out with my hair and makeup. She'd been so sure that this was mine and Ford's moment, and I unfortunately let myself believe that it actually could be. *What a fucking joke!*

As I wipe off my makeup and hastily throw my once perfectly curled hair into a messy bun, I resign myself to the fact that I won't be going out tonight. Honestly, if it were up to me, I'd never go out or be seen in Evergreen Grove again, but given that we're only a few days away from Ronnie's wedding, that unfortunately won't be happening.

Wanting to maximize comfort for a likely long and sleepless night ahead, I change into a pair of biker shorts and an oversized band tee. Hopping into bed, I burrow myself into the blankets. There's nothing I want more than to sleep and escape from this unfortunate reality, even if just for a few hours. Then again, if I could sleep until Saturday and Ronnie's wedding day, that'd be the most ideal. Then I'd only have to see Ford for a few more torturous hours, and then after that, I'll be free of him forever.

The idea of never seeing Ford again is beyond painful, especially after the last few days. Getting a small taste of what a future for the two of us could look like was not only healing, but also so much more than I could've ever imagined. However, it's become obvious that the only way to truly get over him and my feelings is to make a clean break. While I may come back to Evergreen Grove occasionally to visit Miles and Ronnie, there's no longer a need to include Ford in those plans.

Unfortunately, sleep remains elusive as I lie in the dark, my mind consumed by a constant looping replay of every single moment from tonight's date. No matter how much it hurts, I do my best to only focus on the more painful events, but my heart and head have other plans as they unfortunately linger on the good ones, too. Why did Ford have to be so perfect and why does it all have to hurt so damn bad?

My phone pings on my bedside table, jolting me out of my thoughts. Despite knowing I should ignore it, the fact that I'm nowhere near close to sleep has me reaching over.

> **Ford:** I know you're upset and you're hurting, but can we please talk?

Reading his message, I sit up straight. I'm even more convinced that I should ignore it, especially with the way my heart immediately reaches for the possibility of him knowing just what to say to make all of this better. Other than Ronnie, he's always been the person who knows how to soothe my thoughts whenever I go into one of my downward spirals, but this is different. I deserve to feel like this; it's the only thing that will keep me from going back on my already-made decision to leave him and Evergreen Grove behind for good.

Biting on my thumbnail, I inwardly debate with myself. I know I shouldn't, but I can't help it as I finally type in a response. Before I can second guess myself again, I hit send.

> **Blair:** I don't know if that's a good idea. Maybe it would just be easier if we only saw each other when we have to. Wedding events only and that's it.

Three bubbles pop up, and his reply comes through almost immediately, leaving me little to no time to panic.

> **Ford:** Please, Blair.

> **Ford:** I know how you think, and I know you think tonight was a sign, but that's not true.

> **Ford:** I can fix things. I'm actually outside of your brother's place. Will you please come outside?

My eyes go wide as I glance toward the window, which is ridiculous since it's not like I can see him from my spot in bed, given that we're located on the second story.

A part of me is so desperate to be done with this that I almost entertain the thought of not responding and leaving him on read, but deep down I know what I have to do. We should talk, especially since maybe I can explain to him why this needs to be done and over with for good.

> **Blair:** Fine. I'll be out in a minute

I fling myself out from under the covers, flipping on the light as I give myself a quick glance in the mirror. I look like I've been rolling around in bed, but that's fine. For once, I'm not looking to impress him. Plus, it's not like he hasn't already seen me at my worst. Hell, we both saw each other during those weird awkward phases as we grew up.

Adjusting the oversized shirt that constantly slips off my shoulder, I make my way out of my room. I once again find myself blessed by the big brother gods, as Miles is thankfully, nowhere in sight. However, as I open the front door, that feeling quickly vanishes when I come face to face with a pacing Ford.

My heart betrays me as I'm hit with an overwhelming feeling of desire and crushing sadness as I look him over. While he normally looks clean and put together, his brown hair is completely disheveled, as if he's been frantically running his fingers through it.

"Blair," he starts, coming toward me as I hold up a hand to stop him.

"We'll talk, but first, let's go somewhere else."

My nosey-ass brother may not have been in the living room, but that doesn't mean he isn't lurking nearby. I'm not counting on this turning into a loud or heated exchange, especially considering Ford and I have never had that sort of relationship. Nevertheless, I'd rather err on the side of caution right about now, especially since my nerves are already on edge.

I'm also not looking to taint my brother's place with any sad, lingering memories, especially since I know this is the moment when I'll finally have to end things once and for all.

"Oh, okay. Where did you want to go?" he asks, adjusting his glasses.

"Let's go for a drive."

The drive was quiet as we made our way past the Evergreen Grove town limits. Despite his obvious desire to talk, I purposely kept my gaze focused out the window, taking in the sights as he drove.

Unfortunately, I knew I was only biding my time for so long as Ford finally pulls onto the side of the road, picking a destination fairly close to the area where we went for Ronnie's photoshoot. Part of me wants to complain and tell him to pick someplace else, since the last thing I want is for sad memories to pop up when I look at my friend's bridal shoot pictures, but since this area is deserted and will give us some much-needed privacy, I figure this battle isn't one I want to fight.

Letting out a loud breath, Ford unbuckles his seatbelt and turns to face me. "I ended things. Jenny and I are over."

My forehead creases as I try to truly take in what he just said. "What?" I ask, my voice edged with panic. "You guys weren't already separated?" Well, now, it definitely makes sense why Mrs. White was so damn pissed when she saw me and Ford. Hell, now I'm Team Jenny here, too.

"No, I mean yes. Yes, we're separated, but after I dropped you off, I went to Jenny's place and told her we need to make things official. On Monday, we're meeting with our lawyers and ending things once and for all. We're officially getting divorced."

A fleeting sense of relief washes over me, but it dissipates almost instantly. "Was she upset?" Contrary to what others may believe, I never wanted to hurt Jenny in any of this. She may never have been my favorite person, but that doesn't mean I wanted her to get caught in the crossfire, especially since I know all too well what it feels like to be someone's second choice.

"Only because this is truly the end, but she gets it. She wasn't happy with me either," he says, tentatively reaching for my hand, which I let him take—for now.

"Ford," I say, looking down at our entwined fingers. "I don't think we should do this."

"Why not? You can't tell me that what we have between us isn't real. We were made for each other. You're my person. I know it, and I know you know it, too." I feel a tender touch beneath my chin, guiding my gaze upward to meet his. "Tell me that what we have isn't real," he challenges.

I stare, our eyes locked in an intense battle. I know what I should say, and I'm so tempted to lie, but it's impossible. "I can't."

"Then be with me," he begs.

"But it's not that easy."

"Blair, being with you is the easiest thing in the world. Who cares what anyone says or thinks? Because I sure as hell don't. The only thing that matters to me is you and your happiness, and I know that I can make you happy. Please, let me be the one who makes you happy. Let me be your person, because I sure as hell want you to be mine," he further pleads as he drops the hand from my chin before lifting the one with my hand as he presses a soft kiss to my knuckles.

"I'm pretty sure I've always been yours," I confess, giving in as my fingers quickly unbuckle my belt and my hand finds its way to the back of his neck, urging him closer as our lips collide.

Maybe I'm weak, or maybe I'm tired of fighting what I've always known to be true. He's right—he's always been mine, and I know without a doubt that my heart has always been his.

It belonged to Ford Hastings well before I was ready to admit that out loud or even to myself.

He slowly releases my hand, his touch shifting to the side of my neck, his thumb brushing soft circles against my cheek. The sweet and careful kisses soon ignite into a fiery passion as I eagerly open my mouth to him. I long to be near him again, my body buzzing with anticipation, almost like a shaken soda bottle on the verge of exploding.

As if our minds and bodies are in sync, our reluctant lips pull away from each other. As I forcibly push myself out of my seat and clamber over the center console, he quickly reaches down and pushes the seat back as far as it will allow. This would definitely be much easier if he were like many of the other guys in Evergreen Grove, boasting of their manliness with a truck. However, at this moment, I couldn't care less.

All that matters is being close to him, and as I climb into his lap, it works, bringing us even closer, especially as I feel him straining against his zipper through my thin pair of biker shorts.

"Say it again," Ford commands as his lips press into mine once more before they make a desperate trail of kisses up toward my ear.

"Say what again?" I somehow manage, my eyes closing as I relish the sensation of his kisses, the gentle pressure and tingling sensation making my skin come alive.

"That you're mine," he whispers against the shell of my ear before nibbling on my lobe.

"I'm yours," I whisper freely, a soft moan leaving my lips as I softly, but urgently, buck my hips into his, needing to feel the pressure against my already wet and aching core.

Before I can say anything else, his lips capture mine once more, as our tongues meet and tangle together. The intensity and desperation of my longing for him is evident in the way my body twists against his, my fingers seeking solace as they sink into his disheveled brown locks.

With one hand possessively clutching my ass, the other hand languidly explores my body, gliding achingly slow beneath my shirt as his fingers make a trail across my stomach to my ribs, finally halting as his fingertips hover just below the sensitive skin of my bare breast. Craving his touch to go just a little higher, I grind my hips into his once more, feeling his groan vibrate against my lips as he realizes my braless state.

We seem to once again be on the same page as he reaches down below us and unbuckles his jeans before working on unzipping his zipper. The space may be tight, and I'm sure I'm not the most graceful, but I do my best to lift myself up to make it easier. Even more, I too want to feel closer to him as I work on removing my shorts, and he realizes that I'm once again, not wearing any panties.

"Fuck, Blair," he breathes out, his voice strained as I lower my body and press against him, the sensation heightened given that we only have his thin pair of boxer briefs between us. "You're so fucking perfect," he adds, and I have to say, I love this side of him. During the day, he's the most polite man you'll ever meet, and it's rare to hear him utter a single curse word, but when we're like this, a new side of him peeks through.

Wanting to impress him even more, I lift my shirt over my head, leaving myself completely bare to him.

He eagerly scans my figure with hungry eyes, a wicked smile forming on his lips before he finally leans closer to capture my mouth once more. While one of his hands works its way toward my breast where he palms it before rolling my nipple between his fingers, he moves the other lower, between us as he moves toward my aching center. "You're so fucking wet," he whispers appreciatively against my lips.

"All for you," I whisper back before his finger finds and rubs against my clit and a loud moan escapes from deep within.

As Ford skillfully uses his fingers, the pressure builds, propelling me closer to the edge with each passing moment. With a firm grasp on his curls, I press my teeth into his bottom lip, eliciting a chorus of rapid breaths, pants, and moans.

His hands don't stop, and while I'm sure it's not the most comfortable position in the world, he continues on as his fingers move lower and he easily slips a finger inside me, before adding another, expertly finding my G-spot as he curls his fingers just right.

"That's it, my beautiful greedy girl. Take what you need," he whispers against my mouth as I buck more forcefully into his fingers and his touch. Without any means of control, a powerful orgasm consumes me as I call out his name. Thankfully, he persists with his rhythmic movements, slowly guiding me back to reality as I come down from the very powerful high.

Leaning forward, a quiet, contented laugh escapes as I bury my forehead in his chest. Instead of speaking, Ford wordlessly communicates his feelings as he places a tender kiss on top of my forehead.

Once I manage to catch my breath, I raise my head, our gazes locked as we share a mutual smile. "Told you I could make you happy," he teases as I let out a small, breathy laugh and shake my head.

"That's fine, just as long as I get to make you happy, too."

"You always make me happy," he states seriously as he once again lifts his hand and gently runs the pad of his thumb along my lower lip, sending a jolt of electricity down my spine. The passion inside me only ignites even more, as I watch him lift the fingers he'd just used to bring me pleasure as he sucks all traces of my excitement for him clean.

Feeling an overwhelming need for him all over again, I lean in and press my thirsty lips against his, savoring the tender way they part over mine.

Instead of feeling hurried or rushed, our lips glide leisurely and deliberately. As I wrap my hands around the back of his neck, he softly cradles the back of mine, his fingers gently caressing my fallen blonde curls.

Breaking our kiss for a few brief seconds, I gently lift his shirt over his head, enjoying the warmth of his bare skin against my own. In sync once more, I lift my hips, as he reaches down to remove the final barrier between the two of us.

Ford nods toward the glove compartment. "I think I have a condom in there," he says, a sheepish grin on his lips, but I don't question it.

Not wasting time, I adjust in his lap and reach in, where thankfully, under some papers, I find a solo condom. "Got it." I smile, ripping the wrapper with my teeth before doing the honor as I slide it down his lengthy and sturdy cock.

Looking up, our eyes connect, and I'm struck by the intensity of his gaze, a combination of longing and adoration that transcends mere physical attraction. This is more than just sex for us, which only makes me crave and long for him to be inside me even more.

Part of this scares me, but I don't let it hold me back. Not only wanting to explore this feeling but also having the intense need to, I lift my hips as his hands on my hips slowly guide me down onto him.

A mutual gasping fills the air of the car before our bodies move in sync. His hands remain on my hips as I rest mine on his shoulders for support, his eyes never straying from mine. Our bodies move in perfect synchrony, and although I don't want to look away, I can't resist the overwhelming pleasure that causes my head to tilt back as my back arches against the steering wheel.

"Ford," I gasp, my breath catching in my throat as I teeter on the edge once more, the anticipation mounting like the final, stomach-churning drop on a roller coaster. The rhythm of his thrusts accelerates as he pushes into me with greater speed and strength.

"You're almost there, baby," he encourages with a low growl.

Hearing him call me "baby" is what does me in as I unravel on top of him, my fingers and nails digging deep into his shoulders. As he thrusts into me, a symphony of pleasure fills the car—his loud groan merging with my own moans as we reach the pinnacle of ecstasy, leaving me shaking on top of him.

As we both come down from the incredible high that we've found together, I once again collapse onto his chest and his hand slides up my back, rubbing slow, lazy circles.

"God, Blair. I'm so glad you're mine," he says in a breathless whisper as he rests his head on top of mine, our chests rising and falling together as one as we both work on calming our racing hearts.

As much as I want to be his, and in so many ways already am, there's still so much that we need to work out. Sure, we have amazing chemistry; the sex is mind-blowing, and he's officially getting divorced, but how does a relationship between traveling photographer and a man living in her nightmare of a town actually work?

However, I push those thoughts aside—at least for now. "Me too," I say instead, needing to savor this moment for as long as I can.

28

FORD

I CAN HONESTLY SAY that I've never been invited to a bachelorette party before, and if this ends up being my one and only, I'm more than okay with that.

It doesn't help that Gemma and Maeve, the other two bridesmaids, are my coworkers. Gemma is a few years younger than us and works as the drama and dance teacher, and Maeve is at least a couple of years older and is one of the school counselors. After all the dick memorabilia I've already seen at the "the pre-party", I'm not so sure I'll be able to look either of them in the eye ever again. Without a doubt, the women found it utterly hilarious, which only adds to the fact that I couldn't keep my cheeks from turning a bright shade of red.

You'd think that being the only one at tonight's event with an actual penis would make me okay with seeing them everywhere, but nope, it only added to my utter embarrassment, especially when all the women chanted and coerced me into participating in a game of Pin the Penis on Pete. Ultimately, Ronnie is having the time of her life, though, and that's all that matters.

Even more, Blair officially solidified her position of knowing Ronnie best as she decided that after the pre-party we'd head to the next town over for line dancing, with everyone dressing accordingly.

Despite my efforts to get into character, my red plaid button-up shirt, jeans, boots, and cowboy hat do little to make me stand out, especially compared to the rest of the women in our party. They've given it their all, and Ronnie is definitely the center of attention in her short, white, sparkly dress with the dress's long fringe adding an extra flair that swishes and sways with her every step. Then, of course, she topped it off with a matching white hat and boots. Thanks to the bride-to-be sash provided by Blair, she's spent the majority of the evening bombarded with offers from men to buy her and the rest of the bridesmaids drinks.

Blair is the one I can't keep my eyes off of, though, and for good reason. Dressed in a short black skirt embellished with rhinestone stars, she turns heads wherever she goes. To finish her outfit, she's wearing a black halter crop top that shows a perfect sliver of her porcelain skin, along with a matching cowboy hat and boots.

It's both gratifying and slightly unsettling to have the woman whom so many men fantasize about be mine, evoking a mix of jealousy and an overwhelming sense of protectiveness. I hate being that guy. Blair looks amazing and deserves to show off her body in whatever capacity she wants, but I can't help the primal instinct that wants to throw her over my shoulder, carry her back to my place, and show her why I'm the only man for her.

As much as that is also not me, I know it wouldn't bode too well. It wouldn't just upset Blair; Ronnie would be furious and kill us both if we left her on her big night. On top of that, I'm the designated driver. That's not much of a change, but the fact that I drove all the women here in the back of Maeve's soccer mom van is a new one for me.

"You know, I'm starting to suspect I was only asked to be your bridesman so I could drive you around and be in charge of grabbing drinks," I yell above the loud country music blasting from the speakers as I carefully attempt to set down the shots on the table while doing my best not to spill any.

"That, and the fact that you look so darn cute in your lil' cowboy hat," Ronnie teases, her baby voice coming through as she playfully pinches my cheek, clearly feeling some of the effects of the free shots she's been gifted.

"Yeah, yeah," I say, pushing her hand away as I adjust the hat on my head.

"That, and the fact that we're likely going to need a big strong man to carry us all to the car if we keep taking all these shots," Gemma adds with a small laugh.

I can't disagree. These ladies are well on their way to getting drunk, especially since they're getting dangerously close to that point of being more than just a little buzzed.

"Well, I'm not so sure one would actually classify me as a big strong man, so if you did decide to slow down I wouldn't be opposed," I joke. Obviously, I'm not about to police anyone, but I am only one man, after all.

"Well, maybe you should take a break from drink-grabbing duties and come dance with us instead," Blair suggests, reaching for my hands as she walks backward, pulling me with her toward the dance floor.

I vehemently shake my head as I dig my heels into the floor. "Sorry. Not a chance. You know I'm not a dancer. Hell, I'm pretty sure the last time we danced was at senior prom, and I almost broke your ankle in the process."

She scoffs. "Oh, come on. You aren't that bad. Please," she begs, pouting out her bottom lip for dramatic effect. Between that and her beautiful blue puppy-dog eyes, I almost give in, but instead, I pull my hands out of hers.

"Sorry. I'll do just about anything for you all tonight, but that is where I draw the line."

"Boo!" Ronnie chants before the others chime in as well.

"Fine, be lame," Blair gives in, sticking out her tongue at me before reaching for Ronnie's hand, who gladly accepts. Ronnie reaches out, interlocking her fingers with the other ladies as they form a small, human chain. They make their way to the dance floor, their footsteps immediately stepping into sync with the beat of the blaring music as they catch on quickly and immediately join the rest of the dancers in a synchronized dance to some Ed Sheeran song.

I watch in awe as the people move on the dance floor, truly not understanding how everyone can move so in sync. Admittedly, some newcomers take a bit longer to catch on, but it's remarkable how soon they seem to find their rhythm and join the group so seamlessly.

I, on the other hand, was not blessed with any sort of rhythm. I've always struggled with the physical stuff, especially those that require any sort of strength or coordination. There's definitely a reason that I stuck to books and science; dance moves on the other hand—not my thing.

I wish things were different, and that I could be the kind of guy who couldn't care less about how I'd look out there, especially since I know Blair would love it. Not only is her face currently beaming with enthusiasm and pure joy, but whenever she's around music, it's like she enters an entirely different universe where she can let go and forget about everything else as a truly carefree side of her emerges.

On the bright side, as I sit on the outskirts at our table, I have the absolute best view in the room as my eyes refuse to leave Blair. I've always found it easy to get lost in staring at her, but now, as she moves her body to the music, it's even more captivating. Somehow, she manages to hit every step perfectly, and in my biased opinion, she is undoubtedly the best dancer out there.

Despite her being completely lost in the moment, our gazes meet from across the room, and the smile on her face somehow grows even larger. I lift a hand and wave, and while she asks once again, beckoning me with a nod to come and join, I laugh and shake my head. She may have me wrapped around her finger in so many different ways, but there's no way she's getting me out there.

I already feel pretty out of place, and my lack of coordination would only make that worse. I'm not sure why I feel so self-conscious, as I'm dressed similarly to a lot of the other males here, but somehow they look like men who should be dressed like that, especially since part of me suspects that many of them dress like this on a day-to-day basis. I, on the other hand, look like some nerdy dude playing dress-up.

Watching a man approach the women, I immediately become more attentive, and I sit up straight. While I know they can handle these sorts of situations on their own, I have also seen the way certain men often act when they've had a bit too much to drink and think they're owed something, and this man gives off that exact vibe.

As I watch him focus his gaze and undivided attention on Blair, my hands involuntarily clench into tight fists, my knuckles turning white. It's clear they aren't interested in what he has to say, especially Blair, as she shakes her head, her face filled with obvious disinterest as she turns her body away from him, focusing solely on her dancing. This, however, doesn't seem to dissuade him at all.

How is this fucker not getting the message? I stand, watching more intently as he continues to talk and tries to gain their attention by stepping between Blair and Ronnie, inching in even closer.

Even from this far away, I can see Blair's frustration reach its peak as she abruptly stops dancing and launches into a scathing tirade before motioning for the other women to join her on the opposite side of the dance floor.

It's always been the joke that I'm the lover, not the fighter. When you have two feisty friends like Blair and Ronnie, they've always been the first to handle any trouble that came our way. But as the man forcefully grabs Blair's arm and yanks her toward him, a surge of fury courses through me.

I'm seeing red, and before I realize what I'm doing, I've charged my way through the crowded dance floor. I probably should've known that the women could handle this on their own, but why should they have to? No woman ever deserves to be handled like that.

Amidst the clamor of the women's loud reprimands, Ronnie's finger jabbing forcefully into the man's chest, I maneuver my way through the crowd and push to stand in front of him. It doesn't matter that this man towers over me, with bulging muscles that rival John Cena's, or that he appears to look twice my size. All that matters is telling him off.

"Hey, motherfucker, you stay the hell away from them," I shout, and before I can even register what I'm doing, especially since I've never so much as thought of punching someone before, I raise my fist and it connects with this man's intensely strong jaw.

From there, all hell breaks loose.

29

BLAIR

I FIND MYSELF TEETERING between annoyance and appreciation as Ford lands a punch on the irritating creep who insisted on grabbing my attention by any means necessary.

If there's one thing I'm sure of, it's that Ronnie and I easily could have handled this on our own. Between the two of us, we're more than capable of dealing with a handsy asshole. However, Ford rushed in out of nowhere, like some kind of modern knight in shining armor on his white horse as he attempted to swiftly take matters into his own hands—literally.

Sure, very deep down, yes, it's cute to know that he cares, especially since he's normally the guy who wouldn't hurt a fly. Hell, I've witnessed him carefully catch spiders and release them outside, valuing their freedom over their demise. Normally I'm all for a good smashing, especially when it comes to both spiders and creepy dudes, but this felt more than a little unnecessary.

The last thing we needed was for complete chaos to break out, as many people rushed in, putting themselves between the two men. In fact, Ford was pretty lucky so many intervened, since it was pretty obvious the man was ready to go balls to the wall on Ford to a pulp for taking that hit, and he very much had the capability to do so. There was still plenty of yelling, cursing, and shoving going on, but luckily it all came to a halt pretty quickly, especially once the bar's security took over and escorted the man out.

Thankfully, they didn't kick us out as well, but given that the man had clearly been over-served and had been bothering more than just us, we were issued a stern warning instead.

With things settling down, I feel a powerful urge to unleash my anger on Ford, especially with the risk of Ronnie or another bridesmaid getting hurt amidst all the chaos only days away from the wedding. However, as I glance at Ford, with clear signs of guilt and frustration etched on his face, it's obvious he's already beating himself up enough for the both of us.

My eyes immediately fall to the hand that he's attempting to cradle and hide. My stern demeanor disappears as I take a step forward and pull his hand toward me.

"Shit, Ford." I frown, my eyes taking in the already bruised and swollen knuckles.

"Yeah, I think I may have underestimated the fact that my hand was likely going to end up in just as much pain as the guy's face. Then again, given how strong that guy's jaw was, I'm starting to wonder if I even caused any damage at all," he admits with a forced smile, which he displays in an obvious attempt to disguise the discomfort he's clearly feeling.

"Well, given the fact that the guy and his buddies are gone, it's clear your brutish display of manhood worked to some effect," I offer, nodding toward the exit. "And if anything, you should just be happy that we aren't being escorted out of here tonight with them."

While I'm sure it would've been a memorable story that we'd laugh about in the future whenever we talked about Ronnie's bachelorette party, I have to imagine that current Ronnie wouldn't be all that happy about having to end the night a little early if things had gone differently.

This place has always been special to the two of us, and was even where we got the most use out of our fake IDs when we were younger. Coming here tonight felt like the perfect and only way to celebrate one of my best friend's last nights as a single woman, and I can't bear the thought of something tarnishing the memory of such a permanent fixture in our lives.

Not to mention, she looks absolutely breathtaking in her bride-to-be outfit, and it would be such a shame if she couldn't flaunt it to the fullest.

"I'd hate myself forever if that had been the case," he says, his frown somehow deepening. "I honestly don't even know what I was thinking. One second I was watching that guy approach you from the other side of the room, and the next thing I knew I was marching over there. I just lost complete control, and I'm so sorry."

"Well, next time, before you run out there acting like Rocky Balboa, maybe take some boxing lessons first," I playfully suggest, before reaching for his good hand and lead him toward the bar.

Despite the bartenders' evident displeasure at our disruptive behavior, they begrudgingly provide us with a baggie filled with ice.

"How about you head out back, and I'll go and talk with the girls and meet you in a few?" I suggest, as he solemnly nods his head, all the fight taken out of him.

While he makes his way to the back exit, I take a moment to let out a steadying breath before I head back toward our table.

"How is he?" Gemma asks once she notices me approaching.

"He's fine. His hand and ego are both a little bruised though. Honestly, the guy is lucky he didn't bust his thumb or something," I add, somewhat trying to make light of the situation as I attempt to smile. "How are you, though?" I ask, turning my full attention to Ronnie.

"A little shaken up, but nothing another drink can't fix, right?" she asks, and while she also seems to be making light of the situation, I can tell she is exactly what she just said she is—shaken and on edge.

I nod, especially since I could use a drink myself to settle my frazzled nerves.

Ronnie grabs my hands, as if sensing this is something we both need. "Do me a favor and go take care of Ford, okay?" she asks. "We both know our boy is likely beating himself up right about now, and that is the last thing I want. The night isn't ruined. If anything, we're only getting started."

"And we'll take care of our girl here, so no worries there either," Maeve adds, as she wraps an arm around Ronnie's shoulder.

"Alright. I'll be back," I say, giving Ronnie's hand a reassuring squeeze before I release it and make my way out back to check on Ford and his injured hand.

Opening the door to the back, I immediately spot him leaning against the brick wall of the building.

"Is she pissed?"

I shake my head. "No. She's fine. We're all fine, and if anything, we're all likely more concerned and worried about you. The last thing we need is our one and only bridesman down and out."

"I just feel like an idiot. What if I'd gotten punched, or worse, gotten one of you caught in the crossfire? I can't believe I was so fucking stupid," he growls, kicking at the ground, clearly still beating himself up over all of this.

I reach out and place my hand tenderly on his cheek, letting the pad of my thumb lightly caress it as I force him to look at me. "None of that happened. We're all okay, and that asshole is gone. Please, just stop worrying."

He lets out a loud sigh. "Me? Stop worrying? I'm pretty sure I was built to carry the worry for all three of us."

"Well, maybe it's time you stop doing that, since if anything, you're now the rebel and defender of the crew," I tease, my thumb still spinning soft circles. "Who would've ever expected *me* to be the responsible one?"

"Not me," he jokes, the beginnings of a smile slowly making its way onto his face.

"Honestly, not me either," I laugh. Sure, maybe I've been able to move out and take care of myself these past ten years, but when you spend your life on tour with different bands as you travel the world, you tend to make some pretty stupid decisions, especially when it comes to a certain drummer.

"I can't say I totally hate it. You're here now, and allowing me to be the guy that takes you home and to bed at night, so that's at least a pleasant change."

"I have to say, it is a little weird to finally have your full and undivided attention," I agree, my face relaxing into another smile.

"Honestly, you've almost always had my full attention. As hard as I tried to be a good husband to Jenny, I think she's always been right, whether I wanted to admit it or not. Even with you far away and not even living in Evergreen Grove, I was never able to fully let you go. Deep down, I always knew you were the one for me. My only regret is that I wasted so much damn time fighting my feelings for you when I should've surrendered to them a long time ago."

My heart bubbles over with a comforting warmth, especially since his words reflect my own truth so well. "It wasn't just you." I shrug, dropping my hand from his cheek as I lean back against the wall next to him. "I was so terrified of messing things up like I always seemed to do, and I couldn't do that to us. Our friendship was too important to me."

"Yeah," he nods. "I felt that same pressure. I think that's why I clung on so tightly to Jenny. I never felt for her what I felt for you, but she could occasionally make me think that I could distract myself enough to forget about you for a little while, even if that was incredibly selfish of me. I hate that I hurt so many people by denying what was in front of me the whole damn time."

I wrinkle my nose. While it's nice to hear that I've always been his number one, just like he was mine, I don't exactly love hearing about his time with Jenny. "Can we maybe not talk about your soon-to-be ex-wife?" I suggest. "Don't get me wrong, I'm glad to know where you stood all those years, especially since I felt something similar, but it kind of brings the vibes down, you know?"

A very soft chuckle leaves his lips as he nods his head in agreement. "So, what should we talk about instead?" he asks, a suggestive lilt to his tone as he pins me down with a devilish stare.

"We could always talk about how you're planning on making all of this up to me."

"I could get behind that. I also have a few things in mind that could maybe work."

"While I'm sure that your ways are probably just as fun, I think I already have something pretty specific in mind," I tease, leaning toward him, giving his ear a light nip in the process.

"At this point, I'd do just about anything for you, Blair," he says, closing his eyes as his head leans back against the wall.

"Anything?" I ask, needing to make sure.

"Anything."

"Perfect," I say, grabbing the wrist of the hand holding the ice as I take him by surprise and pull him with me back toward the door. "Because I want you to dance with me."

"Wait," he says, resisting my pull. "When I said anything..."

I blink my large lashes and give him my best, most purposeful pout. "You mean you don't want to make things up to me?"

"Fuck." He gives in with a large, dramatic sigh despite the huge grin on his face. "Fine. I give in. You win. I did say I'd do anything, even if that includes making a fool of myself on that dance floor."

"I mean, you already did it once tonight; what's the harm in doing it a second time?" I joke, and he rolls his eyes.

"Just know, this is a one-time deal only, so you better enjoy it," he says, taking initiative and walking ahead to reach the door first before opening it for me.

"Oh, believe me," I assure him, letting myself inside, "I'm going to enjoy every single second of it."

30

BLAIR

IT'S A PECULIAR FEELING to watch your best friend have such a monumental moment as she walks down the aisle toward the groom, while also knowing that the groom is a narcissistic asshole who in no way deserves her. Okay, so maybe he's not *that* bad, and maybe Ronnie is right—I don't know him as well as I should, but there's something about him that just doesn't sit right with me. Knowing Ronnie as well as I do, I know that without a doubt she deserves a man who treats her like the princess she is, and from what I've seen from Pete—it's not him.

In addition, she looks absolutely stunning in the white midi dress she's wearing. The dress gracefully falls off her shoulders, and the fun little ruffle down the front adds an extra touch of playfulness before the main event tomorrow. I can't believe that we're only one day away from my best friend becoming Mrs. Pete West. God help us all.

Unfortunately, yet not surprisingly, that smile of hers only lasts for so long as Pete does what Pete does best: his incessant complaining, practically foaming at the mouth as he continually yells at everyone for not taking this seriously enough or for making some little mistake before he makes us start all over again.

"Don't worry, babe. It's just a rehearsal." Ronnie tries to calm him down as she places her hands on his shoulders. "We're just working through the kinks now so tomorrow everything will be perfect."

"Don't tell me not to worry," he growls, forcibly stepping back as he lifts his hands out in front of him, making her hands fall. "And I'm not some child that needs to be calmed down, so stop with that bullshit. If I want to be pissed off about this, I'm allowed to be."

"That's not what I'm trying to do," she says, her voice sounding defeated as she seems to shrink into herself.

"Why don't we all just take a break?" I suggest, stepping out from my spot behind my best friend, no longer able to keep my annoyance and frustration to myself. It's not her fault that people keep missing their cues and laughing about it. I mean, what did he expect when his entire line of groomsmen act like the annoying frat boys they once were? "We'll start fresh, and everyone will get it right first try, I'm sure of it."

"I second a break," Ford agrees as I look over my shoulder and give him a grateful smile, even if I'm sure this is more for Ronnie's sake than mine.

"Fine, whatever," Pete grumbles, pushing past Ronnie, seeming to ignore her completely as he walks toward the main doors and lets them slam behind him. While the big event tomorrow is going to take place outside in Ronnie's parents' backyard, tonight we are using Evergreen Grove's vast assembly hall for all of the wedding rehearsal needs.

"Just, uh, take a few minutes everyone," Ronnie suggests, as most people anxiously scan the area, uncertain how to process the explosion caused by that ridiculous man-child.

Gradually, the silence is permeated by a few hushed conversations, bringing the room back to life. "You okay?" I ask, placing a hand on her shoulder as her eyes turn to meet mine.

"No, but it's fine. We're just stressed." She shrugs, her voice strained as she does her best to brush off Pete's uncalled-for behavior.

"Maybe," I try to offer, but there is no way I can let him off the hook that easily. "But I'm sensing a bit of a pattern when it comes to Pete, so it's okay if you're not fine."

"I said I'm fine," she snaps and my eyes go wide.

"Ronnie, I..." I start, but she shakes her head before I can say more.

"I'm sorry," she sighs, looking genuinely apologetic. "I think his attitude is rubbing off on me. I think I might need a minute too."

"Yeah, sure, whatever you need." I nod in acknowledgement. Plus, I'm her maid of honor; I should be making this day easier on her, not more stressful. I might hate her fiancé even more now, if that's even possible, but she loves him and wants to marry him, so my only job is to be the supportive friend she deserves.

I watch with a defeated sigh as she walks out of the room before turning to face the rest of the wedding party. "Alright everyone," I call out, doing my best to grab everyone's attention.

It's possible my best friend is making a giant mistake by marrying the wrong guy, but that's not up to me. What I do have control over, however, is stepping up and taking charge both tonight and tomorrow to make sure that, despite everything else, she has the best fucking wedding day ever.

"You did a good job tonight," Ford whispers next to me as he places a hand on my knee and gives it a light squeeze from our spot at the table where we've gathered for the rehearsal dinner.

"Thanks," I say with a smile, enjoying the comforting touch of his thumb brushing gentle circles. In return, I place a grateful hand on his cheek, relishing the rough texture of his light stubble that only adds to his undeniably handsome good looks. "I still feel like a horrible maid of honor, but at least I saved the rest of us from receiving another verbal beat-down."

"You're not a horrible maid of honor," he assures me, placing his free hand on top of mine as he leans into the touch. "Ronnie is lucky to have you. Sure, you may have been trying to talk some sense into her, just like you did with me at my wedding," he goes on, before leaning in to whisper the rest in my ear so only we can hear. "Just please don't do the same thing you did then and beg her not to marry him and to choose you instead, because now that I have you, I'm not about to lose you to anyone else, not even to Ronnie."

I let out a very soft giggle. "Don't worry. That was only for you," I assure him, just as Pete's best man finishes his speech and the sound of applause fills the air. I clap along too, even if I had zoned out for most of it. Sorry, but there's no convincing me that Pete's actually some fun and charming guy, despite what his best friend just tried to sell us.

"So next up, we have Blair Bennett, who is the beautiful bride-to-be's maid of honor and best friend."

As more claps ring out, I stand, smoothing out my baby blue one-shoulder jumpsuit before reaching for my glass of champagne and making my way toward the microphone.

"Thank you, everyone," I start, giving a small nod as all eyes focus on me, while my gaze settles on my best friend. "But most of all, my true gratitude goes to Veronica for not only choosing to include me in her big day, but most importantly, for choosing me as her best friend." I smile. While everyone in the room is tuning in, this message is truly for her.

"As many of you may know, I wasn't always the most liked kid in town and was written off pretty quickly by a lot of people, but not by Veronica. To her, none of that silly stuff mattered. I still remember how on our first day of kindergarten, when we saw each other on the playground, she marched right up to me, told me who she was, and declared that we were now best friends. I'm not sure if she just sensed what was to become fact, or if she manifested it right there and then, but either way, it became the truth, and there was no denying to anyone that we were best friends and still are to this day. While she may have gone off and found her actual soulmate," I start, adding that for her benefit, since maybe it is time to support what she wants and not what I want for her instead.

"I want her to know that in so many ways, she will always be mine. Obviously not in a romantic sense," I continue, glancing toward Ford with a playful smirk. "I love ya, girl, just not like that," I laugh with the crowd as I look back at Ronnie, who has placed a hand over her heart.

"Seriously though, what I've come to realize is that soulmates aren't always found in romantic partners. Sometimes, as in our case, they come in the form of a most cherished best friend who stands by your side through every single one of life's ups and downs. Without a doubt, you are more than just a friend to me; you're my platonic soulmate. Our friendship transcends time and space, and I'm positive that we've spent many lifetimes together and will continue to do so in the future. For me, you've always been someone I could not only spend the good times with, but the hard ones, too. Ronnie, you've always been there for me through thick and thin, offering a listening ear, a shoulder to lean on, and a hand to hold whenever I needed it, and believe me, I needed it," I emphasize, once again earning a small chuckle from those in attendance.

"This is now the time when I should probably tell an embarrassing story that happened between me and the bride, but given the town we live in, I'm pretty sure the majority of you already know each and every devious act we participated in, so I'll end with this; Veronica and Pete, may your marriage be filled with the same love, laughter, and joy that you've brought into my life. And Ronnie, remember, no matter where life takes you, you'll always have a friend and a platonic soulmate in me. And Pete, I hope you know what a lucky man you are. Hopefully you love and cherish growing old with her just as much as I loved being able to grow up with her."

To finish, I raise my glass in the air. "Cheers to the bride and groom," I conclude before lifting my glass to my lips and taking a sip along with everyone else in the room. I've never been much of a crier, but I'm feeling intensely grateful, and it feels like an utter miracle that I somehow made it through all that without shedding a single tear.

The same can't be said for Ronnie as she and Pete walk toward me. "That was so beautiful, Blair," she gushes as she wraps her arms around me. I do the same, holding her tighter than necessary, but I can't help it.

"I really do love you, Ronnie. I can't even tell you how grateful I am that you've allowed me to be not only your best friend but also your maid of honor," I say, and this time, a traitorous tear does fall.

"I love you too," she assures me, pulling back from the hug as her hands lower to hold on to mine. "And just so you know, I couldn't have said it better. You are without a doubt, my platonic soulmate."

"I don't know. I'm not too sure how I feel about you having another soulmate," Pete cuts in, of course needing to ruin our special moment. "But for tonight and the occasion, I suppose I'll allow it."

"Thanks for the permission," I say through gritted teeth as I do everything in my power to hold back from saying what I really want to say.

"What the..." Ronnie's words trail off as I turn to see what's captured her attention. "Is that Max?" she asks, her brows furrowing in confusion. "What is he doing here? I thought you two broke up?"

"We did."

So what the hell is Max Storm doing here?

Taking a deep breath, I excuse myself from Ronnie and Pete, de-termined to keep my composure and not let Max's unexpected arrival overshadow anything about today.

Leaning against the wall, arms folded, he wears a smug grin that I'm more than ready to wipe off that handsome face of his. It's clear he didn't put too much thought into what he's wear-ing, given the heavily wrinkled black slacks and white button-up shirt that's currently rolled up, perfectly showcasing his heavily tattooed forearms.

While it's somewhat understandable given that he had to fly to be here and that his clothes were likely packed away in his suitcase, it wouldn't have hurt for him to at least attempt to press his clothes before showing up to such an important event.

I'm sure he thinks he's doing me some huge favor and that I'm going to be jumping for joy about him changing his mind to actually join me as my date—but clearly he thought wrong. Maybe if things hadn't changed between Ford and me these past few weeks, a part of me would've been touched by the gesture, but I think it's finally time I no longer accept the bare minimum from men.

With the speeches still in progress, I grab hold of his arm and forcefully drag him out of the small banquet room and outside of the building completely. In a town like this, there's always someone eager to eavesdrop on a private conversation. Given

Max's high-profile status, the last thing I need is to add another mark to my already lengthy record here in Evergreen. This is definitely the kind of thing that people love to gossip about here, and I'm not looking to add any fuel to that particular fire.

"Ready to get me all to yourself I see, but hey, I don't—" he starts.

"Cut the shit, Max," I interrupt. "What the hell do you think you're doing here?"

The surprise in his widened eyes makes it evident that he's taken aback by my sudden outburst, and I can't say I blame him. Once upon a time, I would've been ecstatic over something like this, desperately vying for his attention like a hungry dog looking for nothing more than meager scraps. But no more—those days are officially over.

"What does it look like I'm doing here? I came to make up and show you how sorry I am."

"You're sorry?" A forced laugh escapes my lips, lacking any trace of humor as I struggle to keep my eyes from rolling backward, "So tell me, Max. What is it that you're actually sorry for?"

He lifts his shoulder in a small shrug. "I don't know. Fighting. Not coming. Making you come alone. That was shitty of me, but I'm here now, so I don't see what the problem is," he says, his tone dripping with annoyance, seemingly upset at me for my apparent failure to appreciate his supposed virtuousness amidst everything.

This time, I can't help it as my eyes involuntarily roll in exasperation. "The problem is, it shouldn't have taken you so long to decide to join me. Hell," I say, throwing my hands up in frustration, "you should've been here from day one. I follow you and your band all around the fucking world, yet you couldn't even have the decency to come with me for two weeks to be here for my best friend's wedding?"

He scoffs, holding up his hands. "Chill the fuck out. I don't understand what the problem is."

"This, this is the problem," I start again as I motion between the two of us. "You aren't listening to me or taking me seriously. I just told you why I'm upset and instead of truly apologizing or trying to understand, you're telling me to chill out. That's not okay; don't you see that?"

"I already said I'm sorry, and I'm here now. Can't we just make up?" he asks, taking a step toward me, but I take a step back as well, needing to keep the distance between us. "Blair, what the fuck is wrong with you? Why are you acting like this?"

"I'm acting like this because I'm officially done. I've gotten so used to feeling unlovable or like I deserve to be the second most important thing in someone's life that I let you and others get away with treating me like that, but it's over. In fact, *we're* over, Max." I'm not sure where it came from exactly, but it feels so damn good to have those words leave my mouth once and for all.

Sure, Max and I have broken up plenty of times, but for the first time, I finally know that I actually mean it.

"Are you fucking serious? I just flew all the way here," he rasps, his voice growing louder. However, I'm no longer in the mood to care. He's been granted way too many chances and far more than he ever deserved.

With a casual shrug, I fold my arms and raise one shoulder. "And that's my problem, how? If anything, you should've called. Even a text would have been enough, but you can't even do that."

"Why are you acting like such a bitch? I mean, what am I even supposed to do in this stupid-ass town?" he asks, glancing around.

While I can dislike it for multiple reasons, there's no escaping the prickling annoyance that floods over me upon hearing his words. I understand that it may not look like anything special from the outside, likely resembling the set of some old Hallmark film. But, for the first time, I find myself feeling oddly defensive of this place and the people who call it home.

In fact, there is a part of me that suspects that I may have been a little too hard on it and the many people who live here, myself included. Sure, like most places it has its negatives, but given that most people have welcomed me home with open arms, and it also houses so many of my favorite people, I have to wonder if I wrote this place off a little too easily.

"Once again, not my problem. In fact, I can promise you, Max, you will never be my problem ever again."

He scoffs. "Like I'd want you, anyway. The only reason I came here in the first place was because I was bored and had nothing else to do. If you think I can't find a replacement, you're crazy."

"I hope you do, but for both her sake and yours, I pray that your pathetic and sorry ass treats her better than you ever treated me."

I mean it too. While I've found some clarity in coming home with what I want and deserve, I strangely also want that for Max, too. Maybe he also just needs to find the one person who is right for him in order for him to change—but somehow I highly doubt it. I'm fairly convinced he's not capable of being a decent boyfriend, but for once, he's truly no longer my problem.

"Fuck you," he curses, letting out a sound between a scoff and laugh. "Have fun in your podunk, stupid-ass town," he says before turning around to walk away, his hands in his pockets.

"Oh, don't worry. I will," I call after him, and for the first time, I finally believe that's true.

31

FORD

I'D MEANT EVERY WORD of it when I'd told Blair how proud of her I was for how she'd taken control and ultimately saved the wedding rehearsal. However, my pride swelled even more as I listened to her heartfelt maid of honor speech.

I'm not sure how I got so lucky and convinced her to give in to what we've been fighting since we were kids, but I'm reveling in it. Even more, I feel like I've hit the jackpot. She's undeniably one of the most beautiful women I've ever laid eyes on, but there's an indescribable depth to her that sets her apart from anyone I've ever met. It's always been more than just her looks for me; she's kind, she's brave, and most of all, she's someone who will have your back no matter what.

I know it wasn't easy for her to dedicate some of her speech to Pete, but clearly she put her own emotions and feelings aside, prioritizing Ronnie's happiness above all else—something I've come to realize she does a little more often than she should.

My eyes remain fixed on the heartwarming scene unfolding in front of everyone as the two girls share an emotional embrace. Standing up, I prepare to welcome Blair back at our seats, but my gaze is immediately drawn to their shocked expressions as they both turn their heads toward the entrance of the banquet hall. I follow their stares until my eyes land on the cocky ass embodiment of Max Storm in the flesh.

I'd obviously met him just over ten years ago when he and Blair met at the small music festival during our summer graduation trip, and while I hated him then, I especially hate him now.

I can't stand how effortlessly cool he looks. Even when I make an effort to look nice, I'm pretty sure I'll never look like anything more than the tall, lanky nerd that I am. He, on the other hand, effortlessly exudes a casual swagger and charm with his long, brown, and untamed hair. Even though only a few tattoos are visible, you can sense that his entire body is a canvas of intricate designs. Despite his rumpled attire, he carries himself with such confidence that his chill vibes remain unaffected. While I'd be embarrassed to show up to an event looking like that, he looks completely unbothered.

It felt impossible to compete with him then, and I'm not sure how I can even begin to compare to him now. The guy is a musical genius, with women constantly throwing themselves at him. He's already shown that he can give Blair the world as he's taken her on incredible trips and introduced her to new cultures and people.

What do I have that I could possibly offer her in return? I'm a high school science teacher who lives in a cramped studio apartment above a pizza place in a town that Blair absolutely despises. There's no comparison. Hell, I'd choose Max over me too.

What the fuck am I supposed to do? Do I go over there and assert my place in her life, reminding her that I exist, or is that too pathetic and needy? I probably should give her some space, or at least a moment to think. However, before I can decide, she swiftly crosses the room, taking Max along with her as they exit the building.

The show seems to go on, as the next person stands to give a speech to the "happy" couple. As Ronnie's friend, I know it's my responsibility to stay present and attentive to all of the festivities going on at tonight's event, but my thoughts inevitably wander.

The woman I'm in love with is outside chatting with the guy who took her away once, and what if history decides to repeat itself all over again? It's not like I could blame her. In the past, I had my fair share of chances to go after her, but I let every single one of them slip away—or rather, I let her slip away.

There'd been countless instances in high school where I could've and should've been brave enough to end things with Jenny, but I hadn't. Not to mention the many years after high school where Jenny and I had once again been off-and-on through our college and adult years, but it felt much safer to stay in the bubble where I knew that person wanted me instead of trying to chase after someone who I wasn't so sure wanted to be caught.

Once I finally had confirmation that the feelings were mutual, I could've been smart and brave enough to cancel my wedding when Blair confessed her true feelings, but I hadn't then, either. If I lose her now, then it's once again all on me—I'm the one truly at fault for all of this.

Time seems to slip away as I sit, consumed by worry, completely oblivious to the speeches being given. In fact, the last person I remember talking is now sitting with someone else now standing in their place.

The faint sound of heels lightly clicking on the hardwood floor has me glancing over my shoulder. Relief washes over me as I spot Blair walking back in alone—Max nowhere in sight. As happy as I want to be, a small voice inside warns that this might not mean what I think it does. It's not like there are any open seats for him, and perhaps she just told him to wait a few hours and ultimately plans to bring him as her date to the wedding tomorrow, as originally planned.

Against my better judgment, I stand as quietly as possible, and instead of letting her walk back to her seat, I grab her hand and lead her right back out.

"Ford, what are you doing?" she asks once I've quietly let the door shut behind us, doing my best to not totally disrupt Ronnie's special night.

"You can't choose him. You can't be with him, Blair. I know I've given you so many reasons not to trust me or to think that I'm not serious about us, but I've never been more serious about anything in my life. I love you, Blair. In fact, I've always been in love with you," I ramble, but I can't stop, nor do I plan to until she fully hears me out. "Maybe it was a platonic kind of love when we were just children, and part of me isn't even sure when it turned into something deeper, but it has. I'm so in love with you and I don't want to live a life without you. I refuse to keep going on like this when I've always known it was supposed to be you. We're supposed to be together. I know it."

She lightly bites down on her lip, despite her growing smile. "Ford," she starts, a short, soft and melodic giggle leaving her lips. "I choose you."

"Really?" I eagerly ask, a huge smile of my own breaking through.

"Of course I do. It was never Max. He was only ever a placeholder. If anything, I think the reason I chose him for so long and kept going back to him was because I knew it could never last or go anywhere, and that it could never work with anyone else, either. It's always been you or nobody. There's never been any other choice for me."

Closing the distance between us, I pull her closer, my hand finding its place at the back of her neck, my thumb lightly rubbing her jaw as our lips collide in a passionate yet tender kiss.

Her lips move in sync with mine as her hands land on my chest. The kiss lasts nowhere near as long as I'd like as she pulls back to look at me, her gorgeous blue eyes staring into mine. "Oh, and I love you, too."

"Really?" I ask, a boyish grin creeping onto my face as she nods.

"So, so much," she assures me before pressing her lips into mine once more. I want to get lost in the kiss, and as she deepens it, I do, but luckily I manage to pull away first this time, even if I do sneak in one more quick peck in the process.

"We should probably head back in there, huh?" I ask, my hand instinctively reaching up to fix my slightly askew glasses after our heated kiss.

She lets out a sigh. "Do we have to?" she whines.

"Well, we don't, but we probably should."

"I think you're right," she agrees, letting out a breath as she wrinkles her nose.

"But don't worry," I assure her, slinking my arm around her waist as I slowly guide us back in the direction of the banquet hall. "It's almost over, and afterward we can go back to my place where I can show you just how much I really do love you."

"As tempting as that sounds, I'm supposed to be sleeping over at Ronnie's tonight. Our last sleepover as single ladies."

I place a hand over my heart as if offended. "And you didn't invite me? That's messed up."

"Last I checked, you aren't a lady, and honestly, I'm grateful for that, because tomorrow after the wedding, I'm all yours. I promise."

"Well, as long as you promise," I smirk, leaning in to kiss her one last time before heading back inside. While tonight might not be ending completely how I'd hoped, knowing that Blair loves me just as much as I love her is more than enough to get me through until tomorrow.

32

BLAIR

SITTING ON RONNIE'S COUCH, I pop another piece of popcorn into my mouth as I watch Julia Roberts and Dermot Mulroney on the screen in *My Best Friend's Wedding*. It just seemed fitting, especially since tomorrow is, after all, my best friend's wedding. At least this time I'm no longer mimicking Julia Roberts' character as she tries to steal the groom away from the bride. Then again, I suppose I wouldn't be too upset if the roles were reversed a bit and the bride chose not to go through with it anyway.

"You know, I'm starting to think we messed up by not bursting out into our own rendition of 'I Say a Little Prayer,'" I joke as Ronnie comes back into the room, carrying a glass of wine for each of us.

"Can you imagine?" she giggles, passing me a glass before settling down and pulling her half of our shared blanket over her legs.

"I think we would've totally rocked it," I decide, taking a sip. Sure, neither of us is a singer, and it would've been totally off key, but that's beside the point.

"Oh my God, can you imagine Pete's reaction if we had?" she asks, and while there's still a smile on her face, a tiny knot forms in my stomach.

I've been trying so hard not to think about how wrong Pete is for Ronnie, especially since she deserves to have someone who would've found it just as hilarious and adorable for Ronnie to do something so silly and spontaneous. Even at the bachelorette party, Gemma had suggested we make up a choreographed dance to perform during the reception for Pete, but Ronnie had quickly shaken her head and shut that idea down, knowing just how much her fiancé would hate it.

With all the dumb stuff we did as kids, that totally should have been something she jumped all over and loved. And considering who Ronnie is, her husband should've wanted and expected this from his bride. But nope, it was brushed it off just as quickly as it had been suggested.

"Yeah, I imagine he wouldn't have been too happy." I frown, taking another sip as I do my best to focus my attention on the screen. "I know you mentioned him being stressed earlier, and I totally get that," I start again, doing my best to tread carefully. "But he's not always like this, right? You guys must have your silly and spontaneous moments, too?"

"Sort of." She shrugs as she seems to carefully figure out how to answer my question, which honestly can't be a good sign. This shouldn't be one of those things you have to think about. "I mean, we have fun. He loves to golf, and taught me how, so usually on weekends we do that, or occasionally we meet with his college buddies for dinner or barbecues," she adds, her voice an octave too high as she tries to assure me.

I wrinkle my nose, but quickly stop once I realize what I'm doing. Sure, dinner with friends sounds like fun, but what about *her* friends? What about doing the things *she* likes to do?

"What about going out dancing like we did the other night? What about going to nearby towns to see art exhibits or visit museums? What about going to concerts?" I can't help but push, since those were all the things we did together that I know without a doubt bring her actual joy.

"Well, no, not together, but I can do those things on my own, or with Ford, or obviously with you whenever you come to visit, so it's really not that big of a deal." She shrugs before taking what looks like a much-needed sip of her wine, and I'm not too sure if she's trying to convince me or herself.

"But you go golfing with him?" I ask, raising an eyebrow. "What does he do with you that you want to do?"

"Blair," she whines, tossing her head back as it falls against the couch before she moves to set her glass on the coffee table. "I don't get why you're making this into some big thing. I like golfing. It's fun, or at least it's not as bad as I thought it'd be. Is it my activity of choice? Of course not, but there are worse ways to spend your time."

"I'm sorry," I apologize, and I mean it. "I'm not trying to ruin this for you," I say, lifting my leg on the couch as I tuck it underneath me and angle my body to face her. "I want tomorrow to be the best day possible, if not the best day of your life, but I'm worried. You deserve everything, and as your best friend and platonic soulmate, I sort of feel like it's not only my responsibility but also my duty to make sure your husband is the best one in the entire world and is going to take care of you in the way that you deserve."

"He is going to take care of me. He takes care of me now," she assures me. "I mean, look at the house I'm going to be moving into. It's stunning, right?"

"It is a beautiful house," I agree with a nod. "But as of right now, it doesn't even feel like something that's yours. It's missing something, and it doesn't feel like you at all."

She rolls her eyes. "Of course it doesn't. I haven't even moved in yet. His family is one of those super old-fashioned ones who thought it best that we wait until after we get married to move in together."

"So when you move your stuff out of your place, he's going to let you decorate and add your flair to things?" I ask, especially since being here, in her apartment, it has a completely different and warm feel than his cold and sterile house. While her lease may have prohibited her from painting the walls, which are currently a light gray, the room we're in is a vivid explosion of color. It's not only the artwork that catches your eye, but also the attention to detail in the furnishings and decorations. Everything is colorful and unique, even down to the yellow couch that we're currently snuggled up on with an orange fluffy blanket draped over us.

"Come on Blair," she says, tilting her head to the side as she lets out a breath of air. "Of course I'm going to be adding my flair to things. Obviously we're going to keep most of his furniture and decorations since they're already there and he already paid a professional stylist to come in, but it's not like I'm going to be getting rid of my stuff or putting it all in storage. I'm allowed to bring some of it with me."

I hate the way my mouth falls open, especially as my eyes soften. I hate this for her. "You're having to get rid of your stuff? And he got a stylist? Are you serious? Look at your place, Ronnie," I say, motioning around the room. "You're an artist and a visionary. Your entire apartment looks like a Pinterest board with a style that most people would kill for. Why didn't he ask you to decorate it, especially when you're going to be living there, too?"

Ronnie pushes up from the couch. "Why are you doing this?"

"I told you. Because I care about you, and honestly, I'm worried," I confess as I move forward to the edge of the couch.

"Well, stop worrying. I'm fine," she snaps, folding her arms.

I purse my lips together as I do my best to center myself. I still have so much to say, but maybe she's right. This is her life, and her decisions and as much as I want her to see things from my point of view, in the end, it really is her choice and her choice alone to make. It's not like I ever let her make my decisions; if she had, I never would've left Evergreen Grove in the first place.

"I'm sorry," I apologize again. Standing up, I wrap my arms around her and pull her close. It takes a few moments, but she eventually relaxes and returns the hug, unfolding her arms to fully embrace me back. "I'm done, and I mean it this time," I say, pulling back enough to look at her so she can see the sincerity in my face. "Especially since I'm pretty sure as your best friend and maid of honor it's also my responsibility to make sure you're happy, and if you're telling me you truly are, then who am I to say otherwise?"

She attempts to smile, even if it doesn't quite reach her eyes. "Thank you, because as much as I appreciate your concern, I've got this. I know what I'm doing, and I need you to trust that I know what's right for me."

"You're one hundred percent right," I agree. "Plus," I say, glancing back toward the television that's still playing *My Best Friend's Wedding*, "we're missing the juicy stuff." I nod just as the ring gets stuck on Julia's finger.

"Actually," she begins, stepping back as she reaches down for her glass. "I think I might head to bed."

"Oh," I say, slightly taken aback, especially since it's only ten o'clock and we've barely made it through the assortment of candy and treats spread out across her coffee table.

"Yeah, it's getting late, and I'm starting to get tired, and since tomorrow is going to be a busy day, I should probably get my beauty rest."

"Yeah, of course." I nod vigorously. Obviously I'd love it if we did what we used to do in the past when we stayed up way too late watching movies and giggling endlessly, but I can understand the need to want to wake up ready and refreshed for one of the biggest days of her life. "We're okay, though, right?" I clarify. The last thing I want is for her to feel like she needs to get away from me. "Because I meant it. No more talking about that kind of stuff. I'm done."

"Of course we're good. We're always going to be good. You're my best friend, Blair, and you always will be," she assures me.

"And hey, feel free to stay up watching movies, especially since we never even made it to *Bride Wars*."

"Yeah, okay." I nod once more as I watch her retreat to the kitchen where she puts her glass in the sink. "And hey," I call one last time as she turns around to look at me. "You're going to make the most beautiful bride in the world, and I can't wait to celebrate with you."

"Thanks, Blair." She weakly smiles before heading into her bedroom and shutting the door behind her.

Turning back toward the television, I reach for my wine and down the rest of it. Unfortunately, I have a feeling she's right. Tomorrow is going to be a long day, and while I'm still trying to be supportive, I can't shake the feeling of inevitability that it's going to be so damn hard having to watch my best friend marry someone who isn't right for her. Pete West is not the man for Veronica Prescott, and now more than ever, I know that's true.

33

FORD

I'VE NEVER BEEN MORE glad to be a man when I heard that all the others in the bridal party were arriving at 7 a.m. to get their hair and makeup done for the day's festivities. While I offered to be there in solidarity, I was assured it would be boring and that I should just arrive at ten to get dressed and take pictures before the wedding starts at noon.

I suppose one good thing about arriving early is the fact that I don't have to park too far away, since even now I have to park more than a few houses down the road. Given how beloved Ronnie and the rest of the Prescott family are, I'm sure this place is going to be packed in a few short hours, with most everyone in town in attendance.

After parking, I make my way to the front door, where I'm greeted by Martha, Ronnie's mother. "Oh, my goodness! If it isn't Ford Hastings." She smiles, enveloping me in a warm hug. "You look amazing. Ronnie is going to be so pleased," she adds with motherly affection as she places a hand on my chest, her fingers lightly grazing over my baby-blue tie. Ronnie's parents have not only always been kind and generous, but they have always treated both Blair and me as if we were their own children.

"Thanks, Mrs. Prescott." Despite her comfy pink sweats that say "Mother of the Bride" on the front, and the fact that only her hair and makeup have already been done, she looks beyond stunning. "You look pretty amazing yourself," I assure her.

You know that joke about a mother looking like a sister? Well, in this case, it's actually true. Martha's beauty has always been undeniable, and it's evident that this is exactly who Ronnie inherited her good looks from.

"Oh, stop," she says, a blush creeping up her cheeks as she dismisses my compliment with a small wave. "But I better not keep you. Just head upstairs to Ronnie's old room. That's where all the bridal party is gathered," she explains as I nod my head.

Sending me off with another wave, I head up the tall staircase and make the usual trek to Ronnie's childhood bedroom. Wanting to make sure that everyone is ready and decent, I knock first.

"Who is it?" Gemma's voice calls, before opening the door just a tiny bit as she peeks her head through.

"It's Ford," I say, as she finally opens it to let me inside.

"Aw, Ford. You look so great," she coos.

"Thanks," I say, glancing down at the grey suit that had been picked out for me. Even though I'm on the bride's side of the wedding party, it was decided that I would wear the same suits as the groomsmen—a light grey suit, a baby-blue tie, and some brown Oxford dress shoes.

"You look great yourself," I say, gesturing toward the stunning dusty-blue dress that I'd already gotten a small glimpse of on Blair when she'd tried it on at the bridal shop. I mean it too. She looks incredible, but as my eyes wander around the room and I catch sight of Blair standing in front of a full-size mirror, I'm left utterly speechless. Fuck, she's unbelievably breathtaking—and somehow she's all mine.

There hasn't been a single day in my entire life when I didn't find her beautiful, but now, with her hair and makeup done, I'm utterly mesmerized as I admire her from behind. The dress hugs every single curve perfectly, and the way her wavy blonde hair falls down her shoulders and back is captivating, especially as the hair that's been used to pull some of it back is styled in a braid of sorts.

"You should probably close that mouth of yours, Hastings," Gemma jokes, tapping on the bottom of my stubbled jaw as I comply. Without realizing it, I've become one of those ridiculous comic strip characters with my jaw literally dropping toward the floor, but how can I not? I'm in complete and utter awe of this woman.

As Blair's eyes meet mine in the mirror, I try my hardest not to relive that moment from the dress shop, especially as her face lights up with the most enchanting smile imaginable.

She turns around before we both walk toward each other, meeting halfway. "Looking pretty dapper there, bud," she compliments, her hands lightly pressing against my chest as she sweeps them downward in a smoothing motion.

"Blair, you...you're so goddamn beautiful," I gush. Not the most eloquent reply, but the correct words seemingly elude me as I'm left in awe, completely captivated by her mesmerizing beauty. It's a complete mystery why this woman has chosen to fall in love with a guy like me, but I'm not about to question it. At this point, my only course of action is to treat her with the love and respect she deserves, with the hope that maybe someday she'll feel equally as fortunate as I do.

Her cheeks flush as she averts her gaze downward. "Thanks," she manages, just as the door bursts open and the true woman of the hour walks in.

While it's clear I only have eyes for Blair, there's no denying that Ronnie makes a breathtakingly beautiful bride. Like Blair, I had seen her dress before when she got her last fitting done at the dress shop. Not to mention that I'd been dragged along to all the different places as she tried on dress after dress, and while I'd seen others that felt more fitting of her personality, when she'd said this was the one she wanted, I wasn't about to fight her on it.

Like Blair, the dress and the beauty of the bride are only magnified by the fact that her short chestnut brown hair is curled just right with little white flowers woven into the strands that have been pulled back. Her natural beauty has always been striking, but the makeup she's wearing now somehow makes her brown eyes and lips even more eye-catching.

However, it doesn't take long to realize that something is amiss as her eyes stand wide and alert in pure panic.

"Ronnie," Blair says, taking charge as she rushes toward our friend, pulling her inside, making sure to shut the door behind her. "What's wrong? What's going on?"

Worry takes over as I too rush over. Did Pete call off the wedding? I may have punched a guy recently, but I'm far from being a violent person. However, if that asshole did anything to hurt Ronnie, I'd unleash those punches again without hesitation—even if my hand is still a little sore from the last time.

"Gemma, Maeve," she finally says, looking toward her other bridesmaids. "Can you give Blair, Ford, and I a minute?" she asks.

We clearly aren't the only ones worried, and likely thinking the worst, as Gemma and Maeve exchange concerned glances, but instead of fighting her on this, they nod their heads in unison.

"Yeah, of course, sweetheart," Maeve agrees. "Just let us know if you need anything," she says, reaching out and giving Ronnie's hand a small squeeze before she and Gemma exit the room.

"What's going on? You're worrying me," Blair pleads the second the door is closed.

"I don't know," Ronnie says, her breath coming in short, rapid gasps, her panic escalating. "I just—I was thinking about our conversation last night," she explains as I glance over at Blair for some hopeful insight on what in the hell is going on. "What if I'm making a huge mistake?"

"Oh, honey," Blair begins, pulling Ronnie's hand as she leads her to take a seat on the bed where I join them. "I'm so sorry. I didn't mean to make you worry. I mean, I know I said that I was concerned, but if marrying Pete is what feels right and you love him, then that's exactly what you should do."

"Yeah, what she said," I chime in, moving to take my spot next to Blair. "We're here to support you. No matter what and no matter what you decide to do—or not do," I say, needing to make that second part very clear. While I can only imagine the chaos that would ensue if she decided not to go through with things, if that was ultimately what she needed to do, then Blair and I would both be there for her and help with the inevitable fallout.

"I can't just *not* marry him though, right?" she asks, her eyes frantically darting between the two of us. "Everyone is here. People are already starting to arrive."

"Fuck everyone else," Blair bluntly states, waving a dismissive hand behind her. "Today has always been about you and Pete. The rest of us, we're just confetti. You get to do whatever you want, whether that's marrying Pete or changing your mind. The decision is ultimately yours. Hell, most of the people coming today are only here for a good party; none of them have to live with the consequences, so don't let anyone else's feelings dictate your life choices."

"She's right," I agree. "I don't want to come across like I'm trying to sway you in one direction, but remember, this is coming from someone who did make the wrong decision, even when I knew that I was making the wrong choice that day. I can confidently say that choosing to get married not only hurt me in the long run, but hurt Jenny as well," I explain with a loud sigh. "While I'm sure it would've hurt her to cancel the wedding, I'm pretty sure we'd both now agree that we were far more hurt by going through with it. We wasted so much of our lives being married to the wrong person, and I'd hate for you to make the same mistake I did."

"Oh God, what do I do?" she cries, quickly wiping away the first stray tear. "How do I tell him that I can't do it? Because I think you're both right. I can't marry him. He's not it. He's not my person, and he's *definitely* not my soulmate."

"Do you need me to do it?" Blair asks, as both Ronnie and I turn to look at her.

"I can't ask you to do that."

"Why not? I mean, come on. It's Pete. He's an asshole, but I can handle him. And I'm sorry, but I just don't see him taking the news very well and since you're already a mess," she says, looking Ronnie over. "If anything, I can't ask you to do it either."

"Really?" she asks, sniffling, as she seems to think it through.

"Really."

"I mean, if you're serious, then that would help a lot. I just—I think I need to get out of here," Ronnie finally decides as she stands.

I nod my head. "Maybe I should come with you," I offer, not feeling like she should be alone, especially not after making such a huge and life-changing decision.

"No, stay with Blair because, oh shit," Ronnie curses. "Someone is going to have to tell my family, and everyone else too." She panics even further as she lifts her hands to cover her face.

"Don't worry about it," Blair says, taking Ronnie's hand into hers once more. "We've got this. We'll take care of everything. You just worry about taking care of yourself, but Ford's right. You shouldn't be leaving alone, but don't worry," she offers, as she seems to put together a plan in her head. "I'll take care of that, too."

"I don't deserve you guys," Ronnie's voice quivers as she sniffs and extends her hand toward mine as well, intertwining her fingers with ours.

"You'd do the same for us. It's nothing," I promise her.

"Ford, you sneak her out back, and I'll have someone there to take you wherever you need to go," she tells me before pulling Ronnie into a big hug and then rushing out of the room.

"Am I really going to do this?" Ronnie asks, as the first genuine smile of the day comes to her lips. Worry still lines her features, but it's obvious a huge weight has been lifted from her shoulders.

"I think you are, and more importantly, I think you're making the right choice."

Perhaps I shouldn't be projecting my thoughts and feelings onto her during such a pivotal moment, but I also feel like if they truly were right for each other, and if for some reason it turns out that they do love each other and this is just a case of cold feet, she can come back and they will eventually figure things out. If anything, Blair and I are the perfect example of that. Either way, if she's feeling this uncertain, there's no reason she should be walking down that aisle today.

"Ford, one more thing before we go," she starts, giving my hand a small tug. "Will you tell my parents how sorry I am and tell them that I promise to pay them back for everything? Also, with everything already being paid for and since the entire town of Evergreen Grove is about to show up, can you tell them that I still want the party to go on? Just because I'm not here to enjoy it, and even if Pete's family won't want to either, there's no reason for everything to go to waste, right?"

"I'll take care of it," I promise as I give her hand another squeeze. "And don't worry. Your parents will be fine. Plus, I have to imagine that they'll be just as understanding as Blair and I are.

Your parents are good people and I know that the only thing that's important to them today and always is that their daughter is happy. If running is what makes you happy, then they'd want you to do this too."

"I don't know about that, but I appreciate hearing it," she says through a nervous laugh as she stands on her tiptoes to press a kiss to my cheek.

"Alright, let's get you out of here, Miss Runaway Bride," I quip, attempting to lighten the mood, even if I'm not entirely convinced it's working.

I'm not sure if Blair truly meant to be sneaky and stealthy about things as I help Ronnie make her big escape, but I do it anyway as I crack the door open and peek out first. Luckily, the hallway is empty as I reach backward for her hand before we head out.

Keeping it up, I meticulously scan around each corner before we turn, and, most importantly, sneak her out the side door, especially since the backyard is already filling up with people, and out front, even more guests are making their way up the pathway that's been highlighted by flowers and lanterns.

As we walk through the door, Blair meets us and takes Ronnie's hand from mine. "Miles is going to drive you wherever you need," she explains.

"Your brother?" Ronnie gasps, since it's always been pretty clear that Blair's big brother isn't exactly our best friend's biggest fan.

"Yes, but don't worry. He's going to be on his best behavior, plus you get to ride in style," she explains, motioning toward a red Ford Mustang—which happens to be Miles' baby—where he's currently leaning against the passenger door with his arms folded across his chest.

"Well, desperate times call for desperate measures I suppose," Ronnie mutters before breathing out a large breath of air as she turns to face Blair and me. "I love you guys. I hope you know that."

"We do," I assure her, and suddenly I'm caught in a tight three-way group hug, feeling the intense love and unity of our bond. I truly don't know where I'd be without the two of them, and despite all the craziness of this morning and what's still about to come, everything about this moment just feels right.

"Now go," Blair encourages as she pushes Ronnie toward her brother and the car.

With a slight moment of hesitation, she takes a step forward before she lifts her dress to make her escape easier and rushes toward Miles. He opens the passenger door, offering his hand to help, before carefully tucking the large skirt of her dress inside.

As Blair slinks an arm around my waist, I instinctively drape mine over her shoulder as we watch the car drive away. "I have a feeling today is going to be a really good day," she says, letting out a contented sigh.

"I think you're right."

34

BLAIR

"I HOPE RONNIE'S DOING okay."

"I'm sure she's fine, or at least she will be," Ford assures me as his hand that's resting on the back of my chair reaches out to give my shoulder a small comforting squeeze.

Per Ronnie's wishes, we'd made sure to inform both the groom and Ronnie's parents about the situation, and even took it upon ourselves to be the ones to stand in front of the assembled guests to deliver the news.

Unsurprisingly, Pete hadn't taken it very well, making me even more thankful that I'd been the one to deliver the news, and not my best friend.

As expected, he'd unleashed his fury by fuming, yelling, and hurling objects around the room, looking exactly like a child throwing a temper-tantrum. I'd never felt unsafe for a single moment, though, especially with Ford by my side. Just as Pete was about to direct his anger in my direction, Ford confidently interjected, maintaining a poised and authoritative demeanor. He'd fearlessly informed Pete that he'd no longer tolerate his yelling, and that I was to be treated with the respect I deserved.

I'm not sure if it was his teacher instincts kicking in or what, but there was something undeniably sexy about seeing him step up like that.

After Pete, we'd gone to her parents, and while they were understandably worried and a little panicked, they were in no way angry or upset. If anything, they seemed just as relieved as we were, which only seemed to prove how right about Pete I'd been this entire time—he is *not* the one for our girl.

As for the people of Evergreen Grove, they acted in typical Evergreen fashion and seemed to relish the excitement and buzz of it all. All they cared about was having a new juicy topic to gossip about and were particularly relieved to know that the party was still going to take place despite the broken nuptials.

"While I'm glad she isn't here, I still feel bad that she's missing out on all of this," I say, letting my head fall to rest in the comforting nook between Ford's shoulder and chest.

"It is pretty amazing, huh?" he asks, as his eyes wander across the decked-out property.

When we were kids, Ronnie used to talk all the time about her dream wedding, and this was definitely it. The area where the aisle and chairs had been earlier, offering the most perfect view of the pond, has now been transformed into a lively dance floor for the party tonight. They'd also brought in beams adorned with an abundance of blue and white flowers, to hold up a magical canopy of sparkly lights overhead with a few random tables surrounding it.

The area where we're currently seated is in a spacious white tent, adorned with elegant table settings and vibrant floral arrangements. The whole scene is illuminated by even more magical twinkling lights.

"It's everything she ever wanted," I sigh, watching people hit the dance floor while the DJ plays Whitney Houston's "I Wanna Dance with Somebody."

"Don't worry. When she finds the right guy, she'll have an even better wedding," he promises, pressing a tender kiss to the top of my head.

"Definitely," I agree, tilting my face to look up at him. "She just needs to find herself her own Ford," I joke, especially since I easily feel like I've hit the jackpot. Sure, I wasted a lot of time and this should've happened a long time ago, but I also want to believe that everything happened for a reason. Everything we experienced, and everything we went through to get us to this point, shaped us into the people we are today, and it only makes me love and appreciate him more.

The music changes to a slow song, as "You Are the Reason" by Calum Scott plays across the speakers. With my mouth dropping open, I sit up and turn to face Ford. "We have to dance to this song. It's my favorite," I all but beg as I grab his arm and give it a gentle shake.

"Didn't you learn your lesson the last time?" he asks, his eyes nervously darting between me and the dance floor. "I'm pretty sure I almost broke your foot more than once at Ronnie's bachelorette party."

I scoff and brush his words off with a small wave. "That's because I was trying to teach you a line dance. This is a slow song. All you have to do is hold me while you sway back and forth. You won't even have to worry about leading. I've got us covered."

He scrunches his nose, but as he lets out a large exhale, I know I've got him.

He rises to his feet first before offering his hand to help me up. "Thank you, kind sir," I tease, placing my hand into his before he leads us out toward the lit-up dance floor.

I'm both a little surprised and taken aback as we walk onto the floor and he uses his hand to spin me around in a small twirl. "Are you serious? I thought you always complained about not knowing how to dance?" I ask, my mouth open in pure adoration as we now face each other.

"That truly is the extent of all my dancing knowledge, so tell me: where do I put my hands?" he asks as I let out a soft giggle.

"You really are pathetic," I tease. "But luckily for you, I'm a patient teacher. That, and I find you extremely sexy," I add, lowering my voice at the last bit. I guide his left hand to rest on my hip, while interlocking our right hands together, and gently placing my free hand on his bicep.

"So I'm not supposed to just put both my hands on your hips as you hold my shoulders?"

"Maybe if we were high schoolers, or if you were just trying to cop a feel of my ass."

He tilts his head to the side, his mouth twisting into a devilish smirk. "That doesn't sound all that bad."

We laugh together as I dip my head. "Don't you worry, there will be plenty of time for you to play grab-ass later," I say, lowering my voice once more.

"You know," he starts, and I can sense from the change in tone that this conversation is about to take a more serious turn. "I'm more than grateful to know that I have you tonight, and tomorrow as well, but what happens after Sunday?"

I let out a sigh, especially since there's a reason I've been putting off this conversation. "I'm not sure. I mean, I want to cancel my ticket and I'm nowhere near ready to say goodbye just yet, but what happens after the initial magic and excitement of this new thing wears off? Even more, I'm going to need a job and a way to make money. I can't live off hopes, dreams, and love forever."

"First off, what we have is real and too damn special to ever truly wear off," he confidently says, brushing those worries aside. "I'm always going to be in love with you, Blair, and every single day I plan to fall deeper and deeper in love. There's never going to be a single day where I don't plan on showing you just how deep that love goes."

"Okay, I believe you." I smile, my heart bubbling with excitement as he continues to find new ways to amaze me while I fall deeper and harder for him each and every day, too. "Even so, you never answered my other question. Unfortunately, good vibes and love aren't what will pay the bills."

Luckily, my substantial savings could provide me with some financial security, as the bands I toured with covered a lot of my expenses, like lodging and food. However, I'm aware that relying solely on this money has its limits, and while I appreciate the support my family and friends will likely offer, I've also never been someone who enjoys exploiting the kindness of others.

"We'll figure it out. You're a photographer, and an amazing one at that. People here need pictures too," he points out. "Didn't Ronnie complain to you about how hard it was to find a decent photographer for her wedding, and how she had to find someone a few towns over to travel and make the trip?"

As I mull it over in my head, it isn't the worst idea I've ever heard. "That could be an option," I agree, my lips tightening as I anxiously bite down on my bottom lip.

"What's wrong?" he asks, clearly noting my silence and unease. "Just tell me. We'll figure this all out together. You don't have to do any of this alone. I'm here for you."

"I know, and I really do want to figure something out, especially since the idea of being back around you and Miles is so incredibly tempting. Plus, I feel like Ronnie is going to need a huge support system, but what if I can't handle it here again? I mean, come on. There's a reason I chose to leave in the first place."

"You mean, it wasn't just to get away from me?" He smirks as I roll my eyes.

"Well, maybe that was a small part of it," I acknowledge with a small laugh. "But an even bigger part of me has never really believed that I fit in here. What if I try again, only to realize that all those worries and insecurities were valid as I discover I don't fit in or belong here? I'm already so in love with you, and I worry about giving in only to realize that I have to leave you all over again. That would be beyond devastating—it would truly kill me, Ford."

"First off, you belong here. Second, if for some reason you ever feel like you don't fit in and have to leave, then you're not leaving alone. I'll follow you anywhere. It's you and me, Blair bear. Now that I have you, you need to understand that I'm never, ever letting you go again."

Even if I had just playfully teased him about this position, I release his hand, wrap my arms around his neck, and press my lips against his as his firm hands encircle my waist.

I finally pull back enough for my eyes to gaze into his. "I love you so much," I confess, somehow wishing my words could truly convey the full weight of my emotions.

"I love you too," he repeats, leaning down to press a soft kiss to my forehead. As tempted as I am to kiss him again or find a secluded spot to demonstrate the depth of my love, I acknowledge that this isn't exactly the most appropriate setting. If you don't want to become the talk of the town, it's better to limit your public displays of affection.

We'd also promised the Prescotts that we'd stay the entire time to help and handle any possible drama that arises tonight. The constant questioning about the wedding details and its cancellation has taken its toll on all of us, but thankfully, most people brought their questions to us, and not to the Prescotts. Not that we told them anything interesting—we know better than to feed the monster, and instead insisted that this was a personal matter and that both Pete and Ronnie would prefer their privacy at this time.

"Finally," a familiar voice says next to us as we look over and spot Helen, the official owner of The Steamy Bean, and her husband dancing nearby. "You two make the cutest couple and it's about time you made it official. I'm pretty sure the entire town has been taking bets on when you'd finally get together."

My cheeks redden as I look down and a soft laugh escapes.

"You're officially together now, right?" she presses, clearly here to get the full scope of gossip.

"Yes, we're together," I confirm, and I turn my attention back to Ford, who can't seem to fight the immense grin lighting up his face.

"We are," Ford agrees. "And feel free to let everyone know that Blair Bennett is officially mine and that she's planning on sticking around for a while."

"Can do," she agrees with a nod and a chuckle of her own. "And I better you see guys coming into my shop together on the regular," she playfully teases as she points a not-so-threatening finger in our direction.

"Don't worry, we will. I'm pretty sure I missed your muffins more than I missed Ford when I was away," I assure her with a teasing wink.

She laughs with us. "That's good to know. And Blair," she starts up again as she reaches out a hand and places it on my arm, "it's good to have you back."

"Thanks. It's good to be back," I say, and for once, I truly mean it. I may have a complicated past with this town, but more importantly, there are way too many wonderful memories that outweigh the bad.

Even more, I'm looking forward to making new and better ones with my favorite people by my side. Maybe what they say about home not being a place, but a person is true, because being right here, wrapped in Ford's arms, I officially feel at home for the first time in a really long time.

35

FORD

G OING BACK TO WORK on a Monday is never fun, but leaving my place this morning was especially painful. Luckily, I love my job and it's nice to get out of my tiny apartment from time to time. But damn, it's rough knowing that the girl of my dreams is alone, naked in my bed.

As tempted as I was to fake sick, call in, and request a sub, that dream was squashed pretty quickly when I realized I had no sub plans prepared. Sucking it up, I put on my big-boy pants and went in. Moreover, she made it clear that she's here for good and that we aren't on some timeline where we need to get in as much quality time as we can before she leaves again.

I suppose there's always the chance that she'll decide Evergreen Grove is too overwhelming, and she'll want to book the next flight out of here, but I meant every word I said. If she goes, I go. We're a team now, and I have no intention of letting her go anywhere without me.

I may have also used my lunch break this afternoon to sway her decision, ensuring that she not only stays for my sake and the rest of the town, but also because this is something she truly wants for herself as well.

"Are you seriously not going to tell me where we're going?" she whines as we walk, one arm linked through mine, with her brother's dog, Bubba, on a leash in the other.

We'd apparently underestimated just how serious Ronnie had been when she said she needed to escape, never imagining that she would somehow persuade Miles, of all people, to embark on a much-needed road trip. Although no return date has been set, based on their updates, it sounds like Ronnie is finally getting the well-earned break and vacation she deserves, especially since I can't even imagine the drama that's going to unfold when they get back. Until the two of them return, we have Bubba in our care.

"Just be patient. We're almost there," I assure her, leaning over to press a kiss to the side of her forehead. Maybe it's a bit overkill, but I can't seem to keep my hands or lips off of her. Luckily, she doesn't seem to mind.

"Well, I imagine so. There aren't too many places to go here, but I don't know why you have to be so annoying and secretive about it. It's not like there's anywhere that I haven't been in this town."

Despite her attempts to sound annoyed and frustrated, the smile on her face betrays her true feelings of genuine curiosity and excitement, and this is one secret I can't wait to show her.

"Yeah, you've been here, but it's a little different from what you probably remember," I carefully explain, as we approach a historic brick building, its architecture blending seamlessly with the town's aesthetic.

As we stop, Blair's eyebrows furrow as she looks between me and the abandoned storefront. "The old model train store? This is what you wanted to show me? That it went out of business? I could have told you years ago that this place was never going to make it, especially with how mean and grumpy Mr. Henderson was."

I try not to laugh as I keep a straight face. She's not wrong. That place was never going to last, especially when he yelled at pretty much anyone who got too close to one of the displays. Plus, how many people in a small town are truly into model trains? Okay, so maybe enough since there is still a club that meets weekly in Mr. Henderson's basement, but obviously not enough to keep an entire storefront in business.

"That's not what I want to show you," I say, walking over to where a *For Sale* sign sits in the window and tap at it. Since most of Evergreen Grove has stayed the same over the years, this building has sat vacant for quite some time, but I'm hoping to change that.

"What?" she asks, looking even more confused. "You want to move from above the pizza shop to inside the old train store?"

I laugh and shake my head. "No, Blair. I think you should buy it and start your own photography business here in Evergreen."

Her mouth forms a perfect "O" as she comprehends what I'm suggesting, her head nodding in a slow, deliberate manner as she and Bubba cautiously move forward.

"It would take some work to fix it up, but we have time, and you know that Ronnie, Miles, and I would all be willing to help with that. And I'm sure Miles could help with the business side of things," I excitedly rattle on, hoping she loves this idea just as much as I do. "But we could make sets, and backgrounds, and even build you your own darkroom since I remember you always talking about hoping to own one of your own."

Blair cups her hands around her eyes and presses her face against the glass, eager to get a better view of the inside. I just have to hope that she's seeing the same vision I am. While she did say she was open to trying out living here, I can't help the lingering concern that she might want to leave sooner rather than later. Yet maybe, with this opportunity, she'll discover just how seamlessly she can fit back in.

Pulling away from the window, she faces me; her face and expression blank before a giant smile dances across her face. "I love it," she shrieks before running toward me. Bubba isn't exactly the biggest fan of this sudden change as he gets yanked along with her, but he seems to give in and follows as she jumps into my arms. I do my best to catch her, one hand supporting her ass as she wraps her legs around me. "Seriously, Ford. I love it so much, you have no idea," she squeals. Before I can reply, her lips press against mine, conveying her gratitude in a whole new way.

I manage to pull my lips away from her. "I have one more surprise," I admit as her eyes widen in even more excitement. "You know Mary-Beth Wilson?" I ask, because even though she's older now, she's still the town's only realtor—everyone's go-to person for buying and selling property.

"Yeah..." she trails off, obviously hesitant as she waits to see where I'm going with this.

"I talked to her this afternoon, and she said that since it's been sitting vacant for so long, she's prepared to get us a really good deal," I explain, before slowly dropping my hands as Blair carefully slides back down to the ground. "She also gave me this," I add, reaching into my pocket and pulling out a key.

"We can go inside?" she squeals once again as she excitedly jumps up and down, while Bubba somehow manages to look even more confused and annoyed with all the extra tugging.

"We get to go inside," I nod, handing over the key, since if anyone deserves the honor of going in first, it's her.

Not wasting any time, she hands me Bubba's leash and rushes to unlock the door and hurries inside.

Bubba's gratitude is evident as he happily accompanies me, no longer having to endure being dragged around like before as we follow Blair inside.

It's apparent that there is a lot of work to be done in this space. The walls, with their chipping white paint, and the presence of random old shelves signal a picture of neglect. Even so, I'm optimistic that she'll still manage to see the potential here.

I lean back against a nearby wall, crossing one leg over the other, completely enamored by the way her smile remains bright as she walks around, fully taking everything in. "Back here is where we could put the darkroom," she gushes, pointing toward the far back wall. "And then I could make a few different studio sets over there," she says, pointing to the other side of the room. "And then obviously I could have Ronnie help me pick out all the decor," she further gushes, her fingers intertwining before she spins around to face me.

"So you want to do it?"

"Oh, there's no doubt in my mind that this is what I want to do," she assures as she hurries toward me, leaning in and resting her hands flat on my chest.

"Really?" I ask, my smile faltering just for a tiny second as I drop Bubba's leash, letting him free to wander. "And be completely honest," I beg as I let one of my hands rest on her hip. "Is this truly what you want? Because I know how much you loved touring with those bands and traveling around the world," I say, knowing that unfortunately that has never been something I've personally been able to offer. "As much as I want you here, I want you to stay because it's what you want and not because I selfishly just want to have you closer."

"Ford," she starts again as she reaches up and cups her hands on my stubbled cheeks, making sure that I'm not only looking directly at her, but truly listening. "Yes, I loved doing all that, and I'll carry those memories with me forever, but that was what I needed back then. What I need now is you. More importantly, I'm ready to give this town a fresh start, and this feels so damn right. Crazily enough, I've never been more sure of anything in my entire life. I belong here, and most importantly, I belong here with you."

Smiling, I press my lips into hers, getting all the confirmation I need. There could always be a chance in the future that she'll decide this no longer feels right, but I'm not worried. We've got this: no matter what life throws our way, we'll figure it out together. It's me and her for life.

Thank You For Reading

Thank you for taking the chance on this Indie Author. Being able to write these characters and tell their story is a dream come true, and it means the world to me you have taken the time to read my book. If you enjoyed this story and would like to further help and support me, please consider leaving an honest review on Amazon and Goodreads.

Acknowledgements

A lot goes into not only writing a book, but getting it ready and out there for the public to read, and I couldn't have gotten this book out there without the help of some of my favorite people.

The first person I need to thank is my husband, Rey. Thank you for not only supporting me, but encouraging me to finish and to never give up. It means the world to me that you believe in me enough to not only financially back these projects, but believe that I'll one day be able to repay the favor.

The next people I want to thank are my kids. I know it's not always easy when I need to shut myself in my room to write or edit, but you are always patient, and give me the time I need. I love hearing you talk about my books and asking me questions about them. My hope for all three of you is that you see me following my dreams of doing something I love, and that it will inspire you all to do the same.

Next person I need to acknowledge is my chipmunk bestie, Kaele. There is definitely a reason I chose to dedicate this book to you. One of the biggest themes of this novel is friendship, and I'm so grateful to have a best friend who makes it so easy to write a strong and supportive friendship. I'm so lucky to have you in my life and I'm not sure how I'd make it without you.

Next up, is my close friend, cheerleader, and proofreader Britt. Thank you for always being there for me, even when you have so much going on yourself. I know that I can always count on you to be honest, and it means the world to me that you not only help me with proofreading, but talking to me about my book and characters and what you love about them. In an industry where it's so easy to second-guess yourself or feel insecure, you give me the ability to feel confident in my writing and my work.

ABOUT THE AUTHOR

Kristen Lucero is a devoted mother of three boys and has been happily married for 15 years. They live in Utah, along with their two dogs, Milo and Beans. She has always had a passion for reading and writing. Kristen's love for romance novels and their happily ever afters inspired her to create her own heartfelt stories.

To stay up to date on everything Kristen has going on please follow her on social media.

TikTok: @kristenwritesandreads

Instagram: @authorkristenlucero